PROLOGUE

Addie and I were born into the same body, our souls' ghostly fingers entwined before we gasped our very first breath. Our earliest years together were also our happiest. Then came the worries—the tightness around our parents' mouths, the frowns lining our kindergarten teacher's forehead, the question everyone whispered when they thought we couldn't hear.

Why aren't they settling?

Settling.

We tried to form the word in our five-year-old mouth, tasting it on our tongue.

Set—Tull—Ling.

We knew what it meant. Kind of. It meant one of us was supposed to take control. It meant the other was supposed to fade away. I know now that it means much, much more than that. But at five, Addie and I were still naive, still oblivious.

The varnish of innocence began wearing away by first grade. Our gray-haired guidance counselor made the first scratch.

"You know, dearies, settling isn't scary," she'd say as we watched her thin, lipstick-reddened mouth. "It might seem like it now, but it happens to everyone. The recessive soul, whichever one of you it is, will simply . . . go to sleep."

She never mentioned who she thought would survive, but she didn't need to. By first grade, everyone believed Addie had been born the dominant soul. She could move us left when I wanted to go right, refuse to open her mouth when I wanted to eat, cry *No* when I wanted so desperately to say *Yes*. She could do it all with so little effort, and as time passed, I grew ever weaker while her control increased.

But I could still force my way through at times—and I did. When Mom asked about our day, I pulled together all my strength to tell her *my* version of things. When we played hide-and-seek, I made us duck behind the hedges instead of run for home base. At eight, I jerked us while bringing Dad his coffee. The burns left scars on our hands.

The more my strength waned, the fiercer I scrabbled to hold on, lashing out in any way I could, trying to convince myself I wasn't going to disappear. Addie hated me for it. I couldn't help myself. I remembered the freedom I used to have—never complete, of course, but I remembered when *I* could ask our mother for a drink of water, for a kiss when we fell, for a hug.

<Let it go, Eva> Addie shouted whenever we fought. *<Just let it go. Just go away.>*

And for a long time, I believed that someday, I would.

We saw our first specialist at six. Specialists who were a lot pushier than the guidance counselor. Specialists who did their little tests, asked their little questions, and charged their not-so-little fees. By the time our younger brothers reached

WHAT'S LEFT OF ME

KAT ZHANG

WHAT'S LEFT OF ME

THE HYBRID CHRONICLES

HarperCollins*Publishers*

First published in the USA by HarperCollins *Publishers Inc* in 2012
First published in Great Britain by HarperCollins *Children's Books* in 2012
HarperCollins *Children's Books* is a division of HarperCollins*Publishers* Ltd,
77-85 Fulham Palace Road, Hammersmith, London, W6 8JB.

The HarperCollins website address is
www.harpercollins.co.uk

1

ISBN 978-0-00-747681-7

Printed and bound in England by Clays Ltd, St Ives plc

settling age, Addie and I had been through two therapists and four types of medication, all trying to do what nature should have already done: Get rid of the recessive soul.

Get rid of me.

Our parents were so relieved when my outbursts began disappearing, when the doctors came back with positive reports in their hands. They tried to keep it concealed, but we heard the sighed *Finallys* outside our door hours after they'd kissed us good night. For years, we'd been the thorn of the neighborhood, the dirty little secret that wasn't so secret. The girls who just wouldn't settle.

Nobody knew how in the middle of the night, Addie let me come out and walk around our bedroom with the last of my strength, touching the cold windowpanes and crying my own tears.

<I'm sorry> she'd whispered then. And I knew she really was, despite everything she'd said before. But that didn't change anything.

I was terrified. I was eleven years old, and though I'd been told my entire short life that it was only natural for the recessive soul to fade away, I didn't want to go. I wanted twenty thousand more sunrises, three thousand more hot summer days at the pool. I wanted to know what it was like to have a first kiss. The other recessives were lucky to have disappeared at four or five. They knew less.

Maybe that's why things turned out the way they did. I wanted life too badly. I refused to let go. I didn't completely fade away.

My motor controls vanished, yes, but I remained, trapped in our head. Watching, listening, but paralyzed.

Nobody but Addie and I knew, and Addie wasn't about to tell. By this time, we knew what awaited kids who never settled, who became hybrids. Our head was filled with images of the institutions where they were squirreled away—never to return.

Eventually, the doctors gave us a clean bill of health. The guidance counselor bid us good-bye with a pleased little smile. Our parents were ecstatic. They packed everything up and moved us four hours away to a new state, a new neighborhood. One where no one knew who we were. Where we could be more than That Family With The Strange Little Girl.

I remember seeing our new home for the first time, looking over our little brother's head and through his car window at the tiny, off-white house with the dark-shingled roof. Lyle cried at the sight of it, so old and shabby, the garden rampant with weeds. In the frenzy of our parents calming him down and unloading the moving truck and lugging in suitcases, Addie and I had been left alone for a moment—given a minute to just stand in the winter cold and breathe in the sharp air.

After so many years, things were finally the way they were supposed to be. Our parents could look other people in the eye again. Lyle could be around Addie in public again. We joined a seventh-grade class that didn't know about all the years we'd spent huddled at our desk, wishing we could disappear.

They could be a normal family, with normal worries. They could be happy.

They.

They didn't realize it wasn't *they* at all. It was still *us*.

I was still there.

"Addie and Eva, Eva and Addie," Mom used to sing when we were little, picking us up and swinging us through the air. "My little girls."

Now when we helped make dinner, Dad only asked, "Addie, what would you like tonight?"

No one used my name anymore. It wasn't Addie and Eva, Eva and Addie. It was just Addie, Addie, Addie.

One little girl, not two.

ONE

The end-of-school bell blasted everyone from their seats. People loosened their ties, slapped shut books, shoved folders and pencils into backpacks. A buzz of conversation nearly drowned out the teacher as she yelled reminders about tomorrow's field trip. Addie was almost out the door when I said *<Wait, we've got to ask Ms. Stimp about our make-up test, remember?>*

<I'll do it tomorrow> Addie said, pushing her way through the hall. Our history teacher always gave us looks like she knew the secret in our head, pinching her lips and frowning at us when she thought we weren't watching. Maybe I was just being paranoid. But maybe not. Still, doing poorly in her class would only bring more trouble.

<What if she doesn't let us?>

The school rang with noise—lockers slamming, people laughing—but I heard Addie's voice perfectly in the quiet space linking our minds. There, it was peaceful for now, though I could feel the start of Addie's irritation like a dark splash in the corner. *<She will, Eva. She always does. Don't be a nag.>*

<I'm not. I just—>

"Addie!" someone shouted, and Addie half-turned. "Addie—wait up!"

We'd been so lost in our argument we hadn't even noticed the girl chasing after us. It was Hally Mullan, one hand pushing up her glasses, the other trying to wrap a hair tie around her dark curls. She shoved past a tight-knit group of students before making it to our side with an exaggerated sigh of relief. Addie groaned, but silently, so that only I could hear.

"You're a really fast walker," Hally said and smiled as if she and Addie were friends.

Addie shrugged. "I didn't know you were following me."

Hally's smile didn't dim. But then, she was the kind of person who laughed in the face of a hurricane. In another body, another life, she wouldn't have been stuck chasing after someone like us in the hallway. She was too pretty for that, with those long eyelashes and olive skin, and too quick to laugh. But there was a difference written into her face, into the set of her cheekbones and the slant of her nose. This only added to the strangeness about her, an aura that broadcasted Not Quite Right. Addie had always stayed away. We had enough problems pretending to be normal.

There was no easy way to avoid Hally now, though. She fell into step beside us, her book bag slung over one shoulder. "So, excited about the field trip?"

"Not really," Addie said.

"Me neither," Hally said cheerfully. "Are you busy today?"

"Kind of," Addie said. She managed to keep our voice

bland despite Hally's dogged high spirits, but our fingers tugged at the bottom of our blouse. It had fit at the beginning of the year, when we'd bought all new uniforms for high school, but we'd grown taller since then. Our parents hadn't noticed, not with—well, not with everything that was happening with Lyle—and we hadn't said anything.

"Want to come over?" Hally said.

Addie's smile was strained. As far as we knew, Hally had never asked anyone over. Most likely, no one would go. <*Can't she take a hint?*> Aloud, Addie said, "Can't. I've got to babysit."

"For the Woodards?" Hally asked. "Rob and Lucy?"

"Robby and Will and Lucy," Addie said. "But yeah, the Woodards."

Hally's dimples deepened. "I love those kids. They use the pool in my neighborhood all the time. Can I come?"

Addie hesitated. "I don't know if their parents would like that."

"Are they still there when you arrive?" Hally said, and when Addie nodded, added, "We can ask, then, right?"

<*Doesn't she realize how rude she's being?*> Addie said, and I knew I ought to agree. But Hally kept smiling and smiling, even when I knew the expression on our face was getting less and less friendly.

<*Maybe we don't realize how lonely she is*> I said instead.

Addie had her friends, and I, at very least, had Addie. Hally seemed to have no one at all.

"I don't expect to get paid or anything, of course," Hally was saying now. "I'll just come keep you company, you know?"

<Addie> I said. *<Let her. At least let her come ask.>*

"Well . . ." Addie said.

"Great!" Hally grabbed our hand and didn't seem to notice Addie flinch in surprise. "I have so much to talk to you about."

The TV was blaring when Addie opened the Woodards' front door, Hally following close behind. Mr. Woodard grabbed his briefcase and keys when he saw us. "Kids are in the living room, Addie." He hurried out the door, saying over his shoulder as he went, "Call if you need anything."

"This is Hally Mul—" Addie tried to say, but he was already gone, leaving us alone with Hally in the foyer.

"He didn't even notice me," Hally said.

Addie rolled her eyes. "I guess I'm not surprised. He's always like that."

We'd been babysitting Will, Robby, and Lucy for a while now—even before Mom had reduced her hours at work to care for Lyle—but Mr. Woodard still had moments when he forgot Addie's name. Our parents weren't the only ones in town with too much work and too little time.

The living room TV was tuned to a cartoon featuring a pink rabbit and two rather enormous mice. Lyle used to watch the same thing when he was younger, but at ten, he claimed to have outgrown it.

Apparently seven-year-olds were still allowed to watch

cartoons, though, because Lucy lay on the carpet, her legs waving back and forth. Her little brother sat beside her, equally engrossed.

"He's Will right now," Lucy said without turning around. The cartoon ended, replaced by a public service announcement, and Addie looked away. We'd seen enough PSAs. At the old hospital we'd gone to, they'd played them on a loop—endless rounds of good-looking men and women with friendly voices and nice smiles reminding us to always be on the lookout for hybrids hiding somewhere, pretending to be normal. People who'd escaped hospitalization. People like Addie and me.

Just call the number on the screen, they always said, displaying perfect white teeth. *Just one call, for the safety of your children, your family, your country.*

They never said exactly what would happen after that call, but I guess they didn't need to. Everyone already knew. Hybrids were too unstable to just leave alone, so calls usually led to investigations, which sometimes led to raids. We'd only ever seen one on the news or in the videos they showed us in Government class, but it was more than enough.

Will jumped up and headed for us, casting a confused and rather suspicious glance at Hally. She smiled at him.

"Hi, Will." She dropped into a squat despite her skirt. We'd gone straight to the Woodards' from school, not even stopping to change out of our uniforms. "I'm Hally. Do you remember me?"

Lucy finally looked away from the television screen. She

frowned. "I remember you. My mom says—"

Will jerked on the bottom of our skirt and cut Lucy off before she could finish. "We're hungry."

"They're not really," Lucy said. "I just gave them a cookie. They want another one." She climbed to her feet, revealing the box of cookies she'd been hiding from view. "Are you going to play with us?" she asked Hally.

Hally smiled at her. "I'm here to help babysit."

"Who? Will and Robby?" Lucy said. "They don't need two people." She stared at us, daring someone to say that she, at seven, still needed a babysitter.

"Hally's here to keep me company," Addie said quickly. She picked Will up, and he wrapped his arms around our neck, setting his tiny chin on our shoulder. His baby-fine hair tickled our cheek.

Hally grinned and wiggled her fingers at him. "How old are you now, Will?"

Will hid his face.

"Three and a half," Addie said. "They should be settling in a year or so." She readjusted Will in our arms and forced a smile onto our face. "Isn't that right, Will? Are you going to settle soon?"

"He's Robby now," Lucy said. She'd grabbed her box of cookies again and munched on one as she spoke.

Everyone looked at the little boy. He reached toward his sister, oblivious to our scrutiny.

<She's right> I said. *<He just changed.>* I'd always been better at differentiating between Robby and Will, even

if Addie denied it. Maybe it was because I didn't have to focus on moving our body or speaking to other people. I could simply watch and listen and notice all the tiny little ticks that marked one soul from the other.

"Robby?" Addie said.

The toddler wriggled again, and Addie set him down. He ran over to his sister. Lucy dangled what remained of her cookie in front of his face.

"No!" he said. "We don't want that one. We want a new one."

Lucy stuck her tongue out at him. "Will would've taken it."

"Would *not*!" he cried.

"Would too. Right, Will?"

Robby's face screwed up. "No."

"I didn't ask *you*," Lucy said.

<Better hurry> I said. *<Before Robby pitches a fit.>*

To my surprise, Hally got there before we did, plucking a cookie from the box and dropping it into Robby's outstretched hands.

"There." She crouched down again, wrapping her arms around her knees. "Is that better?"

Robby blinked. His eyes shifted between Hally and his new prize. Then he grinned shyly and bit into the cookie, crumbs cascading down his shirt.

"Say thank you," Lucy told him.

"Thank you," he whispered.

"No problem," Hally said. She smiled. "Do you like chocolate chip? I do. They're my favorite."

A small nod. Even Robby was a little subdued around strangers. He took another bite of his cookie.

"And what about Will?" Hally said. "What kind of cookies does he like?"

Robby gave a sort of half shrug, then said softly, "Same kind as me."

Hally's voice was even quieter when she spoke again. "Would you miss him, Robby? If Will went away?"

"How about we go into the kitchen?" Addie jerked the box of cookies from Lucy's hand, inciting a cry of outrage. "Come on, Lucy—don't let Robby eat that in the living room. Your mom will kill me if you get crumbs on the rug."

Addie grabbed Robby's hand, pulling him away from Hally. But she didn't do it fast enough. Robby had time to turn. He had time to look at Hally, still crouching there on the ground, and whisper, "Yes."

TWO

It was getting dark by the time Mr. and Mrs. Woodard came home, the sky a layered wash of gold, peach, and blue. Addie insisted on splitting the babysitting money with Hally. When I commented on it, she shrugged. *<Well, she was more helpful than I expected.>*

I had to agree. Robby and Will—they switched twice more during the course of the afternoon—both adored her. Even Lucy had followed us to the door, asking if Hally was coming back next time. Whatever her mother had said about Hally—and, judging from the way the woman looked at her when she came home, it hadn't been anything good—seemed to have slipped from Lucy's mind.

Turned out we lived in the same direction, so Hally said she'd walk with us. We set out into the evening sun, the air dripping with humidity and mosquitoes. It was only April, but a recent heat wave had driven the temperature to record highs. The collar of our uniform flopped damply against our neck.

They walked slowly, silently. The dying sunlight lifted

traces of red from Hally's black hair and made her tan skin seem even darker. We'd seen people with her coloring before—not often, but often enough to not make it overly strange. But we'd never seen anyone with quite her shape of face, her features. Not outside of pictures, anyway, and hardly even then. We'd never seen anyone act like she'd acted toward Will and Robby, either.

She was half-blood. Half-foreign, even if she herself had been born in the Americas. Was that the reason for her strangeness? Foreigners weren't allowed into the country anymore—hadn't been for ages—and all the war refugees who'd come long ago were now dead. Most foreign blood still existing in the country was diluted. But there were groups, people said. There were immigrants who'd refused to integrate, preserving their bloodlines, their *otherness*, when they should have embraced the safety the Americas offered from the destruction wreaked by the hybrids overseas.

Had one of Hally's parents come from a community like that?

"I wonder," Hally said, then fell quiet.

Addie didn't press. She was too wrapped up in her own thoughts. But I was listening, and I waited for Hally to continue.

"I wonder," she said again after a moment. "I wonder who's going to be dominant when they settle, Robby or Will."

"Hmm?" Addie said. "Oh, Robby, I think. He's starting to control things more."

"It's not always who you think it is," Hally said, lifting her eyes from the ground. The little white gems studding her glasses frames caught the yellow light and winked. "It's all science, isn't it? Brain connections and neuron strength and stuff set up before you're even born. You can't tell those things just by watching people."

Addie shrugged and looked away. "Yeah, I guess so."

She changed the subject, and they chatted about school and the latest movie until we reached Hally's neighborhood. There was a big black wrought-iron gate leading into it, and a skinny boy about our age stood beyond the bars.

He glanced up as we neared, but didn't say anything, and Hally rolled her eyes when she noticed him. They looked alike; he had her tan skin and dark curls and brown eyes. We'd heard about Hally's older brother, but we'd never seen him before. Addie stopped walking a good dozen yards from the gate, so we didn't really get a close look at him today, either.

"Bye," Hally said over her shoulder and smiled. Behind her, the boy finished inputting something into a keypad and the gate yawned open. "I'll see you tomorrow."

Addie waved. "Yeah, tomorrow."

We waited until Hally and her brother were almost out of sight before turning and heading homeward, this time alone. But not really alone. Addie and I are never alone.

<*What was that all about?*> Addie kicked our feet as she walked. <*Inviting herself babysitting with us? We hardly know her.*>

<*I told you. Maybe she's lonely*> I said. <*Maybe she wants to be friends.*>

<*All of a sudden? After three years?*>

<*Why not?*>

Addie hesitated. <*Well, we can't be. You know that, Eva. I can't be friends with her. Not at school.*>

Not where people might see.

<*And what was that with Robby and Will?*> Addie's irritation mounted inside us. She let a car rattle by, then darted across the street. <*Asking Robby about Will? Where was she going with that? They're about to settle. Confuse them, and they might get delayed. They might—*> She didn't complete her sentence, but she didn't need to.

They might turn out like us.

For years, our parents had struggled to discover why their daughters weren't settling like normal. They blamed everyone from our preschool teacher (too unstructured) to our doctors (why was nothing working?) to our friends (had they settled late? Were they encouraging this strange behavior?). In the darkest hours of the night, they fired blame at each other and themselves.

But worse than the blame was the fear—the fear that if we didn't settle, there would come the day when we weren't allowed home from the hospital. We'd grown up with the threat of it ringing in our ears, dreading the deadline of our tenth birthday.

Our parents had begged. We'd heard them through hospital doors, pleading for more time, just a little more time: *It will happen. It's already working. It'll happen soon—please!*

I don't know what else happened behind those doors. I don't know what convinced those doctors and officials in the end, but our mother and father emerged from that room exhausted and white.

And they told us we had a little more time.

Two years later, I was declared gone.

Our shadow was long now, our legs heavy. Strands of our hair gleamed golden in the wan light, and Addie gathered them all into a loose ponytail, holding it off our neck in the unrelenting heat.

<*Let's watch a movie tonight*> I said, fusing a smile to my voice. <*We don't have much homework.*>

<*Yeah, okay*> Addie said.

<*Don't worry about Will and Robby. They'll be fine. Lyle was fine, wasn't he?*>

<*Yeah*> she said. <*Yeah, I know.*>

Neither of us mentioned all the ways in which Lyle wasn't fine. The days when he didn't want to do anything but lie half-awake in bed. The hours each week he spent hooked up to the dialysis machine, his blood cycling out of his body before being injected back in.

Lyle was sick, but he wasn't hybrid sick, and that made all the difference.

We walked in silence, inner and outer. I felt the dark, brooding mists of Addie's thoughts drifting against my own. Sometimes, if I concentrated hard enough, I fancied I could almost grasp what she was thinking about. But not today.

In a way, I was glad. It meant she couldn't grasp what I was thinking about, either.

She couldn't know I was dreading, dreading, dreading the

day Will and Robby *did* settle. The day we'd go to babysit and find just one little boy smiling up at us.

Lupside, where we'd lived for the last three years, was known for absolutely nothing. Whenever anyone wanted to do anything that couldn't be taken care of at the strip mall or the smattering of grocery stores, they went to the nearby city of Bessimir.

Bessimir was known for exactly one thing, and that was the history museum.

Addie laughed quietly with the girl next to us as our class stood sweating outside the museum doors. Summer hadn't even started its true battle against spring, but boys were already complaining about their mandatory long pants while girls' skirt hems climbed along with the thermostat.

"Listen up," Ms. Stimp shouted, which got about half the class to actually shut up and pay attention. For anyone who'd grown up around this area, visiting Bessimir's history museum was as much a part of life as going to the pool in the summer or to the theater for the monthly movie release. The building, officially named the Brian Doulanger History of the Americas Museum after some rich old man who'd first donated money for its construction, was almost universally referred to as "the museum," as if there were no others in the world. In two years, Addie and I had gone twice with two different history classes, and each visit had left us sick to our stomach.

Already, I could feel a stiffness in our muscles, a strain in Addie's smile as the teacher handed out our student passes.

Because no matter what it was called, Bessimir's history museum was interested in only one thing, and that was the tale of the Americas' century-and-a-half-long battle against the hybrids.

The blast of air-conditioning as we entered the building made Addie shiver and raised goose bumps on our skin but didn't ease the knot in our gut. Three stories tall, the museum erupted into a grand, open foyer just beyond the ticket counter, the two upper floors visible if one tilted one's head back and stared upward. Addie had tried it the first time we'd entered. We'd been thirteen years old, and the sight of it had crushed us with the weight of all that history, all the battles and wars and hatred.

No one looked up now. The others because they were bored. Addie because we never again wanted to see.

Addie's friend had abandoned her for someone who could still laugh. Addie should have gone after her, should have forced a smile and a joke and complained along with everyone else about having to come to the museum *yet again*, but she didn't. She just drifted to the back of the group so we didn't have to hear the guide begin our tour.

I said nothing, as if by being silent I could pretend I didn't exist. As if Addie could pretend, for an hour, that I wasn't there, that the hybrid enemies the guide kept talking about as we entered the Hall of Revolutionaries weren't the same as us.

A hand closed around our shoulder. Addie whirled to fling it off, then flinched as she realized what she'd done.

"Sorry, sorry—" Hally put her hands up in the air, fingers

spread, in peace. "Didn't mean to scare you." She gave us a tentative smile. We only had this one class with her, so it hadn't been difficult for Addie to avoid her since last night.

"You surprised me," Addie said, shoving our hair away from our face. "That's all."

The rest of the class was leaving us behind, but when Addie moved to catch up, Hally touched our shoulder again. She snatched her hand back when Addie spun around, but asked quickly, "Are you all right?"

A flush of heat shot through us. "Yes, of course," Addie said.

We stood silently in that hall a moment longer, flanked by portraits of all the greatest heroes of the Revolution, the founders of our country. These men had been dead for nearly 150 years, but they still stared out at Addie and me with that fire in their eyes, that accusation, that hatred that had burned in every non-hybrid soul all through those first terrible warring years, when the edict of the day was the extermination of all those who had once been in power—all the hybrid men, women, and children.

They said that zest had died over the decades, as the country grew lax and trusting, forgetting the past. Hybrid children were permitted to grow old. Immigrants were allowed to step foot on American soil again, to move into our land and call it their own.

The attempted foreign invasion at the beginning of the twentieth century, during the start of the Great Wars, had put a stop to that. Suddenly, the old flame burned brighter than ever, along with the new vow to never forget—never, ever forget again.

Hally must have seen our gaze flicker toward the oil paintings. She grinned, her dimples showing, and said, "Can you imagine if guys still went around wearing those stupid hats? God, I'd never get done making fun of my brother."

Addie managed a thin-lipped smile. In seventh grade, when we'd had to write an essay on the men framed in these paintings, she'd tried to convince the teacher to let her write about the depictions from an artistic viewpoint instead. It hadn't worked. "We should get back to the group."

No one noticed as Addie and Hally slipped into place at the edge of our class. They'd already made it to the room I hated most of all, and Addie kept our eyes on our hands, our shoes—anywhere but on the pictures hanging around us. But I could still remember them from last year, when our class had studied early American history and we'd spent the entire trip in this section of the museum instead of just passing through, as we were now.

There aren't a lot of photographs salvaged from back then, of course. But the reconstructionist artists had spared no detail, no grimace of pain or patch of peeling, sunburned skin. And the photos that did exist hung heavily on the walls. Their grainy black-and-white quality didn't hide the misery of the fields. The pain of the workers, little more than slaves, who were all our ancestors. Immigrants from the Old World who'd suffered back there for so many thousands of years before being shipped across a turbulent ocean to suffer anew in another land. Until the Revolution, when the hybrids finally fell.

The room was small, with only one entrance and exit. The crush of the other students made Addie hold our breath. Our heart thumped against our ribs. Everywhere she turned, we bumped into more bodies, all moving, some shoving each other back and forth, some laughing, the teacher scolding, threatening to start taking down names if they didn't show a little more respect.

Addie shouldered our way through the room, for once not caring what the others might think. We were one of the first to get through the door. And we were going so fast, lurching past the others, that we were the first to hit the water.

THREE

Addie slammed to a halt. The girl behind us couldn't stop her momentum quite as well and plowed into us. We crashed forward onto the ground, our skirt and part of our blouse immediately getting soaked in the stream of water gushing through the room. *The water?*—

"What the *hell*?" someone said as Addie scrambled back onto our feet, our knees and elbow aching from taking the brunt of our fall.

The water barely reached our ankles now, but there was no saving our shirt, though Addie hurried to wring it out. No one was paying attention anyway; everyone stared openmouthed at the flooded exhibit hall. This was one of the largest rooms in the museum, filled with artifacts from Revolutionary times encased under glass and period paintings on the walls. Now it was also filled with several inches of murky water.

The guide whipped out a walkie-talkie and sputtered something. Ms. Stimp tried her best to usher everyone back into the room we'd just left, which was connected by a low step and remained dry—for now. Wherever the water was coming from, it was getting worse, spilling over the ground, soaking people's socks—dirty water that would surely stain the white walls.

The lights flickered. People screamed—some sounding genuinely terrified, others with almost a laugh in it, like this was more excitement than they could have hoped for.

"It's those pipes," the guide growled under her breath, stalking past us. Her cheeks were flushed, her eyes so bright they seemed almost wild. "How many times have we said to get those pipes fixed?" She clipped her walkie-talkie back to her skirt, then raised her voice and said, "Please, if everyone would just come back around through this room—"

The lights went out, cloaking everything in darkness. This time, they didn't come back on. But something else did—the sprinklers. And with them, the earsplitting blare of an alarm. Addie clapped our hands over our ears as water sprayed down into our hair and ran over our face. Somewhere in the museum, something had caught on fire.

It took nearly fifteen minutes to get everyone back onto the bus. There weren't too many other visitors at the museum on a hot Friday afternoon, but enough to form a sizable crowd as everyone poured out of the museum doors, confused and still clutching ticket stubs in their hands, mothers herding small children before them as they went, men with dark stains on their pant legs where they'd dragged in the water. Some of them were soaked through. All of them were complaining or demanding answers or refunds or just staring dumbly at the museum.

"Electrical fire," I heard a woman say as Addie made our way back to the bus. "We could have all gotten electrocuted!"

By the time we got back to the school, our blouse was still damp and no longer completely white, but talk had turned from the museum flood to the end-of-year dance, still more than a month away. And when Ms. Stimp, frazzled and irritated, turned off the lights in the classroom and popped in a video, a quarter of our class went surreptitiously to sleep, even though we were supposed to be taking notes.

<I hope there's irreparable damage> I said as Addie stared blankly at the screen. Bessimir was proud of so many things in that museum—those paintings; sabers and revolvers salvaged from the Revolution; an authentic war poster from the beginning of the Great Wars, dated the year of the first attack on American soil. It urged citizens to report all suspicions of hybrid activity. Teachers didn't mention it in class, but I could imagine the finger-pointing that must have occurred. People back then couldn't have been so different from people today. *<I hope the foundation collapses. I hope the whole building comes crashing down.>*

<Don't be stupid> Addie said. *<There was all of two inches of water. It'll be fixed in a week.>*

<There was fire. And I said I hope.*>*

Addie sighed, resting our chin in one hand and doodling the girl in front of us—who slept with her mouth half-open—with the other. It wasn't like we needed to actually watch the movie to fill out a page or two of notes. We'd covered the Great Wars of the twentieth century so many times we could recite the major battles, rattle off the casualty counts, quote the speeches our president had given as we'd fought off the attempts at invasion. Eventually, we'd proven too strong for them, of course, and their attention had turned back to their own continents, chaotic and ravished. That was what war did. What hybrids did. What they were doing, even now.

<*Yeah*> Addie said finally. <*Me too.*>

On television, an airplane dropped bombs on an indistinct city. The boy sitting beside us yawned, his eyes drooping shut. We didn't have much footage of the latter part of the Wars, since they'd happened so far away, but what we did have was shown over and over again until I wanted to scream. I could only imagine what we'd be subjected to if there had been such a thing as TV news during the invasions a few decades earlier.

<*Eva?*> Addie said.

I shoved my emotions away from Addie, shielding her from my frustration. <*I'm fine*> I said. <*I'm fine.*>

We watched as fire swept across the chaos-stricken city. Officially, the last Great War had ended when Addie and I were a baby, but the hybrids occupying the rest of the world had never stopped fighting among themselves. How could they? Addie and I had enough arguments, and we didn't even share control. How could a society founded on two souls in each body ever be at peace? The individuals making up the country weren't even at peace with themselves, and that led to all sorts of problems—*constant frustration, lashing out at others, and, for the weaker-minded, eventual insanity.* I could see the bleak prognosis on the pamphlets at the doctors' offices, printed in boldface.

So I understood why the Revolutionary leaders had founded the Americas as a hybrid-free country, why they'd worked so hard to eradicate the existing hybrids of the time, so they could start clean and fresh and untainted. I could even understand, in the most rational parts of me, why people like Addie and me couldn't, on the whole, be allowed free rein. But understanding a thing and accepting it are so very different things.

Addie dashed off some halfhearted notes as the movie came to a close and the bell rang. Normally I would help her, adding the facts I remembered to hers, but I was hardly in the mood now. We were out the door before our paper reached the front of the room.

We'd only made it a few steps down the hall when a second person shot out of the classroom and called Addie's name.

"What is it, Hally?" Addie said, holding back a sigh.

To my surprise, Hally's smile slipped a notch, but only for a moment. Enough, though, for me to say *<Addie, don't snap at her.>*

<She keeps following us around> Addie said. *<First babysitting, then at the museum. I—>*

"Want to come over for dinner?" Hally said.

Addie stared. The hall was filling with people, but neither she nor Hally moved from their spots in the middle of the corridor.

"My parents are going out," Hally added after a moment. Her thick hair still wasn't completely dry, and she wrapped a finger around a curl. "It's just going to be my brother and me." She raised her eyebrows, her smile returning to full force. "I'd rather avoid eating alone with him."

<*Addie*> I said. <*Stop staring. Say something.*>

"Oh," Addie said. "Oh, well—I—I can't."

I'd never heard Addie turn down an invitation to go to someone's house before—not without a very good reason. Many of the students at our school had attended classes together since primary; entering late had meant hitting a lot of walls when trying to make friends. Everyone already had a place, a group, a seat at the lunch table, and Addie had learned to grab on to what fingerholds she could. But Hally Mullan just plain being Hally Mullan was, I guess, enough reason to decline any offer of friendship.

"It's my shirt," Addie said, looking down at the stain in the white fabric. "I've got to get home before my parents and wash it. If they—" If they see it, they'll ask what happened. And where. And then that look will fall over their eyes, the one that snuck onto their faces every time they saw another news report about a hybrid being discovered somewhere, or a reminder to watch your neighbors, to be forever on the lookout for the hidden enemy. It made our gut wrench. Made us want to leave the room.

"You can wash it at my house if you don't want your parents to see," Hally said. Her voice was softer now, less brilliant in its cheerfulness, but gentler. "I've got stuff you could wear while it dries, no problem. You could change back before you leave, and no one would ever know."

Addie hesitated. Chances were, our mom was getting ready to drive home. We'd certainly get back before she did, but no way would our shirt be dry before then, and I told Addie so.

<I could lie> Addie said. *<I could say I fell and got dirt on it. I could—>*

<Why not just go?> I said.

<You know why.>

Hally took a step toward us. We were almost the same height, mirroring each other—or inverting each other. Hally's dark, almost black hair to our dirty blond. Her olive skin to our pale, freckled arms. "Addie? Is something wrong?"

Again that question. Are you okay? Is something wrong?

"No," Addie said. "No, nothing."

"Then you can come?" Hally said.

<Come on, Addie> I said. *<Go. No one will know. Nobody even talks to her. What can it hurt?>*

I felt her waver and pushed harder. Addie might not have appreciated this girl who questioned Robby about Will and didn't flinch from talking about settling, but I did. If nothing else, she intrigued me. *<It's Friday. Nobody's going to be home for dinner anyway.>*

Addie chewed at our bottom lip, then must have realized what she was doing and said quickly, "Well . . . all right."

FOUR

Addie had to run to the pay phone to tell Mom we wouldn't be home for dinner, so by the time we reached the arranged meeting spot, most of the other students had gone. Hally stood alone by the school doors. She didn't notice us until we were right next to her, and then she jumped as if we'd startled her from some quiet reverie.

"You ready?" she asked as soon as she found her voice.

Addie nodded.

"Great. Come on, then."

The solemn contemplation of a moment ago disappeared. She was all bubbles and energy. Addie hardly got a word in edgewise as Hally blabbered on about how glad she was that it was finally Friday, how nice it was that it was almost summer break, how tiring the first year of high school had been.

Yes, said Addie. Yes, except for the mosquitoes and the humidity. Yes, but it had been fun, hadn't it?

Neither she nor Hally brought up the ruined trip to the history museum.

We'd expected Hally's house to be larger than it was,

especially after all the pomp and circumstance of the wrought-iron gate guarding the neighborhood. It was bigger than ours, of course, but smaller than those of the other girls we'd visited after school. Whatever its size, the place was impressive, all worn brick and black shutters and a slender, pink-flowered tree in the front yard. The lawn was manicured and the door looked recently painted. Addie peeked inside a window while Hally rummaged for her keys. The dining-room table inside shone a deep mahogany. The Mullan family certainly didn't need scholarship money to send Hally and her brother to our school.

"Devon?" Hally called, pushing the door open. No one answered, and she rolled her eyes at Addie. "I don't know why I bother. He never answers anyway."

I remembered the boy we'd seen at the gate yesterday, standing behind the black bars. Since he was two grades higher, Devon wasn't as common a topic of gossip as Hally was, but our teachers mentioned him from time to time, and we knew he'd skipped a grade.

Hally slipped off her shoes, so Addie followed suit, undoing the laces and setting our oxfords side by side on the welcome mat. By the time we looked up again, Hally was in the kitchen with the refrigerator door open.

"Soda? Tea? Orange juice?" she called.

"Soda's fine," Addie said.

The kitchen was beautiful, with polished dark wood cabinets and granite countertops. A small, lushly colored statuette stood in one corner, a half-burned candle serving sentinel on either side. A tiny clementine lay at the figurine's feet.

Addie stared, and I was too curious myself to remind her not to. Hally's looks were one thing—she couldn't help those. But to broadcast the family's foreignness like this . . .

"I was thinking we'd get takeout," Hally said. Addie turned just in time to catch the soda can she tossed at us. It was so cold we almost dropped it. "Unless you're a brilliant cook or something."

"I'm all right," Addie said.

<Liar. We're terrible.>

"But takeout sounds good," she added.

Hally nodded without looking at us. She'd turned her head a little, her eyes focused on some point in the distance. Addie snuck another glance at the small altar. Was it Hally's mother or father who'd so carefully arranged the candles and the statuette?

"Devon?" Hally called again. But there was still no answer. I thought I saw her mouth tighten.

"I've never actually met your brother before," Addie said, looking away from the altar as Hally's attention returned to us.

"No?" Hally said. "No, I guess not. You'll meet him tonight, then. He really ought to be home. . . . I don't know why he'd be late."

Addie set her soda on the counter and pulled at the bottom of our shirt. "Well, while he's not here, could I . . ."

"Oh, right," Hally said. She blinked and brightened, all smiles again. "Come on. You can choose something from my room. That stain shouldn't be too hard to wash out."

Addie followed her up the stairs, which were covered with a rich, cream-colored carpet that extended to the upstairs hallway. Our socks, I realized, had been soaked in that water, too. They seemed too dirty for this house, this whiteness. Addie checked behind us to make sure we weren't leaving marks on the carpet. Hally didn't seem to care at all. She bounded on ahead, toward what must have been her room at the end of the hall, leaving Addie trailing behind.

<*Look*> I said, whispering though it wasn't like anyone else could hear. <*They've got a computer.*>

We could see it in one of the rooms on the way to Hally's, a large, complicated-looking thing sprawled over a desk. We'd used computers once or twice at school, and Dad had mentioned, a long, long time ago, getting one once they got cheaper, but then we hadn't settled and Lyle had gotten sick and there was no more talk of computers.

Addie paused to stare at it and, by extension, the rest of the room. A bedroom, I realized. A boy's room with an unmade bed and . . . screwdrivers on the desk. Even more strangely, there was a gutted computer in the far corner—at least I thought it was a computer. I'd never seen one with all the wires hanging out, bright silver parts naked and bared. This was Devon's room. It had to be, unless there was another member of the Mullan family I'd never heard about. But what sixteen-year-old boy had computers in his room?

"Addie?" Hally called, and Addie hurried away.

Hally's room was ten times messier than her brother's, but she didn't seem the least bit embarrassed as she invited us inside and closed the door. She threw open her closet and waved a hand at the clothes hanging inside. "Pick whatever you want. I think we're about the same size."

Her closet was full of things Addie would never wear. Things that said *Look at me*—too-big tops that hung off one shoulder, bright colors and flashy patterns and jewelry that might have gone well with Hally's black-framed glasses and dark curly hair but would have looked like dress-up clothes on us. Addie looked for something plain as Hally perched herself on the edge of her bed, but Hally didn't seem to own such a thing.

"Can I just, I don't know . . . wear your spare uniform blouse or something?" Addie said, turning.

That was when I noticed something was wrong.

Hally looked up at us from her bed, but there was something in her eyes, something dark and solemn in her stare that made me stop, made me say <*Addie. Addie*> without hardly knowing why.

And then slowly, so slowly it was like something deliberate, there was a *shift* in Hally's face. That was the only way I could put it. Something minuscule, something no one would have caught if they weren't staring straight at her as Addie and I were staring now, something no one would have noticed—would have even *thought* to notice—if they weren't—

Addie took a step toward the door.

A shift. A change. Like how Robby changed to Will.

But that was impossible.

Hally stood. Her hair was neat and tidy under her blue

headband. The tiny white rhinestones set into her glasses twinkled in the lamplight. She didn't smile, didn't tilt her head and say, *What are you doing, Addie?*

Instead, she said, "We just want to talk with you." There was something sad in her eyes.

<*We?*> I echoed.

"You and Devon?" Addie said.

"No," Hally said. "Me and Hally."

A shudder passed through our body, so out of either Addie's or my control it might have been a shared reaction. Another step away from the closet.

Our heart thrummed—not fast, just hard, so hard.

Beat.

Beat.

"What?"

The girl standing in front of us smiled, a twitch of the mouth that never reached her eyes. "I'm sorry," she said. "Let's start over. My name's Lissa, and Hally and I want to talk to you."

Addie ran for the door, so fast our shoulder slammed into the wood. Pain shot through our arm. She ignored it, grabbing at the doorknob with both hands.

It refused to turn. Just rattled and shook. There was a keyhole right above the knob but the key was gone.

Something indescribable was rising inside me, something huge and suffocating and I couldn't think.

"Hally," Addie said. "This isn't funny."

"I'm not Hally," the girl said.

Only one of our hands grabbed the doorknob now. Addie pressed our back against the door, our shoulder blades aching against the wood. Words squeezed from our throat. "You *are*. You're settled. You're—"

"I'm Lissa."

"No," Addie said.

"Please." The girl reached for our arm, but Addie jerked away. "Please, Addie. Listen to us."

The room was growing hot and stuffy and way too small. This wasn't possible. This was *wrong*. Someone should have reported her. This couldn't be real. But it *was*. I'd seen it. I'd seen her change. I'd seen the shift. And oh, oh, but didn't it make sense? Didn't it make sense for Hally to be—

"*You*," Addie insisted. "*You*, not *us*."

"*Us*," she said. "Me and Hally. *Us*."

"No—" Addie twisted around again. The doorknob rattled so hard in our hands it seemed ready to jerk right off the door. Lissa started tugging at us, trying to make Addie face her.

"Addie," Lissa said. "Please. Listen to me—"

But Addie wouldn't. Wouldn't stay still, wouldn't take our hands from the doorknob. And I was just there, stunned, unable to believe, until Hally—Lissa—Hally finally gave up pulling at our hands and shouted, "Eva—Eva, make her listen!"

The world shattered at the sound of her voice, the name that leaped from her tongue.

Eva.

Mine. My name.

I hadn't heard it aloud in three years.

Addie locked eyes with the girl staring at us. Everything was too clear, too sharp. The headband slipping from her hair. Her perfect, glossed nails catching the overhead light. The furrows between her eyebrows. The freckle by her nose.

"How . . . ?" Addie said.

"Devon found it," Lissa said. Her voice was soft now. "He got into the school records. They keep track of everything if you haven't settled by first grade. Your oldest files list both names."

They did? Yes, they must have. Back in the first years of elementary school, when Addie and I were six, seven, eight, our report cards had come home with two names printed on the top: *Addie, Eva Tamsyn*. In later years, *Eva* had been left out.

I hadn't realized my name had survived the four-hour drive, the transfer of schools.

"Addie?" Lissa said. And then, after a long, shuddery hesitation, "Eva?"

"*Don't.*" The word exploded from our chest, burned up our throat, and hit the air with a crackle of lightning. "Don't. Don't say it." A pain slashed at our heart. Whose pain? "My name's Addie. Just Addie."

"*Your* name," Lissa said. "But it's not just you. There's—"

"Stop," Addie cried. "You can't do this. *You can't talk like this.*"

Our breaths shortened, our vision blurring. Our hands

squeezed into fists, so tight our nails bit crescent moons into our palms.

"This is the way it's supposed to be," Addie said. "It *is* just me. I'm Addie. I settled. It's okay now. I'm normal now. I—"

But Lissa's eyes were suddenly blazing, her cheeks flushed. "How can you say that, Addie? How can you say that when Eva's still there?"

Addie started to cry. Tears ran into our mouth, salty, warm, metallic.

<*Shh*> I whispered. Everything spun in confusion. <*Shh, Addie. Please don't cry. Please.*>

"What about Eva?" Lissa's voice was shrill. "What about *Eva*?"

Misery. Misery and pain and guilt. None of them mine. Addie's emotions sliced into me. No matter what happened, what we said or did to each other, Addie and I were still two parts of a whole. Closer than close. Tighter than tight. Her misery was mine. <*Don't listen to her, Addie*> I said. <*She doesn't know what she's saying.*>

But Addie kept crying and Lissa kept shouting and the room packed to the brim with tears and anger and guilt and fear.

Then the world gave out.

Someone must have opened the door, because all of a sudden we were falling—falling backward, and I was screaming for Addie to catch us before we slammed onto the ground, and she was flailing, and I was bracing for the both of us, bracing for the pain, because that was all I could do, until the falling stopped. The falling stopped, and we were staring up, up at the ceiling, and Addie was still crying in her—our—fear, and because she was crying, I was crying, and everything was secondary to our tears. But someone had caught us. His arms were around our body, holding us up.

"What the *hell* did you do?" he said.

FIVE

<*Shh, Addie*> I kept saying. <*Shh, shh. It's okay. It's gonna be okay.*>

We weren't so much crying as just taking small, sharp breaths now. Addie wouldn't—couldn't—speak to me. But her presence pressed against mine, hot and limp with tears.

<*Shh*> I said. <*Shh . . . Shh . . .*>

"I didn't mean to," someone was saying. "She wouldn't listen to me. I didn't know what to do. You wouldn't have done any better, Ryan, don't tell me you would've—you weren't even home, and you said you were going to be—"

"I would've done better than *this*."

I heard them speaking, but Addie had closed our eyes, and our pain overrode everything else in the world.

<*Addie, say something. Say something, please.*>

"Addie? Addie, please stop crying. I'm sorry. Really, I am." It was Hally. Or was it Lissa? It didn't matter. All that mattered was Addie. Addie, who finally took one long, shaky breath and rubbed away the last of her tears. "Are you okay?"

Addie said nothing, just stared at the ground, hiccupping.

I felt the heat of her rising embarrassment, of her horror for having broken down like this in front of someone, for having reacted the way she had.

<It's all right> I said over and over again. *<Don't worry. Don't think about it. It's all right.>*

Finally, Addie looked at the girl crouched beside us, who smiled shakily.

"Hally?" Our voice was hoarse.

The girl's forehead wrinkled. She hesitated, then shook her head once.

"No," she said softly. "No, I'm Lissa."

<I don't think she's lying, Addie> I said. But she didn't need me to tell her that.

"And Hally?" Addie whispered.

"Here, too," Lissa said. "Hally walked home with you. Hally stopped you after class." She smiled a sad, crooked smile. "She's better at those kinds of things. I wanted her to tell you, but she said I should do it. She was wrong, obviously."

Our mouth kept opening and closing, but nothing came out. This was out of—of a dream. What kind of dream? A nightmare? Or . . .

"That can't—" Addie shook our head. "That can't happen."

"It can," said Hally's brother. He stood a couple feet away, still dressed in his school slacks and shirt, tie not even undone. I barely remembered jerking away from his arms, barely remembered seeing him at all, just the screwdriver in his hand and the doorknob gleaming on the floor. He'd dismantled it. "We—" *We*, I thought wondrously. Did he mean him and Hally? Or him and Hally and Lissa? Or him and his sisters and some other boy also inside him, some other being, some other soul? Looking at him, seeing the way he watched us, I knew it was the last. "We know Eva's still there," he said. "And we can teach her how to move again."

Addie stiffened. I trembled, a ghost quivering in her own skin. Our body didn't move at all.

"Do you want to know how?" the boy said.

"Now *you're* scaring her, Devon," Lissa said. Devon. Right, her brother's name was Devon. But I was sure she'd used a different name a few minutes before.

"That's illegal," Addie said. "You can't. They'll come; if they find out—"

"They won't find out," Devon said.

The public service announcements. The videos we watched every year on Independence Day, depicting the chaos that had swept across Europe and Asia. The president's speeches. All those museum trips.

"I have to go," Addie said. She stood so suddenly, Lissa remained crouching, only her eyes moving up with us.

"I have to go," Addie repeated.

<Addie—>

She shook our head. "I have to leave."

"Wait." Lissa jumped to her feet.

Our hands flew up, palms outward, warding her off. "Bye, Hally—Lissa—*Hally*. I'm sorry, but I'm going home now, okay? I have to go home." She backed up, stumbling all the way to the end of the hall. Lissa started forward, but Devon grabbed her shoulder.

"Devon—" Lissa said.

He shook his head and turned to us. "Don't tell anyone." His eyebrows lowered. "Promise it. Swear it."

Our throat was dry.

"*Swear it,*" Devon said.

<*Addie*> I said. <*Addie, don't leave. Please.*>

But Addie just swallowed and nodded.

"I promise," she whispered. She twisted around and darted down the stairs.

She ran the whole way home.

"Addie? Is that you?" Mom called when we opened the front door. Addie didn't reply, and after a moment, Mom stuck her head out from the kitchen. "I thought you were eating at a friend's house?"

Addie shrugged. She cleaned our shoes on the welcome mat, the rhythm of the action grinding the bristles flat.

"Is something wrong?" Mom said, wiping her hands on a dish towel as she walked over.

"No," Addie said. "Nothing. Why aren't you and Lyle at the hospital yet?"

Lyle wandered in from the kitchen, too, and we automatically looked him over, checking his skinny arms and legs for bruising. We were always terrified each bruise would develop into something worse. That was the way it always seemed to be with Lyle—food poisoning that had developed into kidney trouble, which had resulted in kidney failure. He was pale, as always, but otherwise seemed okay.

"It's not even five yet, Addie," he said, throwing himself on the floor and pulling on his shoes. "We were watching TV. Did you see the news?" He looked up, his face a mix of anxiety and excitement, eagerness and fear. "The museum caught on fire! And flooded, too! They said everybody could have gotten all electrocuted, like *zzzzz*—" He tensed and jerked back and forth, miming the throes of someone being zapped by electricity. Addie flinched. "They said *hybrids* did it. Only they haven't caught them yet—"

"Lyle." Mom gave him a look. "Don't be morbid."

We'd gone all cold.

"What's *morbid* mean?" Lyle said.

Mom looked like she was about to explain, but then she caught sight of our face. "Addie, are you all right?" She frowned. "What happened to your shirt?"

"I'm fine," Addie said, fending off her touch. "I—I just realized I've got a lot of homework tonight." She avoided the second question altogether. We'd been so worried about our shirt before. Now it hardly seemed to matter.

Hybrids? Hybrids were responsible for the destruction at the museum?

Mom raised an eyebrow. "On a Friday?"

"Yeah," Addie said. She didn't seem to realize what she was saying. We both looked at Mom, but I didn't think Addie saw a thing. "I—I'm going to go upstairs now."

"There are leftovers in the fridge," Mom called after us.

"Dad will be home around—"

Addie shut our door and fell into bed, kicking off our shoes and burying our head in our arms.

<*Oh, God*> she whispered, and it was almost a plea.

If hybrids were being blamed for the flood and fire at the history museum, and if said hybrids hadn't been caught yet, then . . . I couldn't even imagine the frenzy that would sweep the city. It would reach us here in the outskirts for sure. Everyone would be on alert, nerves raw, quick to accuse. That was the thing about hybrids. You couldn't tell just by looking at them.

The Mullans would be the first to have fingers jabbed in their direction, with their foreign blood and strange ways. No one with a shred of sense would have anything to do with them now.

But still, but *still*.

I could see Hally's brother standing in the hallway, could remember his eyes on us, remember every word that had come out of his mouth. He'd said I could move again. He'd said they could *teach* me.

What if he and his sister *were* taken away? I might spend every burning second of the rest of my life thinking back on this day, ruing the things I did not say, the action I did not take, the chance I failed to seize.

<*We're going back*> I said quietly.

Addie didn't even reply. We lay there, our face pressed into the crook of our elbow.

<*We're going back, Addie*> I said.

Devon's words were red-hot coals inside me, searing away three years of tenuous acceptance. The fire screamed to get out, to escape from the throat, the skin, the eyes that were mine as much as Addie's. But it couldn't.

<*Can you even hear what you're saying?*> Addie demanded.

Normally, I wouldn't have responded. I'd learned not to speak whenever I felt like this. To stay quiet and make myself pretend I didn't care. It was the only way I could keep from going insane, to not die from the want—the *need*—to move my own limbs. I couldn't cry. I couldn't scream. I could only be quiet and let myself go numb. Then, at least, I wouldn't have to feel anymore, wouldn't have to endlessly crave what I could never have.

But not today. I couldn't stay quiet today.

<*Yes*> I said. <*I hear it, and you hear it. But no one else does, do they?*>

Addie shifted so we faced the wall. <*Eva, can . . . Can you imagine what would happen to us if anyone found out?*>

<*I know*> I said. <*I know, but—*>

<*We're safe*> Addie said. <*For the first time since we were six years old, we're safe, and you want to throw that away?*>

My voice had turned pleading, but I was too desperate to care. <*This could be my only chance, Addie. I have to risk it—*>

<*It's not just your risk*> Addie said.

<You don't understand, Addie> I said. *<You can't. You never will.>*

Our eyes squeezed shut. *<I can't go back>* Addie said. *<I just can't. I can't.>*

<But I have to!>

<Well, you don't really have a choice, do you?> Addie said.

It was as if she'd sliced the tendons connecting us, leaving me raw and reeling. For a long, long moment, I couldn't find any words.

<Fine> I finally spat. *<Whatever you want. Obviously I don't matter at all.>*

Once, a few months after our thirteenth birthday, I disappeared.

Only for five or six hours, though it had seemed timeless to me. This was the year Lyle fell sick. The year we found out his kidneys were failing him, that our little brother might never grow up.

Suddenly, we were right back in those hospital hallways. Except this time, Addie and I weren't the patient—Lyle was. And as terrible as the former had been, the latter managed to be ten times worse. The doctors were all different, the tests different, the way they treated him different. But our parents were just as wild with worry, and Lyle, sitting on the examination table, just as pale and silent as we'd been.

One night, he'd whispered a question in our ear as Addie sat at the edge of his bed, reaching to turn off his lamp.

If he died, did that mean he'd be with Nathaniel again?

Addie had to fight past the stopper in our throat before she could breathe, let alone answer. As was customary, no one had spoken of Nathaniel since he'd faded away three years prior. *You're not going to die*, she'd said.

But if— Lyle had said before she cut him off.

You're not *going to die, Lyle. You're going to be fine. You're going to get better. You're going to be fine.*

She was short-tempered the rest of the night, and we'd argued over stupid things that had escalated until she shouted at me that our little brother was *sick*, couldn't I be *human* and lay off her, and I'd screamed back that she'd gotten through the death of one little brother just fine, hadn't she? Because I'd wanted to hurt her, as she'd hurt me.

And I was so scared, so scared.

So scared that just for a moment, I didn't want to be there beside Addie. I didn't want to know what tomorrow would bring, what Addie would say next, what would happen to our little brother, who'd asked us today if he'd ever see Nathaniel again.

I'd spent my whole life clutching on. To suddenly go the opposite direction—to curl up smaller and smaller, to sever my ties to our body and to Addie—it had been terrifying. But I'd been so angry, so hurt, and so scared—

And before I even fully realized what I was doing, it was done.

I spent those hours in a world of half-formed dreams while Addie panicked and screamed for me to come back. This she admitted to me more than a year later, but I'd felt her fear when I returned, cloudy-eyed and confused. I'd tasted her relief.

And I never disappeared again, no matter how hard we fought. No matter how scared I was.

But tonight, I got close. I flirted at the edge of it, too frightened to make the leap but angry enough to think I might.

I don't know who suffers more when Addie and I don't speak to each other. For me, staying silent all Friday night and Saturday made the time dreamlike. The world swam by like a movie, distant and intangible.

On the other hand, Addie had no one to remind her about the little things. She forgot to get a towel before getting in the shower. Our alarm clock blared us awake at seven o'clock on Saturday. She looked everywhere but the bookshelf for our hairbrush. I said nothing. Hadn't I always known she couldn't do without me?

I studied when she was too busy daydreaming or stressing to do anything but keep our eyes on the text and flip pages when I told her to. I put words on our tongue when she was too flustered to speak.

And so whenever we fell into sullen silences and refused to talk to each other, it was always Addie who broke down after a few hours—a day at most—and spoke first.

But Saturday melted into Sunday, and Addie stayed mute. I felt the emptiness beside me, the hard, blank nothingness that meant she was struggling to keep her emotions bound.

"Are you all right?" Mom asked when we came down

for breakfast Sunday morning. I felt her eyes on us as Addie opened the cabinet and grabbed a cereal bowl. "You've been acting funny all weekend."

Addie turned. Our cheeks tightened, stretching our lips into a smile. "Yeah, Mom. I'm fine. Kinda tired, I guess."

"You're not coming down with something, are you?" she asked, setting down her mug to feel our forehead. Addie pulled away.

"No, Mom. I'm fine. Really."

Mom nodded but didn't stop frowning. "Well, don't share cups with Lyle or anything, just in case. He—"

"I know," Addie said. "Mom, I live here, too. I know."

Our cereal stuck in our throat. Addie dumped the rest in the trash.

When she went back upstairs to brush our teeth, I stirred enough to stare at our reflection in the bathroom mirror. Addie was looking, too. There were our brown eyes, our short nose, our small mouth. Our wavy, dishwater-blond hair that we always said we'd do something with but never quite dared to. Then Addie shut our eyes, and I couldn't look any longer. She rinsed with our eyes still closed, felt for the washcloth, and pressed it against our face. Cool. Damp.

<*You can't. You can't want to go back, Eva.*>

Addie always gave in first. I waited for some kind of satisfaction, some kind of relish that once again I had won and she had lost. But all I felt was a great sigh of relief.

<*Think about what could happen*> she said. Our face stayed buried in the cloth. <*We could be normal now. We*

could just be like this.>

<I don't want to be like this> I said.

<Settling happens to everyone. It—>

<But we didn't settle> I said. *<Not completely. I'm still here, Addie.>*

We stood there in the stillness of that Sunday morning, a barefooted girl in a T-shirt and faded red pajama pants, water dripping down her chin, a terrible secret in her head.

<What if someone finds out, Eva? What if they take us away and—>

<Addie> I said. *<If it had been you—if it were you trapped inside. If you were the one who couldn't move, I'd go back. I'd go back in a second.>*

The washcloth was suddenly hot with tears.

SIX

All Monday morning, no one talked about anything but the Bessimir museum flood. Those of us in Ms. Stimp's history class suddenly became the most sought-after students in school, even among the upperclassmen, who usually paid attention to the freshmen only when they wanted us to get out of the way.

Addie hid from everyone's eager questions as best she could, but she couldn't avoid them all. Again and again, she had to describe the scene at the museum, estimate the amount of water there'd been, how our guide had reacted, had anyone screamed? Had she suspected it was an attack? Did she see anyone suspicious? Daniela Lowes said she had. What about the fire? Had anyone seen the fire? Oh, you're the one who fell, aren't you?

They always seemed disappointed by Addie's answers. Apparently, everyone else had gotten soaked up to their knees and seen shady men in the corners—or at least caught sight of a tower of flames.

Hybrids, ran the whisper in the corridors, the bathrooms,

the classrooms, while everyone pretended to pay attention to the teachers. *Hybrids.* Hidden, free hybrids. *Here.*

"They could be next door and you'd never know it," said the girl sitting in front of us in math, her voice full of wonder and excitement. Others weren't so bold. We found an upperclassman crying in the bathroom after second period, convinced that her father, who worked at Bessimir's city hall, was in terrible danger. Addie fled from her tears.

By third period, we were pale, almost shaking. Our hands gripped the sides of our seat to stay still, to keep ourself in our chair until lunch. We'd both forgotten our money that morning, but neither of us was in the mood to eat, so it didn't matter.

Finally, the bell rang. Addie all but ran into the hall. Shouting filled the air, bouncing off posters, banging into dented metal lockers. Addie jumped aside to avoid a boy's elbow as he yanked off his tie.

<*Where's Hally's room?*> I said. I almost didn't dare to ask, considering everything that had happened that morning, considering how tightly our fists were clenched. But I had to.

Addie looked down the hall. <*506*> she said softly.

We pushed our way there, gathering speed as the crowds thinned. Addie walked stiffly, planting one foot in front of the other with the deliberate force of someone who had to keep going forward, never stopping, for fear of never starting again if she did. Soon we were jogging, then running, through the halls.

We crashed into room 506 with such a clatter and a bang

that the teacher cried out and leaped to her feet. Addie threw out our arms, bracing against a desk to keep from falling.

"Sorry, sorry," she said. She bent to right a chair we'd knocked over. "I'm—I'm looking for Hally Mullan. Was she here?"

"She just left," the teacher said. Her hand was still pressed against her chest. "Really, is it such an emergency?"

Addie was already halfway out the door. "No, it's not. Sorry."

<Where now?> she said, and I felt a rush of gratitude. The school crawled with anti-hybrid sentiment. Our chest was so tight I felt each breath squeezing in and out of our lungs. Addie could have said, *She isn't there. I tried. Maybe tomorrow.* Instead she just asked, *Where now?*

<I don't know. The cafeteria, I guess. Then outside. Then maybe that café across the street.>

We scanned the faces in the lunchroom for Hally's black-rimmed glasses, searched for a glimpse of her long, dark hair among the café's coffee drinkers and newspaper readers. But she was nowhere to be found. By the time we left the café, lunch was more than half over.

<We'll wait by her classroom> I said. *<She has to go back there.>*

<We'll be late.>

<I don't care.>

Hally's teacher eyed us as we reentered her room. Addie slid into a seat by the door, crossing our arms on the desk. We waited. And waited.

<The bell's going to ring, Eva.>

<Just a little longer> I said. *<She'll come. You'll see.>*

But she didn't. The minutes passed, long and silent. Hally's teacher cleared her throat. We ignored her. Finally, Addie stood.

<Addie, let's just stay a few more—>

But Addie shook her head and gripped our skirt, wrinkling the cloth in our fists. Taking careful, measured steps, she walked out the door. *<She's not here, Eva. That teacher probably thinks we're crazy. And—>*

<Stop, Addie.>

<We're leaving> Addie said. *<I don't care what—>*

<No—no. Stop. Look—it's Hally.>

Addie froze. I felt her mind go white. Hally hadn't seen us yet. She stood by her open locker, fiddling with her books. Where had she been? How hadn't we found her? That didn't matter now.

<Addie, say something.>

But Addie didn't budge.

<It's Hally, Addie. Please. Speak.>

Our feet stayed glued to the floor, our lips stapled shut. There were only half a dozen feet separating us and Hally, but it seemed like the world.

<Addie, for me.>

A fist closed around our heart. Addie took a painful step forward.

"Hally?" she said. Our sweaty hands fidgeted at our sides.

Hally's head lifted just a little too quickly, her lips twitching upward. "Oh, hey, Addie," she said.

Addie nodded. She and Hally stared at each other. I wrestled with my impatience. If I pressed her, it might snap her already slingshot-tight nerves. But if I didn't, she might lose her courage.

Come on, Addie, I prayed. *Come on. Please.*

"I . . ." Addie said. "I . . . um—" She looked around, ensuring there was no one listening. "Eva," she said, so quietly I feared Hally wouldn't hear her. "Eva wants to learn."

Our voice gave out. Addie wasn't even fidgeting anymore, just staring straight ahead, not quite meeting Hally's eyes.

"Oh, great," Hally whispered. "That's great, Addie. Just fantastic."

Addie gave her a rigid smile.

The end-of-lunch bell rang. Hally grabbed one last book, then banged her locker shut. Her smile lit up her eyes. "I'll meet you by the front door after school, okay?" she said. "We'll go to my house. You'll meet Devon and Ryan properly. It'll be great. I promise."

Ryan. The name of the second soul dwelling in Devon's body. I tucked it away, another piece of these past few days that I just knew were going to change everything.

"All right," Addie managed to say.

Some boys were already coming up the hall, chatting and laughing. Addie stood by Hally's locker, watching her walk back to her classroom. But just as Hally was about to enter, she turned and darted back. The group of boys was almost upon us, but Hally leaned in and whispered with a laugh, "This is fantastic, Addie. Really. You'll see."

This time, Devon was sitting at the kitchen table when Hally opened the door. He had a screwdriver in one hand and what looked like a small black coin in the other. A mess of tools lay scattered across the table, half encircling him like some sort of wall. He looked up when we appeared in the doorway, then returned to his tinkering with only a nod hello.

"Hi," Addie said. Her voice had none of the spark she usually pumped into first meetings. With other boys, she could craft a mask of smiles and laughter. She seemed to hardly want to glance at this one.

Why? Because he wasn't really one boy, but two? Because hidden inside his body were twin souls, nestled side by side?

If so, then Addie looked away for exactly the same reasons I wanted to stare until I memorized the shape of his face. But I wasn't the one in control.

"Want some tea?" Hally asked. She'd bustled inside after kicking off her shoes and was already halfway to the fridge.

"Tea?" Addie said.

"Yeah. It's good. I promise."

Addie bent to untie our shoes, picking at the thin laces. "Okay, sure."

Nobody said anything about why we were here. Addie stood by the doorway, our arms crossed, our hands gripping our elbows. <*What now?*>

I wasn't sure. We looked to Hally, but she was too busy rummaging in the cabinets to notice. Devon tightened something in his coin, frowning as he did so. Addie and I might as well have not been there.

Finally, Hally turned and laughed. "Well, don't just stand there, Addie. Come on, sit down." She pointed to the chair across from her brother. "Devon, entertain her while I get something from upstairs."

The boy raised an eyebrow without even looking at her. "Isn't she your guest, though?"

Hally rolled her eyes. "Ignore him," she whispered as she passed us en route to the stairs. "He's just rude and antisocial like that."

"Ignore her," Devon said, still intent on . . . whatever he was doing. "She's just upset Ryan took apart her doorknob."

Hally pulled a face at him, and then she was gone, leaving us and Devon alone. Addie still hadn't moved.

"You *can* sit down, if you want," he said, finally raising his head.

Addie nodded and, after another awkward second, walked over to the chair. She sat. Devon turned back to his tinkering and tools. The seconds ticked by.

<Say something, Addie. For the love of all that is holy, you have to say something.>

<Can you think of something to say?> she snapped. Our body tensed, irritation flickering to our eyes and mouth.

Devon looked up.

<Great, now he's staring at us. What do I say?>

"So, um . . ."

He didn't speak. Didn't say *Yes? Do you want to ask me something*? He just watched us, his face still half tilted toward his hands.

<Think of something> Addie said. *<You wanted to talk, right? Well, think of something to say.>* She writhed in the

silence. I racked my mind, but Addie's irritation made it hard to think. It was like trying to brainstorm next to a thrashing bird.

<Just say—>

"So are you really Devon right now, or should I be thinking of you as Ryan?"

The question burst from our lips, and no matter how fast Addie shoved our fist against our mouth, she couldn't take it back. I was too shocked to speak.

Devon blinked. Or *was* he Ryan? No, he couldn't be; he'd just referred to Ryan. The boy frowned, looking more nonplussed than truly annoyed. "No, I'm Devon. But if you'd prefer Ryan, we can—"

"No," Addie said, leaning back. "No, that's quite all right, thanks."

Her coldness wiped the quiet puzzlement from his face, made his expression blank again. Devon nodded and turned back to his tinkering. Silence reigned, broken only by the click of his screwdriver when his hand slipped.

<That was smart> I said. *<Make him hate us. Always a good plan.>*

Heat rushed to our face. *<You want me to leave, Eva? Because I will. Right now.>*

I fell silent. A wall slammed down between Addie and me, sealing her emotions to her half of our mind. But she didn't do it quickly enough. I'd sensed the tendril of guilt.

The kettle started to shriek.

"Coming!" Hally called, thumping down the stairs. She skidded to a stop by the kitchen counter and reached over to switch off the stove. The kettle's screech puttered into a low whistle, then silence. There were a few moments of quiet, interrupted only by the clinking of mugs and what was probably a spoon.

Addie tore our eyes from Devon's hands. "What kind of tea is it?"

"Oh, um, something my dad gets. I forget the name," Hally said. She bent over one of the mugs, sliding the spoon out against its rim so it didn't drip, then brought the steaming mugs to the table. "I put a little cold milk in it, so it's not that hot. Try it. It's good."

She watched as Addie took a sip. We'd hardly ever had hot tea before. This tasted sweeter than I expected, milky and spiced.

"Lissa's obsessed with tea at the moment," Devon said. "A month ago it was those ornate pocketknives."

Lissa. Was she Lissa now? Addie threw a sideways look at the girl sitting next to us, but of course she looked exactly the same. Same dark hair, same dimples, same brown eyes. I didn't know her and Hally well enough to discern between them.

"I'm not obsessed," Lissa said, taking a long drink from her own mug. "And I'd still collect the pocketknives if Mom would let me."

"The tea does taste good," Addie said quietly.

Lissa smiled at us. A bright, overeager smile. "It does, doesn't it?"

A moment crawled by. Addie fingered the handle of our mug. Even through the wall in our mind, I could feel her tension mounting. It leaked through the cracks like steam.

"Why me?" she said.

Both Lissa and Devon looked up, the former from her tea, the latter from his tools. The strength of their stares, identical in so many ways, made Addie falter, but she soldiered on.

"Why did you choose me? How did . . . how did you know I was different?"

Lissa spoke slowly, as if weighing each word. "Remember last September, when you dropped your lunch tray?"

Of course we did. We'd been arguing about something or other, screaming at each other in our mind until the outside world faded away. The lunchroom had fallen silent as our tray slipped from our hands and smashed to the ground, mashed potatoes and milk flying through the air.

"Sometimes it seemed like you were talking to someone else, you know? Like someone else was there, fighting." Lissa paused. "I don't know. Maybe it was just a feeling." She flashed a tentative grin at us. "A kinship?"

Addie didn't smile back.

"Anyway," Lissa said quickly. "We got Devon to check your files, and they said you hadn't settled until you were twelve. That was a big clue that something was up."

Addie hunched over our tea. The soft, sweet steam soothed our frayed nerves. "So you could tell. Just like that."

"What do you mean?" Lissa said.

"It was so obvious I was different?"

"Well, it's not like anyone could have hacked into your school files, so—"

"Is there really something so wrong with that?" Devon said. His voice was low. He'd finally set down his screwdriver, his attention completely focused on us. "With being different from the others?"

"You sound like a bad after-school TV special," Addie said, laughing even as our fingers tightened around our mug. She twisted our voice into a mockery of a chirpy happiness. "*It's okay to be different.*"

"Isn't it?" he said.

"Not like this, it isn't."

"But you still came," he said.

Addie was quiet. Then haltingly, she said, "Eva wanted to."

Devon's expression didn't change, but Lissa smiled.

"I—" Addie frowned. Our head felt strange. Stuffy. Cottony. A little dizzy. She pushed away the mug of tea, but it wasn't steaming *that* much, so that couldn't be it. "I, um . . . I think—"

We swayed.

<Eva?> Addie cried. One solitary, frightened word.

And then she was gone.

Darkness. We slumped forward, knocking our temple, *hard*, against the table.

I screamed.

<Addie? ADDIE?>

Nothing.

It wasn't just the silence. It was the emptiness, the lack of—of *anything* where Addie should have been. Even when we ignored each other, even when Addie tried her absolute hardest to hide her emotions, I could feel the wall she put up. There was no wall now. There was a chasm.

Nausea slapped against me.

"Move the mug. Thank God she didn't knock into it."

"She pushed it away herself. It was like she knew—"

"Well, you were being so obvious about it. I'm surprised she drank anything at all."

The voices faded into murmurs. I delved as deep as I dared into the darkness and searched frantically for signs of Addie. The warmth of her presence, her thoughts, were gone. There wasn't a scrap to show she'd ever existed.

Our body felt incredibly empty. Hollow. Too big. Of course it was too big. Our body had always held two. Now there was only one.

"Eva?"

<Yes?> I shouted.

"Can you hear us, Eva?" Lissa said.

<Yes!—Yes, I can hear you. Where's Addie? What happened to Addie?>

But of course they heard nothing at all.

"Let's lay her down first," Devon said. "I'll bring her over."

Hands grabbed our arms and tilted us back in our seat. Someone pulled our chair away from the table. Then more hands, around our waist now. Finally, there was a heave and we were in the air, being carried slowly toward some unknown destination. And I, trapped inside this body that was and wasn't mine, couldn't even say a word aloud.

Where were they taking us? Had this all been a trick? A

trap? Was this how the government rooted out hybrids who'd escaped institutionalization? By pretending they had friends, had people who understood? By letting them feel like they weren't alone and then snapping them up while they were vulnerable? We'd walked right into it. Or I had, and I'd dragged Addie down with me.

I'd been so stupid. So trusting. So desperate to believe I might move again.

"Could you get that pillow, Lissa? That one . . . and just put it here . . ."

I felt something soft and solid below us. The hands let go. They weren't taking us out of the house, then. Maybe they weren't planning on kidnapping us. I didn't even feel anything akin to relief—just a little less sick.

<Addie> I said. *<Addie, what have they done to us?>*

"Eva?" It was Devon. "Eva, listen."

I was listening. I was listening, but they couldn't know because Addie wasn't here to tell them.

"Eva, if you're freaking out, you have to stop. You have to listen to us. Addie's fine. She's just . . . asleep right now because of the medicine. We didn't think she'd take it if she knew—"

They'd drugged us. They'd really drugged us. A flash of anger seared through me, singeing away just a little of the fear.

"Eva, can you move?"

Of course I couldn't move!

"The medicine will help, Eva," Lissa said. "Try and wriggle your fingers."

I tried. I tried like I'd been trying for years—if only so I could get the hell away from here. Nothing happened. I was trapped in a dead prison of skin and bones, shackled to limbs I couldn't control. What sort of plan was this? Were they trying to help us? Like *this*?

<*Addie?*> I said. <*Please, Addie, wake up.*>

A hand enveloped mine, and I couldn't jerk away.

"Eva," someone said. "Eva, this is Ryan."

Ryan. Devon's voice, but Ryan's, just as Addie's voice was also mine. Had been mine.

"We haven't really met yet, but we will. Right now we just want you to try and move your fingers. Move the fingers of the hand I'm holding right now."

The gentle pressure on our right palm helped orient me. I mentally traced up to the tips of our fingers. Then I tried again to curl them. I tried. I really did.

"It's been years, I know," Ryan said. "It's been a long time, but not too long. You can still do it, Eva."

<*I can't*> I said. <*I can't. I can't. Not like this.*>

Not alone in the dark like this.

"Eva? Are you still trying?"

<*Yes*> I said, almost crying. <*Yes. Yes.*>

"I know it's hard," he said.

<*Do you?*> My voice reverberated shrilly in the chasm that had stolen Addie. <*Have you ever been like this? Drugged and alone?*>

He didn't hear, so he couldn't respond. Instead, a new voice broke through the darkness. Lissa? Hally?

"Eva, trust us."

Trust them!

"The medicine will wear off in a little bit," she said. "So please, please try."

I tried. I lay there in the dark, listening to them talk at me, and tried for what seemed like hours. Finally, exhausted and ready to scream, I stopped.

"That's right," Lissa said. "That's good. Keep going."

"You've almost got it," Ryan said. He'd said it at least ten times.

<I'm not> I raged. *<I'm not close at all.>*

I couldn't do it. I couldn't. I wasn't strong enough, wasn't good enough, wasn't tough enough. It had been too long. And Addie—Addie was gone. I couldn't do it without her. I had never done anything without Addie.

I'd dreamed so long of being able to move again, every fantasy tasting equally of longing and terror. But I'd never dreamed I would be alone like this. That it would happen like this.

"Come on, Eva."

No. No—

"You can do it."

Shut up. Shut up shut up *shut up*. I can't do it. I ca—

"Eva—"

"I can't!"

Silence.

"Eva?" Lissa breathed. "Eva, was that you?"

Me?

Oh.

Oh.

"*Ryan*—did you hear that? Did you hear her?"

My head spun.

"Can you do it again?" Ryan said.

I'd spoken. I'd formed words and moved our lips and tongue and *spoken.*

They'd heard my voice.

<Addie?> I said. *<Addie, I spoke. I spoke.>*

From far within the abyss, a pulse.

<Addie?>

Again the pulse. Then came a feeling like the drawing of a breath. A tendril of something as light and insubstantial as dawn haze floated from the chasm.

<Eva> it whispered, warm and frightened. *<Eva?>*

Then she was back, bleary-eyed and weak and confused, but back, back, back, filling that terrible hole inside us. Making us whole again. Making us how we were meant to be.

<Eva> she said. *<What happened?>*

<Shh> I said. I was laughing, almost crying in relief. *<Shh, it's okay. We're okay. Don't worry. Don't worry.>*

She believed me. She kept our eyes closed, and she relaxed little by little.

<Eva> she murmured. *<I had the strangest dream. Did you have it, too?>*

SEVEN

Addie was still woozy five minutes after she awoke, swaying when she tried to sit up. She moved as though through syrup, each limb thick and unwieldy.

<*I . . . I can't raise our arm*> she said. We could see Lissa and Ryan now, and they were crouched by the sofa. They kept talking, their words washing over us but barely sinking in. Addie wasn't listening at all. I heard enough to know the drug would take a little longer to wear off completely.

<*Don't worry*> I said. <*It'll be okay in a bit.*>

<*It was the tea, wasn't it?*> she said.

<*It was*> I didn't tell her anything she didn't ask about. I didn't tell her what had happened while she slept. I didn't tell her I had spoken.

I didn't think she was ready to know.

Addie strengthened, her presence growing less tenuous beside mine. She kept blinking, like someone trying to clear away a dream.

"Addie?" Lissa said. She reached toward us, then pulled her hand away again at the last moment. "Are you okay now?"

Addie started, as if noticing her for the first time. "You—you drugged me." Her words were slurred.

The siblings looked at each other.

"We had to," Lissa said. "It's so much easier with the drug—"

"What's easier?" Addie said.

Another glance between Ryan and Lissa. The sofa was solid against our back. Our fingers dug into the rigid fabric.

"Didn't Eva tell you?" Ryan said.

Addie's frown deepened. "How would Eva know?"

"Well . . ." Lissa tugged on a curl of her hair, wrapping it around her finger. "Eva was awake, right?"

"Of course not," Addie said. "That's not pos—"

<*I was*> I said.

The rest of Addie's sentence lodged in our throat. It hurt to breathe around. <*What?*>

I hesitated. Lissa and Ryan watched us, studying our face. But I knew Addie wasn't paying them any attention.

<*I was awake*> I said.

<*But . . .*> Addie faltered. <*How?*>

<*I don't know. The drug did it. They put you to sleep, but I—I was awake, Addie.*>

Stunned silence. Her astonishment swirled bright and wild around me.

<*But*> she said <*But—no, that's—*>

<*I talked, too*> I said, unable to stand it any longer. The very knowledge pushed at our bones. <*I talked, Addie. When you were asleep.*>

<*Oh*> she said. Then again, softer. <*Oh.*>

"Addie?" Lissa said. Her fingers hovered above our arm.

Addie looked up. Our lips parted. Then the sound came, hoarse and crackly. "Eva talked?"

Lissa smiled. "She did."

Addie stared. She didn't speak, not even to me. I matched her silence. I didn't know what to say. And then, suddenly, she tried to stand. Our legs felt too frail to support our weight. "I'm . . . I'm going to go home."

Lissa grabbed our arm as we wobbled. "No, Addie, stay. Please stay."

"Wait a little longer. I'll walk you back," Ryan said. Addie looked at him. She didn't even know he was Ryan, I realized. She thought he was still Devon.

"I'm okay," she said. She tugged out of Lissa's grasp and sleepwalked toward the kitchen. They hurried after us, their feet slapping against the hardwood floor.

"I'm coming with you," Lissa called. "Just wait a second, Addie. I'm—"

Addie seemed not to hear.

<*Maybe we should let someone walk us back*> I said quietly as we stumbled and had to grab the counter. Addie didn't respond. I didn't mention it again.

She slipped into our shoes without tying the laces. But when she reached for our book bag, Ryan was already holding it. He nodded for us to go through the door first.

"I'll go, Ryan," Lissa said. "I can go—"

I didn't know how the argument ended. I couldn't hear because Addie had already stepped over the threshold, our shoelaces clacking as we walked. I heard the door close behind us. Then a voice by our ear: "You should tie your shoes or you'll trip on them."

Addie bent down and did the knots. Our fingers fumbled with the laces. When we stood again, Ryan was watching us.

"Well, come on," he said, not unkindly. "I don't know where you live, so you're going to have to lead the way."

They walked the first two blocks in silence, the mosquitoes out in full force. The humidity made it feel like we were slogging through sheets of suspended rain. The sky was straight out of a picture book, so perfect summer-spring blue it hurt to look at.

I couldn't tell what Addie was thinking. Her mind was blank, her emotions boxed. The few cars on the road rushed by us as if we didn't exist. They didn't know who we were. What we'd done.

What I'd done. Spoken.

I'd *spoken.*

"What did she say?"

"Sorry?" Ryan said, turning to face us.

It took Addie a moment to repeat herself. "What did she say?"

"Who, Eva?" he asked.

She nodded.

Ryan frowned. "What do you mean?"

It didn't make sense to him why Addie would ask him instead of me. I didn't know, either. I didn't think Addie knew.

"I want to know what Eva said while I was asleep," Addie said. Our voice was low, almost raspy.

He was quiet for a second before answering. "She said: 'I can't.'" He inflected the last two words to show they were mine.

"Can't what?"

"Why don't you ask her?" he said.

Addie didn't reply. Ryan looked away again, but he said, "Does that make you happy? That she spoke?"

"*Happy?*" said Addie.

Ryan stopped walking. Our eyes dropped to the ground.

"Happy," Addie said again, softer. The lukewarm, waterlogged air swallowed our voice.

"It's okay," Ryan said. "It's okay if you aren't."

Slowly, Addie looked up and met his gaze.

"I think she understands if you aren't," he said.

They started walking again, taking their time in the heat even though the mosquitoes attacked with a vengeance. It wasn't a day built for things like walking quickly.

Little by little, our house came into view. Squat, off-white, with a black-shingled roof and a row of straggly rosebushes, it had been one of the few we could afford when our parents decided to move. Our room was smaller than the one we'd had before, and Mom didn't like the kitchen layout, but complaints had been kept to a minimum as we'd walked the halls for the first time. We might have been young, but not nearly so young we didn't understand that doctors were expensive and government stipends only helped so much.

Soon, we stood in our front yard. The soft kitchen lights shone through the strawberry-patterned curtains.

"Here you go," Ryan said, holding out our book bag. Addie looked at it as if she'd forgotten it was ours, then nodded and took it before turning and heading toward the house. "I'll see you later, then, Addie," he said.

He'd stopped at the edge of our yard, letting Addie walk the short distance to the door alone. There might have been a question buried in his words. Or it might just have been a reflex, a meaningless good-bye people passed around. I wasn't sure.

Addie nodded. She didn't look at him. "Yeah. Later."

She was wiping our shoes on the welcome mat when he added, "Bye, Eva."

Addie stilled. The air smelled of dying roses.

<*Bye*> I whispered.

Our hand froze on the doorknob. Slowly, Addie turned around.

"She says bye," she said.

Ryan smiled before walking slowly away.

After that day, Addie and Hally walked together to her house every afternoon after school. Addie no longer drank the tea; it was too hot for that. Instead, Hally dissolved the fine white powder into sugar water, which masked the bitter taste.

Addie and I didn't talk about these sessions. I told myself I didn't bring it up because I didn't want to push my luck. Addie was risking everything by agreeing to go. What more could I ask for? But to be honest, I was scared. Scared of hearing what she might have to say, what she really felt.

Hally and Addie didn't speak much, either, though it wasn't

for lack of trying on Hally's part. Addie fielded all her attempts at conversation with an averted gaze and one-word replies. But as long as we didn't have a babysitting job that afternoon, Addie never missed a day, either. Her friends invited her out shopping or to the theater, but she suggested skipping our trip to the Mullan house only once.

"I've got to go to someone's house today," Hally had said as she stuffed things into her bag that particular afternoon. "We've got a project due—"

Addie hesitated. "Tomorrow, then."

"No, wait," Hally said. She smiled. "I won't be long. Half an hour at most, okay?"

I said nothing. Addie didn't look Hally in the eye. She stared at the half-erased chalk marks on the blackboard, the graffiti on the tops of the worn desks, the bent plastic chairs.

"Devon will walk you—" Hally started to say, but Addie cut her off.

"I remember how to get to your house."

"Oh," Hally said and laughed, which should have eased the tension but only made the silence that followed more pronounced. She slung her book bag over her shoulder, her smile unfaltering but her eyes blinking a little more rapidly than usual. "Half an hour at most," she repeated. "Devon knows where the medicine is. And he'll make sure nothing happens to Eva while you're asleep."

Addie ended up walking home with Devon anyway, since we ran into him by the school doors. It was possibly the most uncomfortable ten minutes I could have imagined. He didn't speak to Addie. Addie didn't look at him. The heat made them both sweat, made an uneasy situation worse, and it was an even bigger relief than usual to reach the cool, airy Mullan house, to swallow the drugged water and lie down and wait for Addie to fall asleep.

It still made me sick to feel her ripped away from me, but I was getting better at keeping calm. She would come back. It was easier knowing that she would come back, that the drug's effects lasted only an hour at most, and sometimes only twenty minutes or so.

Devon had been sitting at the table when Addie went to lie down, but about ten minutes after she disappeared, my name came floating through the blackness.

"Eva?"

He said my name like a secret. Like a password, a code whispered through locked doors.

<*Yes?*> I said, though he couldn't hear. Everything was darkness and the soft couch beneath Addie and me. I could feel the ridges of the fabric beneath our fingertips, the textured grain against the heel of our hand.

I felt the warmth of his palm as he laid it softly on the back of our hand, the pressure of his fingers, the brush of his thumb against our pulse.

"It's Ryan," he said. "I figured you—that you'd like to know there was someone here."

I tried to speak. I focused on our lips, on our tongue, on our throat. I tried to form *thank you* with a mouth that belonged to me yet didn't want to obey. But it seemed I wasn't going to be able to speak this particular day.

So instead, I focused on Ryan's hand, which was easier. He'd slid his palm down over our knuckles, his fingers tucked beneath our hand. I curled our fingers around his and squeezed as hard as I could, which was barely anything at all.

I figured that was as articulate as I was going to get.

But the thought of one day being able to respond to him, to sit and laugh and talk with him as anyone else might have done, was added to my ever-growing list of reasons to keep on coming to the Mullan house. To keep fighting, no matter the cost.

EIGHT

The days passed. Then a week. Then another and another. I used to count my life in weekends or theater visits or Lyle's dialysis sessions. I marked the days with school assignments or babysitting jobs. Now I tallied my life by the improvements I made lying on a couch with Ryan or Devon, Hally or Lissa, by my side. The number of words I managed to speak. The fingers I managed to move.

And for the first time, my mind filled with memories that were mine and mine alone. My first smile while Hally whispered to me all the stupid, crazy things she'd dragged her brother into when they were little. My first laugh, which startled Lissa so much that she'd jerked away before laughing, too. And even on the days when all my progress seemed to backslide and I lay mute and paralyzed on the couch, trapped in the darkness behind our eyelids, I had someone beside me, talking to me, telling me stories.

I learned how the Mullan family had moved to Lupside a year before Addie and I did, when their mother had changed jobs. How Ryan missed their old house because he'd spent twelve years there, had known the position of every book in the library, the creak of every step in the curved stairwell. How Hally didn't miss it because they'd hardly had any neighbors, and the ones they did have had been hateful. How they both had fond memories, though, of the fields behind the house and childhoods spent running through them, pretending to be anywhere but where they actually were.

I remember with perfect clarity the first time I opened our eyes.

Hally had screamed, then scrambled to fetch Devon. "Look!" she'd cried. "Look!"

"Eva?" Devon had said. But it hadn't been Devon.

That was the first time I caught them shifting, caught Ryan pushing through and looking out at me. I couldn't even move our gaze or smile or laugh, could only stare up at his face. He was so close that I could pick out his individual eyelashes, long and dark and curved like Hally's.

I remember that snapshot of him, smiling with only one side of his mouth, hair damp and curlier than normal from that afternoon's rain. It was my first glimpse of him, really, because we hardly ever saw him at school, and even when we did, Devon always seemed to be in control. He rolled his eyes slightly as Hally nudged him aside so I was looking at her instead.

"Soon," Hally said, grinning, "you'll be doing cartwheels."

At times like that, I believed her. Other times, I wasn't so sure.

"Don't worry about it," Ryan said one afternoon. Hally and

Lissa were gone again that day. They seemed to be leaving us with Ryan more and more now, and Addie had stopped asking where they went. I didn't mind. I liked this boy who pulled up a chair next to the couch, who talked to me about wiring and voltage and then laughed and said I was probably bored out of my mind, that this was all incentive for me to get control of my legs so I could escape.

<*What if the control never comes back?*> I said. I talked to him and Lissa like this a lot now, knowing they couldn't hear me but speaking anyway. Sometimes they carried on one-sided conversations for up to an hour. The least I could do in return was speak to them, even if they didn't know it.

Ryan pulled his chair closer. "Devon and I never really settled. There were a few months when we were five or six when I kept losing strength. Everyone was sure I'd be gone by our seventh birthday." His lips twitched into a smile. "But I came back. I don't know how, exactly. I remember fighting it, Devon fighting it . . . and I don't know. Our parents never told anyone. You remember our mom works at the hospital?"

I did. That was where the medicine came from—stolen one day when Hally had gone with her mother to work. Addie had barely kept from shuddering when she'd learned.

"She knows a bit about this kind of stuff. She thought maybe we were just late bloomers or something. Or she hoped, anyway. So she never reported it, and she made sure we hid it—she hid *us*. Donvale—that's where we lived before—is this tiny, rural place, so it was easier to keep to ourselves. Our dad homeschooled us through first and second grade so we wouldn't be in public so much during that time, when everyone's newly settled. Our parents were afraid, you know?"

It took all my strength—all my strength and all my concentration—but I managed to force our lips, our tongue, to form one word: "*Yes.*" And in that one word, I tried to convey everything.

Ryan smiled, like he always did when I spoke, even when it was just a few syllables. But then his smile faded. "The officials wouldn't have been lenient about the deadline—not with us."

I was torn between horror and envy. If you knew your child was sick, wasn't developing naturally, how could you not take him to the doctor? How could you not worry?

"But eventually, *not* going to regular school was attracting more attention than it was worth. Our mom thought Devon showed signs of being dominant, so when she finally registered us, she put only his name. Just pretend, she told us. We'd already learned how important it was that we did."

I stared up at him, wishing I had the words and the strength to tell him I knew exactly what he meant. About the open curiosity and growing fear Addie and I had faced on the playground.

But Ryan knew that, just like he knew how his features reminded everyone who saw him of the pictures in our history books, the foreigners who had to be kept out at all costs to keep our country safe.

"So we pretended." Ryan shrugged. "And we kept on pretending. Hally and Lissa were seven then, and they didn't show any signs of settling, either." He laughed. "I think Mom and Dad were a little more worried the second time around. Hally's kind of hard to keep hidden inside."

<So what did they do?>

"Hally was always the louder one, so they put her name down for school," he said, as if he could guess what I might be wondering just by looking at me. "She pretended so well there, we started pretending she was dominant even for our parents. They were so relieved. And now they . . . well, we never talk about it anymore." He grinned wryly. "We're all such excellent pretenders, I suppose our parents think we're normal. Or they tell themselves that, anyway."

He fiddled with his latest project, a flashlight that didn't need batteries but could be wound up like a clock. He had so many things stashed away in the basement: cassette players linked up to speakers, computers he'd built and others he'd taken apart, even dissected cameras. He'd promised to show me sometime, when I could move.

"I wasn't sure if we'd ever find anyone else," Ryan said. "Even if we did, I didn't know—didn't know if it would be safe. To try . . . to be . . ." He paused. "Hally wanted it so badly. More than all the rest of us. She just had to meet others, you know? To be with other people like us. But I thought—Devon and I thought it would be too dangerous to even try. It took a few months for her to convince us." He looked at me, then back to his flashlight. "I'm glad she did, though."

Me too, I wanted to say. I could have, probably. I could have said it, but somehow it didn't feel like enough. Because if Hally hadn't stopped Addie in the hall that day or insisted on us going to their house after the museum flood—or if Devon hadn't agreed to break into the school's files or if Lissa hadn't made Addie listen or any one of a dozen other tiny things—I'd probably still be counting my existence in weekends and babysitting jobs. I'd still be nothing but a ghost haunting Addie's life.

"Eva?" Ryan said.

I looked up, linking our eyes to his. So strange, to see how different this boy's face could be when Ryan, not Devon, was in control. He had a smile that made me ache to reciprocate.

"Yes?" I said again. It was slightly easier the second time, like playing a song on an instrument after practice.

He took a minute to answer. A frown wrinkled his forehead—darkened his eyes. For a moment, I was afraid he'd shift. Devon hardly ever spoke to me. Ryan shifting now would mean the end of our conversation, would mean my lying on the couch alone until Addie woke up. But Ryan didn't, though his next words were halting and forced.

"You ever wonder what really happens to those kids who're taken away?"

I just stared at him. His frown deepened. His mouth opened and closed wordlessly.

Then: "Ever wonder how many hybrids are really out there—"

His face jerked away from ours and stiffened. And then he was gone. Devon angled his body toward the wall.

"Anyway," he said quietly. "Not like you can answer yet."

Hally came home just then, and Devon withdrew upstairs. I

had no way to call him back, no way to speak with Ryan again.

The days and weeks slid by. I grew stronger at a snail's pace, remaining glued to the couch and dumb except for fragments of sentences that got increasingly longer. But soon I could open our eyes regularly and wiggle our fingers and toes. The first time I lifted our hand a full six inches or so off the couch, Hally squealed and clapped her hands.

When I wasn't worrying about regaining control of our body so slowly, I worried about doing it too quickly. Was it too fast for Addie? Sometimes, Lissa or Hally would tell her what sort of progress I'd made that afternoon. Addie never said much, just nodded and picked up our book bag so she could leave.

I could never help feeling hollow.

NINE

Addie wriggled out of our school uniform as fast as she could, reaching for a pair of shorts even as she stepped out of our skirt. Still, Lyle was pounding at our bedroom door before we finished dressing. "Mom says to hurry *up*, Addie. We're going to be *late*."

I'd been the one to suggest we skip going to Hally's house today and go to the city instead—get a break from the repression drug and the forced sleep. Maybe Addie needed a day off from it all. We were keeping one of the biggest secrets anyone could ever hope to keep. We were stripping away years of counseling and doctors' visits, going against everything we'd ever been told about settling.

And one day, I couldn't help thinking, we might come to regret this. I'd done everything in my power to convince Addie to go to the Mullans' because I'd been afraid of regretting it later if I didn't. But this road was far from safe. Even if we were never discovered, how would Addie and I live as I got stronger and stronger? Would we eventually tear ourself apart, as the doctors claimed? The Mullan siblings seemed to be doing fine but . . . one never knew.

It was normal for her to be unnerved. For *me* to be unnerved, even as I relearned how to smile. So I wasn't surprised when Addie jumped at the chance to tell Lissa we were going with our little brother to the city after school today. I *was* surprised, however, when Lissa asked, with that sideways smile she and Ryan shared, if we'd mind if she met us there. And I was even more surprised when Addie said we wouldn't.

"We are *not* going to be late," Addie snapped. "Go sit in the car and tell Mom I'll be there in two seconds."

He muttered something, but we heard him pound back down the stairs. Lyle always walked like an elephant, though he was built more like a crane . . . a baby crane with a flop of yellow hair and a complete lack of grace.

We and Lyle had both taken after Mom in looks: blond hair—though a bit of Dad's curl had snuck into ours—and brown eyes. Dad, who was brown-haired and blue-eyed, used to say how cheated he felt in the genetics department. We'd all laughed about it, but under our laughter had been the awful wondering: where had our faulty hybrid genes come from?

Everyone knew hybridity carried some sort of genetic element. The rest of the countries were mostly hybrid, after all. The trait was suppressed here only because the victors of the Revolution had not been hybrid, and they'd taken care in their crafting of a non-hybrid country; they'd purged the hybrids who remained after the long war, linked the two continents, and shut down the borders.

Addie finished dressing and jerked a brush through our hair before dashing downstairs and grabbing our shoes. She half hopped, half ran for the car. Lyle was already buckled in back, a small pile of beat-up paperbacks beside him. He always insisted on having at least three whenever he went in for a dialysis appointment, and they were always adventure novels. He ate them up during the long hours he spent hooked to the machine, then made us listen to him recount them all the way home.

Lyle was always the first kid to tire when his class played soccer in gym. The last to finish in races. I guess it made sense that he wanted to lose himself in books about heroes who were forever breaking out of locked rooms and scaling the sides of crumbling buildings.

Mom sighed as we slid into the front seat, starting to back out of the driveway the second Addie slammed the door shut. "I don't understand why you can't just wear your uniform, Addie."

Addie didn't reply. She was too busy tying our shoes, and besides, she'd already told Mom a million times that no one wanted to be seen outside of school in their school uniform, especially not in the city. "Can you drop me off at that boulevard with the crafts store? The one near—"

"Yes, yes, I know, Addie," Mom said.

Lyle strained against his seat belt, leaning forward between Mom's seat and ours. "Can I go, too, Mom? After my appointment? Please?"

We nearly ran a red light, zooming through the intersection just as it changed.

"If there's time, Lyle," Mom said.

Lyle had dialysis at a clinic in the city three times a week. Addie and I used to hitch a ride with him and Mom once a week or so, but lately we'd been too busy going to Hally and Devon's house instead. Bessimir was a welcome relief from Lupside's bland suburbs. It wasn't nearly as big as Wynmick, where we'd lived before moving here, but it was something, at least. Even if the presence of the history museum darkened everything.

Talk had died down a lot in the month since the museum flooded, but the building was still closed, roped off with yellow police tape, a stark reminder of what had happened. And almost every night, the local news station mentioned the ongoing investigation or replayed clips from past hybrid attacks. These always ended with shots of the men and women tracked down and brought to justice, their hair messy and limp, the women with smeared or runny makeup, like clowns. Hybrids. The ones who'd hidden, as we were hiding.

Compared to the bombing in San Luis or the fire that had blazed across the Amazonia in the southern Americas, both also ultimately discovered to be caused by hybrid violence, a couple of inches of water and a few licks of flame at the Bessimir museum hardly seemed noteworthy. But it was discussed over and over and over again.

And each time, no matter how hard I tried, I couldn't help remembering what the guide had said as Addie had pushed us up from the dirty water. *It's those pipes. How many times have we said to get those pipes fixed?*

Mom dropped us off at the boulevard, reminding us to be back in three hours. We both knew it would take longer than that to get through Lyle's session. It always did. But Addie promised to be here anyway.

Hally met us at the end of the street, wearing a bright yellow sundress with what seemed to be white puffed sleeves from a long-gone century. Somehow, she made it look good. We were so distracted by her clothes, we almost didn't notice the boy standing a few feet away from her until we'd reached the corner.

"He wanted to come *shopping*," Hally said. She managed to laugh with just a twitch of her lips and a lift of her eyebrows.

"I needed to come," Ryan said. "I've got to get—"

"He's lying," Hally whispered, bumping her shoulder against ours. Ryan pretended very hard that he hadn't heard.

If I could have, I would've smiled.

"Well, you lead the way, Addie," Hally said. She grinned. "What did you need to get?"

"Art supplies," Addie said, sounding like she was regretting having agreed to company.

Hally grabbed our hand as if she and Addie were friends, as if they were normal and safe, as if people weren't already sliding looks out of the corners of their eyes at Hally and Ryan, at the foreign blood written into their faces. Both were so good at pretending they didn't notice.

"I didn't know you did art," Hally said, forging ahead.

Addie quickened our steps to keep up. Ryan seemed content to let us walk ahead of him. "Oh. I—I don't really do it so much anymore. I used to. When I was younger."

"Why did you stop?" Ryan asked. So he was listening to their conversation after all. With Addie turned the other way, I couldn't be sure if he'd even been looking at us.

Our shirt had rumpled a bit at the hem. Addie smoothed it down. "No reason, really. Because I got busy."

Because she'd gotten good. She'd won two competitions before we turned twelve, before we realized winning meant attention, and attention was something we could never have. If attention lingered on something with imperfections long enough, the imperfections were sure to show, however small they were. And ours were far from small.

Addie still drew, but more privately. If anyone saw, even our parents, they always made a big deal of it, always called other people over to see. And sooner or later, someone would ask why we didn't enter a contest. She no longer painted. That was harder to hide. And canvas was expensive, anyway.

Walking down the boulevard with Hally took twice as long as walking it alone. She was drawn to every second store window, fascinated by every bauble and length of fabric, every glimmer of jewelry or cleverly made toy. By the fourth or fifth time she demanded we pause, Addie stopped following her into the shops and just waited outside with Ryan, who somehow bore all this without comment. Addie was fairly humming with the desire to just get to the crafts store and get things over with.

<*We've got tons of time*> I was saying, trying to calm her down, when Ryan said, "You know, Eva can move her

hands now. Did she tell you?"

Her hands. Not *your* hands but *her* hands. My hands. Of course, *her hands* was safer to use, in case anyone was listening, but a warmth spread through me anyway.

"No," Addie said.

He smiled. "Not all the time, but sometimes. And we're working on talking more. It's nice to . . ." He paused, then laughed a little before continuing. "I mean, I'm sure she's sick of hearing me going on all the time. And she's got to have so much to say—"

He was looking at us, looking right at *me*, it seemed, and I said <*Yes*> before I knew what I was doing, before I could remember I wasn't on his living room couch, that Addie wasn't asleep. She tensed.

"And—"

"Look, we shouldn't be talking about this," Addie said. "Not here." She took a quick, shallow breath. "And stop talking about her like she's a baby. Like it's some big miracle she can make a fist and spit out words."

Ryan blinked. "That's not what I meant—"

"And she *does* have a lot to say," Addie snapped. "I know because she says it to me."

She slipped past him into the store, where Hally was getting the salesgirl to take down a ridiculously ornate clock from the very top shelf.

<*You know he didn't mean it like that*> I said.

<*Then he ought to be more careful with his words.*>

Hally smiled at us as Addie drifted closer, then looked over our shoulder and lost her smile a little. "Did something happen?" she said. Or started to say, anyway, because just as the words left her mouth, the sirens blared over them.

The first police car sped past before Addie even left the store, going so fast our hair whipped into the air. A second car soon followed. All along the street, conversations stopped as sirens stole sentences from mouths before they could reach anybody's ears. People stilled. Turned. Stared. We were among them.

We couldn't hear, but we could read the lips of the old woman a few feet from Ryan. "*Hybrids*," she said, her face contorting. Addie almost lurched away from her. But the woman was talking to the man next to her, not us; she wasn't looking in our direction.

A pair of boys ran past us, following the trail of police cars. They were farther away now, the siren wails fading but still ringing in our ears. And then something—someone—shot past us and darted after the boys.

"Hally," Ryan shouted, running after her. "Hally, stop!"

Fear turned our limbs to stone. Was it true? Had someone made a mistake? Or lied, just to cause a commotion?

<Addie> I cried. I didn't know what I wanted her to do—run, yes, but where? After Ryan and Hally? Or in the other direction? All I could say was *<Addie, move!>*

She did. She spun around, life springing into our legs, and ran away from the police cars, away from Ryan, away from Hally. Away from whoever they'd discovered. The streets filled with people running—streaming in or out of shops, of apartments. Somebody shoved up against us. Then another and another. Half were trying to get closer to the scene, filled with some morbid need to bear witness, the other half trying to flee.

In the space of a few seconds, there was hardly any room left to move. News had traveled.

Danger. A hybrid had been found, and the police had come collecting.

Addie whirled from one direction to another, fighting against the crowd. Bodies crushed against ours. <*Eva*> she cried and stumbled, falling backward. Someone's elbow smashed against our cheek. Another rammed just below our ribs, knocking what breath remained from our lungs.

The crowd surged forward and swept us along with it, a river of bodies with Addie floundering in the current, fighting just to stay afloat. I was so disoriented I didn't know which direction we were going until we hit a line of police officers, powerful in their dark uniforms, shouting for everyone to *keep back, keep back*. Their voices barely made it over the mob's cacophony: the furious screaming, the cries of those who fell. Addie and I pinballed from left to right, wanting to close our eyes but not daring to.

<*Eva*> Addie kept crying in the whiteness of our mind. <*Eva—Oh, God.*>

A leg tangled with ours, wrenching us off balance. We jerked forward—we would fall—

A hand closed around our arm. An officer's hand. He yanked us back onto our feet before pulling us through the crowd—a fish on a line, a bird on a string—and depositing us across the street. We breathed in gasps. When the officer looked at us, we stopped breathing altogether.

Did he know? He couldn't know. Could he?

"You okay?" he said, releasing our arm. He was a big man. He could knock us down in an instant, and he had a look on his face like he'd do it. Addie nodded, unable to speak. Our eyes moved back to the protesters, drawn almost against our will.

"Idiots," the officer said. "Don't know how dangerous it is." Dangerous? Did he mean the mob, or did he mean the captured hybrid, hidden somewhere in the center of that screaming throng, so crushed by the mass of humanity we couldn't even see him? "You get away from here, got it?"

Addie nodded again. Our breath was returning, our lungs unclenching. The officer plunged back into the fray, joining the others struggling to contain the crowd.

We ran as far as we could from the screaming and the shouting and the sweating bodies. We didn't go to the crafts store. We didn't look for Ryan or Hally, who'd both been swallowed by the mob. We didn't stop moving until the three hours were up and we had to return to the rendezvous spot.

By the time Mom pulled up nearly half an hour later, we were no longer shaking. All the police cars were long gone, their backseat prisoner subdued, the crowd dispersed.

"Didn't you buy anything, Addie?" Lyle said as we climbed, blank-faced, into the front seat.

We just shook our head.

We didn't sleep that night, and we didn't whisper to each other like we usually did when sleep didn't come. Instead, we lay silent in the darkness. I could still hear the shouting, the sirens. The crowd's angry faces were emblazoned on the ceiling, and, when Addie finally closed our eyes, on the backs of our eyelids.

The raid was on the evening news, but they'd somehow managed to make it look different, make it look as if the crowd had gathered like spectators at a blood sport, jeering at the handcuffed man in the center, instead of being the fighters themselves in the ring. There were no shots of the police struggling to get them under control.

If the officer hadn't grabbed us—if the officer hadn't rescued us—we'd have slipped right under that crowd, been stomped into dust beneath their furious feet. Would he have saved us if he'd known our secret? If he'd known what we were doing every day after school? Maybe he would have let us fall, then dragged our broken body into the back of his police car. Locked us inside.

Everyone at the dinner table had fallen silent as we watched, even Lyle. He'd sat clutching his fork in his hand, his eyes unmoving from the small TV screen. He'd been seven when the doctors declared Addie settled. Only five when I lost the majority of my strength, and though he had to remember the fear that had prowled the house back then, all the doctors' visits, all the days Mom would just wake up in the morning and cry as she made breakfast, I wondered how much he actually remembered *me*.

The neighbors, those stupid, nosy neighbors, had warned our parents to separate Addie and me from him as much as possible, especially as he neared settling age. Some said it was just an urban legend that the presence of a hybrid affected unsettled children, but with things like hybrids and settling, one could never be too safe.

As was obvious on the TV screen. The ring of policemen. The mob. All for one man who we hadn't even managed to glimpse in the city but saw now in the fuzzy recording. We stared at his face. He didn't try to block it like other criminals sometimes did when on camera. Other criminals . . .

Because he was a criminal.

For being hybrid and free.

For putting others in danger with his very presence.

For the flooding and resulting fire at the Bessimir history museum, which, we heard with a certain numbness, had been found to be his doing. In an attempt to destroy history? To vandalize past heroes? Or just the mad thrashing that resulted from a crumbling hybrid mind?

Had he worked alone? Sometimes, the more daring kids at school spread stories about a secret network of hybrids across the Americas, like some kind of Mafia or conspiracy theory. They would be the real reason for everything bad that happened in the country, from shark attacks to economic downturns.

It was a stupid idea. If hybrids really had that much power here, people like Addie and me wouldn't be so scared.

The news cameras followed the man and the policemen flanking him as they ducked into the police cars. Did he seem like someone who would vandalize a museum? Maybe. He was perhaps forty, with brown hair and a short beard and strong-looking hands. But he also reminded me, in some shots, of our uncle on Mom's side. The one who'd stopped speaking to her after our parents had begged the officials to give Addie and me more time instead of sending us away, as was dignified. As was expected. As was right. The one Mom no longer mentioned and who no one ever mentioned to her.

Neither of our parents met our eyes that night. Everyone went to bed early, though judging by the light leaking under closed bedroom doors, no one slept.

Addie spoke only once as she curled up under the covers. *<Eva . . . Eva, we have to stop. We can't keep going with things like this. If we get caught . . .>*

I said nothing. Could I stop the lessons? Could I give them up now that I knew I could one day learn how to walk again? Could I give up listening to Ryan tell me about his inventions? Telling me stories about his past?

Could I give up the chance that one day, I'd be able to tell my stories, too?

<I'm going to tell Hally tomorrow> Addie said. *<Eva, we have to stop.>*

But the next day, Hally and Lissa weren't there.

TEN

Our history class felt oddly empty without her, though everyone else seemed to take up twice as much room as usual, caught up in the frenzy of yesterday's raid. Addie told no one we'd been there, and we faded into the background.

<*Something's happened to her*> I said.

<*Don't be overdramatic*> Addie said. <*Did you hear anything about them taking a girl? Did you see her on the TV? She's probably just sick. Or she stayed home, like—*>

Like we wished we had.

<*What if she got hurt?*> I said. <*What if she got . . . trampled or something?*>

Addie flinched. <*God, Eva, you're so morbid. What are the chances?*>

But her unease mingled with mine, and I caught her scanning the crowds in the hall between classes, searching, perhaps, for Devon. He would know. But we'd never run into him much in the halls before, and today was no exception.

We walked home alone. Addie's old friends had long since

given up asking her to go with them, and no one had waited for us today.

We slept a little better that night, mostly out of pure exhaustion, but we dreamed of flashing red and blue lights and wailing sirens.

Hally wasn't at school the next day, either.

<*Maybe we should drop by*> I said on the way home.

<*She's sick*> Addie said, but she couldn't hide the waver in her voice. Not from me. <*No one really wants visitors when they're sick.*>

And she wouldn't budge, no matter how much I argued.

When history class convened on Thursday, Hally's seat was once again empty.

<*We're going. Today*> I said.

But Dad needed someone to help at the store while he ran errands that afternoon, so he picked us up from school. He returned wondering if we would restock the canned goods. That led to organizing the receipt book and tallying up the store's sales for the past week.

It was almost sundown by the time we finished. Dad dropped us off at home with a kiss on the forehead and a promise to be back before we went to bed. Perhaps, he said, smiling, once school let out, he and Mom would take a few days' vacation and we'd all drive up to the mountains. Go camping.

Addie smiled back.

I wondered if he ever thought about the first time we'd gone camping, back before Lyle was born. Addie and I had been four years old, and Dad had spent what seemed like forever and a half sitting with me on a log in front of the fire, the stars staring down at us, teaching me how to put my thumbs together and whistle through a blade of grass.

"Lyle's having trouble with his math," Mom said as Addie walked into the kitchen. "Go help him while I finish dinner?"

And so passed the night. I thought about making Addie call, then realized we didn't even know the Mullans' phone number. We'd never had cause to use it before.

<It's been three days> Addie said. *<She'll be back tomorrow.>*

She wasn't. But as we picked up our book bag and tried to slip out of the classroom at the end of the day, someone blocked our way. Not Hally, not Lissa.

Devon.

Addie halted, staring at him. He stared back. Our fingers wrapped around the doorframe.

"Hey," Addie said. "What're you doing here?"

Ms. Stimp watched us from behind her desk. Devon frowned at her, and she looked away, fussing with her papers, her hands flashing white, her face red.

Devon's mouth tightened, but he turned back to us. "Come on, we'll talk outside."

Addie followed him out of the building, out of the parking lot. We kept on walking until we reached a quiet grove of trees on the very edge of school property. Addie struggled to keep up with Devon's long strides. It had rained this morning, and the soft earth squelched beneath our patent-leather shoes. The scent of wet grass weighed down the air.

"What's going on?" she said finally. "Devon, tell me—"

He spun to face us, stopping so suddenly Addie nearly ran into him. "Hally and Lissa are gone."

Gone. The word smashed into our chest. Addie swallowed. "What do you mean, *gone*?"

Devon glanced around us before speaking again. He was so tense he practically shook, a spring bound by fishing wire ready to snap. "She should have known better. She just wanted to see. But she should have known—" He broke off and looked away. The trees stood still and silent, glistening with rainwater. "We're not like the rest of you. We can't be seen around things like that. Raids. We can't be caught too near. They took her. They questioned her." A wave of different emotions rippled across his face, too fast to decipher.

"They took her away," he said.

"The police?"

Rough hands. Flashing red and blue lights. Sirens wailing and wailing and wailing.

Devon still didn't look at us, just kept staring at the slender white tree trunks, trembling. The wind was picking up. The leaves rustled. "At first. Then the man from the clinic."

"What cli—"

Devon jerked around to face us. "All because she wanted to see!" His voice dropped, a rumble of distress locked in steel. "I told her to stop. Ryan told her to stop. She never, ever listens." He pressed his fingers to his temples. When he spoke again, his voice was tight but toneless. "They came to our house and told us she's mentally unstable." His eyes were black. Cold.

"They say she needs intensive, specialized care before it's too late to save her. They want to *correct* her. They want to *correct* my sister, Addie."

Unstable. Special care.

Too late.

I felt Addie twist and turn beside me, her anguish bleeding into me, mine seeping into her.

Something must be done before it's too late.

That was what the doctors, the specialists, that guidance counselor with the bobbed gray hair had told our parents while we listened with our ear pressed against the door.

"But—" Addie said. "But how? They can't—"

"They did tests. Scans. They had papers. Signatures from officials. They scared our parents, convinced them she was in danger—would *be* a danger. We couldn't do anything."

We stared at him, our hair tangling as the wind blew it across our face.

"They're going to take me, too," Devon said.

Our fingers choked the nearest tree trunk.

"Just like that?" Addie whispered.

<*They can't*> I said. <*No. They can't.*>

Devon and Ryan stared at us. One pair of eyes, two people. "We might not be settled. That's enough reason for them."

Our throat was thick, our lungs molasses-soaked sponges.

And then Devon shifted—a sudden, harsh change like a jerk sideways. Nothing subtle.

"Run," Ryan said.

Addie dug our nails into the tree. "What?"

"They're going to be checking files, Addie." His voice was softer now, almost like the one I'd heard sometimes when he sat by me on the couch, talking about his various projects, showing me how each one worked. The little robot man that was balanced well enough to walk across a table. The metal box that wouldn't open unless you pressed all the buttons in the right order. "They're going to ask who we've been seen with. Who comes over. Who we've done projects with. And your file—your file is going to be very, very interesting to them."

The wind moaned, making the trees sway. We swayed with them.

"Run, Addie." There was a current of fear in Ryan's voice that made our insides twist. "Don't go home today. Just leave."

"Just *leave*," Addie said. "*Leave*? My parents? Lyle?"

"You'll be leaving them behind either way!" he said, his voice tight and hoarse—as if crushed down from a shout. "Addie, they'll *take* you away."

"They'll give me back," Addie cried. "They always gave me back. I'm settled. I always came back home."

Silence. Head-pounding, heart-throbbing silence.

"And you?" The words cracked as they left our lips. "Will you run?"

He shook his head. "I can't. They've already taken Lissa and Hally. But you have to. Addie, *please*. Run. You can't—Eva—"

"Devon?" someone shouted. "Devon Mullan!"

Ryan stiffened. Addie twisted around just in time to see a man in a white button-down shirt slam his car door shut. He strode toward us, his lips thinning as his shoes sank into the mud.

"There you are, Devon." The man was tall—lean, with a strong jaw and short, light brown hair. He looked about our parents' age, no more than forty-five. A good-looking man. Crisp. Official. "I was just about to give up and see if you'd gone on home. Didn't we agree to meet by your locker?"

"I forgot," Ryan said, his voice flat.

The man looked at us. Glanced, to be more precise. But a glance that made me feel naked, as if he was looking straight past our eyes and seeing Addie and me curled in the nebulas of our mind.

"Well, no real harm done," he said, sounding as if real and grievous harm had been done indeed. He gestured to his car. It gleamed on the side of the road like a black monster in wait. "Are you ready to go now?"

"One moment," Ryan said. He shifted on his feet, stepping forward—toward us. Before we knew what was happening, he'd pulled us into a hug. Addie flinched and tried to jerk backward. He held us still. I was caged in our body and caged in his arms and, somehow, the former was the real prison.

"*Run*," he whispered into our ear.

Then he let go and walked toward the car, his hands in his pockets, his movements unhurried. We stared after him.

"Well," the button-down man said. He gave us a smile, a threat wrapped in a promise. Tied with a bow. "Are you Addie, then?"

Addie swallowed.

<He already knows> I said. *<He's not really asking.>*

"Yeah," Addie said. "That's me."

"Nice to meet you, Addie," said the button-down man. He nodded at us, then turned and walked off. His shoes left muddy footprints all the way to his car. Ryan looked at us one last time before opening the passenger-side door and ducking inside.

We watched them drive away.

Run. The word reverberated inside us.

I will always wonder what might have happened if we'd listened.

ELEVEN

He came for us that same night.

Mom had just changed into her waitressing uniform after sending Lyle to his last dialysis session of the week. A coworker had begged her to take over her shift at the restaurant, and after Lyle told her a million times he'd be fine alone at the clinic for an hour or so—a nurse would be within calling distance the entire time—she'd bitten her lip and agreed. Dad was heading in the opposite direction. He'd come home from work a little early so he could drive to the city and sit with Lyle for the remainder of his session.

Addie and I sat at the table, about to eat dinner. The only ones not in motion.

The doorbell rang just as we took our first bite. The fork froze in our mouth, tines hard and metallic against our tongue.

Mom frowned, caught in the middle of putting up her hair. "Who could that be?"

"It's probably someone selling something," Addie said slowly. "They'll go away if you ignore them."

But the bell rang again, followed by a bout of knocking.

Each blow seemed to shake the pictures on the walls, the figurines on the mantelpiece.

"I'll get it," Dad said.

"No!" Addie said. He jumped and turned to us.

"Something wrong?"

"No," Addie said. Our fingers tightened around our fork. "Just—it's just . . ."

The bell interrupted her. Dad started toward the door, frowning. "Whoever it is, they aren't very patient."

Mom hummed as she twisted her hair into a bun, using the back of a pan as a makeshift mirror. We could barely hear her over the blood roaring in our ears.

"Hello," said a familiar voice as the door opened. "I'm Daniel Conivent, here from Nornand Clinic."

There was the briefest of pauses.

"Let's go outside," Dad said. His voice caught, just slightly—a tremble we noticed only because our nerves were strung so tight. "Please, let's talk outside."

"A clinic," Mom said. "Can't imagine what they'd be selling."

Run echoed Ryan's voice in our head. *Run*, he'd pleaded, but we hadn't listened. Where would we have gone?

Now it was too late.

There was nowhere to run, nowhere to hide. We sat frozen in our chair, staring at our peas and carrots. Our fingers curled around the edge of our seat.

"Addie?"

Our head jerked up, our fork clattering onto the table.

Mom frowned. "You're pale, Addie. What's wrong?"

"Nothing," Addie said. "I, um, I—"

The door opened again. Our eyes flew to the hallway.

<Breathe> I said. *<You have to breathe, Addie.>*

Air struggled into our lungs. Addie gripped the chair so tightly our arms shook.

Dad came into view first. His eyes kept flitting everywhere but our face, his hands hanging limply at his sides. Behind him came a man in a stiff-collared shirt.

<They won't let him take us> I whispered fiercely. *<Mom and Dad won't let him take us.>*

But we both knew it wasn't true. Dad was a tall man. We'd never seen him look so small and helpless.

"Addie," Dad said. "Mr. Conivent says he met you today at school?"

"You remember me, don't you, Addie?" the button-down man said.

Addie managed to nod. Our eyes kept shifting from Mr. Conivent to Dad, Dad to Mr. Conivent. Both men towered over our chair. *Stand*, I thought, but I couldn't manage to say it.

Dad shifted. "He says—he says you've been hanging out with Hally Mullan a lot."

"Not . . . not a lot," Addie said.

"I'm sure this Hally talked with plenty of girls," Dad said, his voice tight. "Are you going to each of them one by one?"

His anger comforted and frightened us all at once. Did it mean he would fight for us? Keep that man from taking us away? Or was he angry because he already knew he had no choice?

Mr. Conivent ignored Dad's question. His eyes stayed intent on ours, a smooth, slick smile on his lips. "What exactly have you been doing at Hally's house, Addie?"

Addie tried to swallow and couldn't. Our mouth opened, but our voice had gone, as if someone had reached down our throat and tangled our vocal cords.

"Addie?" Mr. Conivent said.

<Homework> I said. It was the only thing I could think of. It was what we'd been telling our parents.

"Homework," Addie said.

Mr. Conivent laughed. He was all sleek confidence and aplomb, a summer day compared to the oncoming thunderstorm that was our father next to him.

"I won't drag things on," he said, and held up a manila folder. I hadn't even noticed it in his hand. "These are Addie's medical and school files. Your daughter had . . . problems settling as a child, am I right?"

Mom stepped forward, her knuckles shining white against her black slacks. "How—you can't have access to those."

"In cases like this, we do get a little special authority," Mr. Conivent said.

He opened the file. The top sheet was a black-and-white copy of what looked like our elementary school report card. He shuffled that aside, flipping through the pages until he found a sheet full of charts and figures. "She didn't fully settle until she was twelve. That's rather unusual, isn't it?" His eyes passed from Mom to Dad. "Very unusual, I'd say. Only three years ago."

Again, silence.

Mom's voice broke the stillness. "What do you want?" Her voice made me hurt, made me want to reach out and grab her hand—squeeze until we were both numb.

"Just to do some tests."

"Tests for what?" Dad said.

Mr. Conivent's stare kept us fixed in our seat; his smile kept us dumb and disbelieving. "To see if Eva's still there."

My name slammed into the room like a hurricane, rocking the chairs, rattling the silverware. Or maybe it just felt that way to me. I'd gotten used to Hally and Lissa saying it. Ryan and Devon saying it. But this—this was a strange man. And our parents . . .

"Eva?" Mom said. The word crawled from her lips, frightened and blinking at the harsh light.

Yes. Eva, I thought. *The name you gave me, Mom. The name you never, ever say anymore.*

Dad's hand crushed the back of our chair. "Addie's settled. She settled a little late, but she's settled." Neither of our parents looked at us.

But Mr. Conivent did. "That's what we'd like to verify," he said. "We fear the process never quite finished—that there might have been an oversight when she was younger. There have been great improvements in technology over the past three years. Astounding, really. And I truly believe everyone would benefit from a few more tests." He looked at Dad, then

Mom. He smiled and said pleasantly, "I'm afraid, you see, that your daughter might have been lying to you all this time."

<Addie, say something!>

"That's not true," Addie said, the words tumbling from our lips. "That's not—that's not true."

Mr. Conivent spoke over us without even raising his voice. "Your daughter might be a very sick child, Mr. Tamsyn—Mrs. Tamsyn. You have to understand the consequences inaction now could have on her life. On all your lives." Neither of our parents said anything. Mr. Conivent's voice hardened. "A child suspected of hybridity is, by law, obligated to undergo the proper tests."

"Only if there's real reason to suspect—" Dad said. "You need due cause—"

Mr. Conivent dropped a Xeroxed sheet of paper onto the table. "You signed an agreement, Mr. Tamsyn, when Addie was ten. When she *should* have been taken away. They only agreed to let her stay because *you* agreed to allow any and all necessary examinations—"

<No> I said. *<No, no, Addie. Say something. Say something, please.>*

"But she *settled*," Dad said. His eyes finally met ours, wide and desperate. "She *settled*. The doctors said—"

<Addie, Addie, Addie—>

<What?> she said. Her voice was so flat. *<What can I say?>*

But she spoke anyway, and our voice was steadier than I'd imagined. Tiny, so soft it was barely audible, but unwavering. "I'm not sick."

For all the attention our words drew, Addie might as well have screamed.

"She says she's not sick," Dad said. "The *doctors*, they said—"

"I'm afraid it's not that simple," Mr. Conivent said. He shuffled through his papers again and came up with what looked like a computer printout. "Have you ever heard of Refcon?"

Dad hesitated, then shook his head.

"It's what we call a suppression drug, a highly controlled substance. It affects the neural system. Suppresses the dominant mind. Taken in the right doses, in the right circumstances, it could allow a lingering recessive mind to slowly regain control of the body." He passed Mom the paper. She took it as if in a dream.

"What are you getting at?" Dad said. He didn't look at the paper.

Mr. Conivent turned to us. "Do you have anything to say, Addie?" He waited just a second, as if really interested in our reply. Then he continued, in the voice of a disappointed teacher, "We found a bottle of it hidden in Hally Mullan's nightstand. Apparently, she'd stolen it from her mother's hospital."

A frown flashed across his face, the first time tonight he'd looked truly troubled. Then it was gone. His expression turned to one of silky reproof. "Addie, you knew this, didn't you?"

"No," Addie whispered.

"I'm getting confused here," Dad said. "Are you a representative from the hospital or an investigator? Are you trying to help my daughter or accusing her of some—"

"I'm trying to do what's best for everyone," Mr. Conivent said. "Hally Mullan has admitted to medicating Addie in a misguided attempt to bring Eva out—"

"*No*," Addie said, almost jumping from our chair. "No, she didn't—I didn't—" Had Hally really given us up like that? Or was this man lying through his teeth? I couldn't tell at all, and the unknowing left us unable to even defend ourself. Our parents stared at us in silent, terrified horror. "That *never* happened," Addie said, wrangling our voice back under control.

Mr. Conivent's voice was like a chameleon. First harsh. Then condescending. Then righteous. Now it was gentle. "I have all the papers here. It would only take a day or two. She'd have to fly up to our clinic, but—"

"Fly?" Dad said. He barked out a laugh that felt like a wound, raw and hurting. "How far is this place?"

"A three-hour flight. But Addie would be very well taken care of."

"Isn't there someplace closer? When we—" Dad rubbed his forehead, then took a short breath. "When we had her tested as a child, we did it at the nearest hospital."

"Mr. Tamsyn," the other man said quietly. "Trust me, sir. If you care for your daughter like I know you do, you'll let me take her to Nornand, not ship her off to some third-rate facility." He paused. "Let the government help Addie, Mr. Tamsyn. Same way we help care for your little boy."

Dad's head flew up. But Mom spoke before he could. "This girl, Hally. She's already at the hospital?"

Mr. Conivent smiled at her. "Yes, Mrs. Tamsyn."

"And—and they already know she's . . . hybrid?" Her voice broke at the last word.

Mr. Conivent nodded.

Mom took a shaky breath. "What'll happen to her?"

As if she didn't already know. As if we didn't all already know.

Mr. Conivent's smile stayed as steady as ever. "She's going to stay at Nornand a little while. We have some of the best doctors in the country for this sort of thing. They'll look after her. Her parents are being very open to treatment, and things look hopeful."

"She won't be institutionalized?" Dad said quietly.

"Nornand's program is different," Mr. Conivent said. "First in the field. I told you, didn't I, that you'd want Addie there instead of at some other hospital?" He opened his file again and began pulling out sheets of paper. "Here's some more information. And here—here's what you sign."

The last sheet landed on top of the other two, right next to our plate. Mr. Conivent took a pen from his trouser pocket. One of those thick, shining fountain pens that seem to bleed rather than emit ink. "If Addie wants to go pack while you two go over these, I'd be happy to explain anything you don't—"

"Pack?" Mom's face had gone as pale as her knuckles. "You can't mean—tonight?"

"The flight leaves tomorrow morning at five, and the airport is a good two hours from here. We didn't realize Addie would need to come with us until today, you see."

"Then you don't have a ticket for her," Mom said. "She couldn't—"

"She will be accommodated," Mr. Conivent said, and from the way he said it, I imagined people at the airport scrambling to do his bidding.

I didn't want to be accommodated. I didn't want to go—

<Addie, please—>

"But *alone*—she—no, no. I'm going with her."

"That's entirely unnecessary," Mr. Conivent said.

"I'm going," Mom said, but her voice cracked. The words came out as a plea, not a statement.

He smiled. "If you insist, Mrs. Tamsyn, of course that's fine. Unfortunately, we wouldn't be able to provide another ticket."

"Then we'll take Addie there ourselves later." Dad's shoulders relaxed a little as he spoke.

Mr. Conivent sucked in a breath through his teeth. "Not recommended. You know how difficult it is to get tickets, and any that *are* available will be expensive. It might be a month or more before anything even vaguely reasonable comes up." His lips thinned. "A month is a long time."

If only they knew. A month ago, we barely knew Hally. We'd never met Devon and Ryan. I lived without hope.

"We could find something quicker than that," Dad said. He gripped the back of our chair, refusing to look at the papers Mr. Conivent had dropped onto our table. "Give us two weeks—one week. We could—"

"A lot can happen in a few weeks," Mr. Conivent said,

raising an eyebrow. Then, like flipping between channels in a television, his expression flickered—morphed into something cold and hard. "She might get worse, as sick people often do. Think about it. Your little boy, for example. What would happen if he weren't able to get his treatments for a few weeks?"

His words sucked all the air from the room.

"I think," Mr. Conivent said into the vacuum, "it would be best for everyone if Addie came with me. Tonight."

<*No*> I whispered.

Addie said nothing at all.

Mom touched our shoulder with a trembling hand. "Addie. Addie, go pack, all right?"

Addie stared up at her. Our parents stood on either side of our chair like day and night. Mom, with her corn-silk hair pulled back from her pale, half-moon face. Dad gaping at her, his face red, his lips parted but nothing coming through.

"It'll only be a few tests and things. Scans," Mom said. Her voice was so low she might have been speaking to herself. "You had some when you were little, remember? It's not such a big deal. It'll be all right."

Dad looked at us. Addie stared back. *No,* she mouthed. *No. Please.*

"Take that red duffel bag," he said, and he sounded so weary. "Don't pack too much. You'll only be a few days."

<*No*> Addie sobbed, but only I heard. Our face stayed an unbroken sheet of glass. We didn't move.

"Go on, Addie," Dad said.

We had no choice but to obey.

The stairs were mountains. Our heart dragged down our feet.

<Something will happen> I said. *<Don't worry, Addie. Something will happen. They won't sign.>*

Addie pulled out the duffel bag and began folding clothes, grabbing underwear and socks from our dresser, yanking a T-shirt from the closet.

<They won't let us go. We'll go downstairs and they'll have changed their minds. Trust me on this one, Addie. Watch. Just watch.>

But when we finally trudged down the stairs again, duffel bag hanging like a sack of bones from our shoulder, no one said anything about changed minds. Mom's face looked thinner than I remembered. Lined. Weary. Dad had sunk into our abandoned chair, but he stood when Addie slunk into the room. On the table, the dinner we never got to eat slowly got colder.

"There you are, Addie," Mr. Conivent said, smiling. "Your parents have already taken care of everything." He gestured with his folder toward the door. "My car's parked outside. Why don't you say good-bye now and we'll get going."

Our eyes slid to our parents.

"Just give us a moment," Dad said. He grabbed our wrist and pulled us into the far corner of the family room. There, surrounded by happy pictures of us and Lyle at various ages—from babyhood to only last month, he sat us down on the couch and kneeled before us, still holding our hands.

A tingling had started in our nose. Addie blinked. Blinked again. Again.

"It'll only be two days, tops," Dad said. The huskiness in his voice made the tingling worse. "He told us."

"What if he's lying?" Addie said.

"Any longer than two days and I'll come get you myself," Dad said. "I'll fly right up there and kidnap you from under their noses. You got that?" He smiled weakly, and we tried, tried so hard, to smile in response, but couldn't. Instead, we just nodded and wiped at our eyes with the back of our hand. "So just tough it out two days, okay, Addie? You can do that."

We nodded. Held our breath so the tears wouldn't come. Stared at the ground because it hurt too much to look at Dad's face.

He pulled us into his arms, pressing us against his chest so tight he squeezed tears from our eyes. Addie put our arms around him, and in a moment Mom was there too, hugging the both of us. Dad let go, and we hugged Mom properly. Her eyes were red. They didn't meet ours. But she clutched our hands until they ached.

"You understand, Addie," she whispered in our ear. "You understand, darling. Lyle needs his treatments. They could cut off the treatments, and then—"

She tore herself away so only our hands remained connected, her eyes squeezing shut.

"Mom," Addie said. Our fingers and hers were wound so tight I couldn't tell where ours ended and hers began. "Mom, it's—"

It's okay.

But she couldn't say it. She couldn't force the words out, and so we said nothing, just gripped Mom's hands and held on.

What would they tell Lyle when he came home? Half of me was glad he wasn't here now, that he hadn't been here to witness any of this. The other half wept because I wanted to tell him good-bye.

"He's waiting," Mom said finally. "We shouldn't make him wait."

"He can wait a little longer," Dad said.

But a few minutes more and we had to go. Mr. Conivent led the way to the car, Dad carrying our duffel bag and setting it in the backseat. We were just about to get in, too, when he pulled us aside and hugged us one last time.

"Love you, Addie," he said.

"Love you." Our voice was soft.

We turned again to go. But again he stopped us.

For a long, long moment, he just stared at us, his hand on our shoulder, his eyes tracing our face. Then, just as Addie opened our mouth to say something—I didn't know what—he spoke again. This time it was he who whispered.

"If you're there, Eva . . . if you're really there . . ." His fingers tightened around our shoulder, digging into our skin. "I love you, too. Always."

Then he pushed us away.

TWELVE

The drive to the hotel took an hour and twenty minutes. An hour and twenty minutes of Addie hugging our bag to our chest and staring out the window. An hour and twenty minutes of me wishing we could disappear.

We got our own hotel room with a bed bigger than the one our parents shared at home. The coverlet hung perfectly parallel to the ground. The pillows sat at attention, downy chests fluffed out.

"Order dinner if you like," Mr. Conivent said. "It's covered by the clinic, and room service will bring it up for you."

Addie nodded. Mr. Conivent leaned down slightly and showed us one last thing: our hotel key.

"I'm going to keep this with me," he said. "We're leaving before dawn tomorrow, and I don't want you looking for it early in the morning." He slid the card into his pocket. "Besides, you don't really need to leave the room until then. Just call room service or reception if you want anything. Okay?"

"Okay," said Addie.

"I told the front desk to call at three. I know it's early, but please be ready by three thirty. I'll come get you."

"Okay," said Addie.

He smiled. "Wonderful. Well, good night, then."

"Good night."

Addie didn't order room service. The television screen stayed black and cold-faced like an enemy. The severely tucked bedsheet bound us against the mattress, and Addie curled up beneath it, shivering as the air-conditioning unit blasted under the window.

An hour later, we were still wide-awake, each minute oozing past. Our grip on the pillow tightened. Addie flipped from our side to our back to our other side, then back again. Finally, our eyes popped open.

<*It's going to be okay*> I said, as much for my benefit as hers. <*We're going to be—*>

<*This is your fault*> Addie said.

My words shriveled up.

<*Your fault*> she repeated, whispering. I tasted something sour in the back of our throat. <*Yours.*>

Water in our eyes. Salt on our lips.

<*I never wanted this*> she said, and each word carved into me until I was raw and bloody on the inside, everything scooped out.

I tried to block my pain, but I was never as good as Addie at putting a wall between us. She must have felt it. My pain, my guilt—

My anger.

I wrapped myself around the last one, feeling it heat the

hollow space inside me like a sun.

Addie gave a long, shuddering sigh. Or it started as a sigh. It ended as a sob.

Once upon a time, I had been strong enough to resist fading away. I'd been reduced to smoke, stripped of everything but a voice only Addie could hear. But I'd held on. I'd refused to go.

I prayed now for the strength to face whatever came next.

The phone blasted us from our nightmare of water and coffins. It was pitch-black. The darkness choked us, digging claws into our throat.

Addie groped across the bed. Our fingers met with an endless landscape of pillows and blankets. The phone screamed and screamed. Finally, our hand slammed down on something hard and cool—the nightstand. Addie reached for the black shape beside the taller black shape, which might have been the lamp.

"H-hello?"

"Good mor—well," an unfamiliar voice said. "I suppose it's not really morning yet, is it?"

We were too groggy to form sentences.

"Hello?" said the voice.

Who—? Oh. Oh, right. The wake-up call.

"Yeah—" Addie said. "Yeah, I'm awake." She sat up, propping ourself against the mattress with one arm. "I'm awake," Addie repeated, our voice a little stronger. "Thank you."

"No problem," the receptionist said. "Have a good day."

There was a click, and the line went dead. We sat in the darkness, the phone still pressed against our ear.

<We have to get up> I said softly. I still rang with the reverberations of Addie's words from last night: *Your fault.* My fault. *<He's coming in half an hour.>*

Addie gave no reply. Her silence hurt more than any words.

Slowly, she slid off the bed and padded to the bathroom. The tiles pricked icy needles into the soles of our feet. The sink faucet turned silently—no squeak like the ones in our bathroom at home. The water that came out heated up so quickly Addie almost burned our hands. She had to switch off the hot water completely. The cold water felt more natural, anyway, as it slapped against our face and ran down our cheeks.

She undressed and dressed again without ever turning on the light. There was a change of clothes in our bag, but our school uniform already lay in a rumpled heap on the floor, so Addie pulled it on instead. She brushed our teeth, stuffed our things back into our bag, and then sat on the bed to wait in the heavy, somnolent darkness.

It may or may not have been three thirty when there came a quiet knock. Addie didn't move. She'd been staring at the door since she'd sat down, so she didn't even need to shift our gaze.

"Addie?" he said, intruding on our silence, cracking and burning away the last fragments of our dreams. "I'm coming in."

The door clicked open. Light poured into the room from the hallway, swallowing the darkness wherever the two touched. Mr. Conivent stood blinking in the doorway.

"Are you still in bed?" he said. His voice was lower, harder, sharper than I remembered. He reached inside and flicked on the lights. They seared our eyes.

We stared at him. He stared at us. Our hand tightened on our bag. Then he smiled and laughed a little.

"What are you doing sitting here in the dark? Come on, let's go." He beckoned, and we stood. "You aren't leaving anything behind?"

Addie shook our head.

"Good, because we can't come back."

The ride to the airport wasn't too long, but it was quiet. The radio murmured on and on as the sleeping town slipped by, melting into a never-ending stretch of highway. Each streetlight was a gold flash in the corner of our eyes. We were silent but for one question, which Addie didn't dare ask until the journey was more than halfway over.

"Where's Devon?"

There was a slight pause before Mr. Conivent answered. "I sent him ahead in a taxi." He took his eyes off the road to give us a small smile that only made his next words more chilling. "He's a little upset at the moment, so I think the two of you would be better off separated for now. Don't worry about it. Someone will meet him at the airport."

"We'll be on the same plane, though?" Addie said.

"Yes," Mr. Conivent said, a growing edge in his voice. "But we weren't able to get seats next to one another. You won't see him."

It was still dark by the time we checked in at the airport. Addie and I had never been on a plane before; the excitement we might have felt was replaced by a sharp, twisting pain in our stomach.

"Come on," Mr. Conivent said as we lagged at a window, watching a plane lift off from the runway outside. We couldn't make out details, mostly just flashing lights in the gloom.

Addie followed him through check-in, then to security. We'd seen things like this on television, but never been near one in real life. We'd heard enough about them, though. Whenever someone at school got to go on a plane, they came back bursting with stories and wouldn't shut up for ages.

It was early, the security area almost deserted but for us. Mr. Conivent started emptying his pockets and gestured for Addie to do the same. "Put your bag on the conveyor belt. And make sure there's nothing metal in your pockets."

Addie hesitated, and he motioned with his head again. "Come on, Addie."

Addie eased the duffel bag's strap over our head. The bag began moving away from us as soon as she set it on the belt.

"Nothing metal?" Mr. Conivent said. "No keys? Money?"

She shook our head.

"All right, then," he said. "Go through that archway over there. I'll be right behind you."

Addie walked toward where he pointed, but stole a glance over our shoulder before stepping under the arch. Mr. Conivent was talking with an officer. The latter mumbled into a walkie-talkie between sentences. Before we could catch more than a few words—"here?" "Yes, he—" "three"—a man in uniform on the other side of the arch called for us to come on through.

Addie obeyed, then nearly jumped out of our skin when something started beeping. A step backward brought us back under the arch again. The beeping began anew.

"Hey, hold still," the officer said, grabbing our wrist and drawing us aside. He was dressed a little like Mr. Conivent—dark pants and shoes, white shirt. Official. "Did you empty your pockets?"

Addie pulled our hand against our chest as soon as he let it go. "I don't have anything,"

"Well, hold out your arms—that's right. Straight out like that. I'll just pass this sensor over you, okay?"

The black wand flashed as he bent and moved it along our right leg. But when he passed it up our left one, it started beeping like the arch had.

"You're absolutely sure you don't have anything in your pocket?" the officer said. "Check for me one more time."

"I don't usually put anything there," Addie said, but she reached into our skirt pocket anyway. "I—"

Something small and smooth brushed against our skin. Addie closed our fingers around it and pulled it free: a small black disk, slightly larger than a quarter, with a tiny light set in the middle. Almost—almost familiar, though I couldn't imagine where we'd seen it before.

"See," the officer said. He didn't sound angry, and Addie relaxed a little. "Something like that might set these things off."

<*What is it?*> Addie said. Something inside me unclenched at her voice. She hadn't spoken to me since we'd woken up.

<I don't know> I said.

"Here, I'll hold that for you," the officer said. Addie put it in his hand, and he glanced at it before passing the wand over our body again. This time, the thing stayed quiet. "All done," he said, giving the coin back to us. He even smiled a little.

"Is there a problem?"

Addie spun around. When had Mr. Conivent gotten so close?

"Not at all," the officer said. "You're free to go."

"Wonderful," Mr. Conivent said, and he was smiling the same way he had when he'd seen Addie walking down the stairs back at home. "Get your things, Addie. We're behind on time as it is."

"What was that all about?" he added as Addie grabbed our bag and jogged along behind him.

"Nothing," Addie said. But our hand closed tightly around the coin.

The airport was arranged into gates, each labeled by a shiny black number on a plaque. By the time we reached the correct one, a line of people was already waiting to board the plane. Mr. Conivent strode to the service desk, leaving us behind a young woman and her two children. The boy, maybe seven or eight and looking highly uncomfortable in his dress clothes, stared at us with big blue eyes.

Addie tried not to be as obvious as she watched Mr. Conivent argue with the woman at the desk. The latter kept gesturing to the computer. We couldn't see Mr. Conivent's face, but his shoulders were stiff.

"Your hand's *shining*."

Addie looked down, frowning slightly at the little boy who'd spoken.

"Your hand," he repeated, pointing to our right side. Addie stared. A bright red light pulsed out from between our fingers. The coin. The light we'd noticed before had come to life and was flashing slowly on and off.

"What is it?" the boy asked, leaving his mother's side.

Addie's frown deepened. "I don't know."

The boy stood on tiptoe, trying to get a better view.

"Tyler?" The line had moved. The young woman grabbed her son's arm and pulled him forward, ignoring his protests.

"What's that?" said a voice over our shoulder.

Addie jumped, nearly ramming our skull into Mr. Conivent's chin. He straightened. How did he manage to keep sneaking up on us like this?

"Nothing," Addie said. Our fingers curled shut.

His hand clamped around our wrist. "May I see?"

<Let him> I said quickly. *<He'll only be more suspicious if you don't.>*

Mr. Conivent plucked the black coin from our palm and held it to the light. Our eyes traced his movement, pinpointed on the blinking coin until he returned it to us.

"Funny-looking thing," he said.

Addie tried to smile. "I got it at a joke shop."

"Did you? What does it do?"

"It's—"

I rattled off the first thing that came to mind. <*It's part of a bigger trick.*>

"It's part of a bigger trick," Addie said. "And it never really worked, anyway. I just found it in my bag—I have tons of junk in there."

"All right," he said. He'd already turned away. "Well, let's go, then."

The tunnel leading to the plane echoed with grumbling suitcase wheels. A flight attendant stood by the plane's mouth, smiling at us when we reached the threshold.

We stepped into the plane. Mr. Conivent walked as briskly as he could down the narrow corridor, but he kept having to stop as people found their seats or loaded luggage into overhead compartments. Were Ryan and Devon here already? They had to be; we'd been one of the last people in line.

<*The coin thing's flashing faster*> Addie said.

<*Don't stare at it*> I said. <*He might notice.*>

She raised our eyes and lowered our fist to our side. The woman and her children in front of us finally found their seats, and we heard the mother mutter to herself, "Thank God we're by the bathrooms."

Ahead of us, an older man grappled with his suitcase, and Mr. Conivent had to stop again, his lips thinning. The coin in our hand was warm.

<*Just one quick look*> I said.

Addie turned slightly, hiding the coin in case Mr. Conivent glanced over his shoulder. The light was no longer flashing. Instead, it glowed an unwavering red. She frowned at it, our bottom lip caught between our teeth. We didn't notice when one of the bathroom doors opened.

But when we looked up again, there was no way not to notice the dark-haired boy standing in the aisle. And no way not to recognize who he was.

THIRTEEN

What happened next happened very quickly and almost silently. Devon's finger shot to his lips. He ducked back into the bathroom. The door shut.

"Addie?" Mr. Conivent said, her name half sigh and half warning. "What is it now?"

"Nothing," Addie said. Our heart was thumping, but she turned and kept our expression placid. "I've just never been on a plane before."

"There's not much to see." He beckoned for Addie to close the three or four feet between him and us. "Come on. We need to get to our seats."

She followed Mr. Conivent down the aisle, farther into the belly of the plane. Despite the incredibly early hour, most of the other passengers were as smartly dressed as he was, the women in skirts and pantyhose, the men in pressed shirts. Our scuffed oxfords stood out in a line of heels and leather shoes.

"Thirty-four-E," Mr. Conivent said finally. "Here we go. Give me your bag."

Addie handed it over, then frowned. The seats on either

side of 34-E were both filled by middle-aged businessmen in dark suits. Mr. Conivent was still trying to stuff our bag into the overhead bin. Addie tapped him on the arm. "There's only one seat."

Mr. Conivent nodded as he slammed the compartment shut. "I'm down that way." He gestured back in the direction we'd just come. "On the other side of where we entered. If you need help, call for a stewardess. It's not a long flight."

Addie nodded, the coin hot in our palm. Devon's face was captured in my mind, beckoning for us to be quiet. Addie sat down, and I hoped Mr. Conivent would leave, but he didn't. He stood in the aisle like a sentinel. Eventually the man on our left roped him into a rather one-sided conversation as Addie fidgeted in our seat.

Finally, a stewardess in a blue-and-white uniform told Mr. Conivent he had to sit. Then another woman at the head of the plane began explaining what to do if the plane went down. Addie and I both listened. At least one of us would remember what to do. I'd thought we'd get a chance to run to the bathroom when the stewardess finished, but then the plane began moving and we couldn't go anywhere.

<He wouldn't be there, anyway> I said. *<They would've made him go to his seat.>*

The plane screamed, careening faster and faster down the runway. Then, with a lurch and a pop in our ears, it wrenched itself from the ground. Our legs jellified. Addie squeezed the armrests, our back pressed against the seat. She glanced only once out the window, but it was enough. We saw the dark shape of the airport below, growing smaller and smaller as we left the ground behind.

The seat belt sign extinguished ten or fifteen minutes later, and Addie mumbled an apology to the businessman in the aisle seat as she squeezed past him and stumbled down the aisle.

The bathroom doors were shut, but little panels declared UNOCCUPIED in bright green. Addie looked around before pulling open the door Devon had been hiding behind earlier. The tiny bathroom was empty. The one next to it was empty, too. So was the one next to that.

A man sitting nearby shot us a strange look.

Our hand closed around the handle of the fourth door. Addie jerked it open.

And this one was not empty.

"Shh," Devon said before Addie could speak. He took our arm and pulled us into the bathroom, yanking the door shut behind us. We stood, squished between the sink and the wall, boxed in by the toilet and the door. And Devon. His face was half a foot from ours, his hands by our elbows, one knee pressed against our leg. We were folded together with nowhere to go, backs against walls, trying to breathe. Everything vibrated.

"You didn't run," he said. His voice was quiet, but something in it hummed the same tenor as the plane's engines. The sink's hard edge dug into our back, keeping Addie from shifting away from his touch. "Ryan told you to run. Why didn't you?"

A bout of turbulence rocked the bathroom. Addie squeezed our eyes shut until it was over. The bathroom was too small. Way, way too small.

"Of course I didn't run," she said through our teeth. "Where would I have gone?"

Devon looked like he was going to argue, but the bathroom trembled again and by the time Addie reopened our eyes, he'd swallowed what he was going to say. "You didn't admit anything?" The words were hardly a question, more a confirmation. "You played dumb?"

"I'm not stupid," Addie said. We couldn't focus, not in this tiny, rattling place, with the door behind us and Devon so close. Sweat pricked the back of our neck, heat rushing through us in waves. Our chest constricted, a band cinching tighter and tighter and tighter until every breath was a war.

Devon frowned. "Are you okay?"

<Concentrate on his face> I said. *<Don't think about anything else.>*

"I'm fine," Addie said. Our voice was rough, but she listened to me, keeping our eyes on Devon's face. "And I didn't run. And now I'm here." Our hands clenched.

Neither she nor Devon said anything for a moment. Our muscles trembled from the effort to keep still. Our gaze stayed firmly straight ahead. Was Addie separating Devon's face into brushstrokes? Into light and shadow? I would never see the world in terms of colored dabs on a palette, the way Addie sometimes seemed to, but I'd seen her draw enough people to imagine how she might sketch the hard, smooth line of this boy's jaw, the straight sides of his nose. How she might shade his hair curling across his forehead, almost brushing against his eyebrows.

I could picture some of the hues she would pick and mix—yellow ocher, burnt sienna, violet—to color in Devon's face, which was also Ryan's, as Addie's was also mine.

"You brought the chip, at least," Devon said finally.

"What?" Addie said.

Devon stared at us. "The chip. The black chip. Ryan put it in your pocket when he—you have to have it."

Addie uncurled our fist finger by finger. She raised the chip but didn't look away from Devon's eyes. "You mean this?"

He didn't look down, either, just kept staring back at us. Wondering, maybe, at our shallow breaths and the tension in our limbs. Finally, Addie lifted our hand higher, almost to the level of our mouth. The light glowed red between us and Devon, a Cyclops's eye on a round, black face.

This seemed to snap Devon back to attention. "Yes, that."

He dug an identical circle from his pocket and raised it next to ours. It also shone red. Every shift he made meant Addie had to move as well, a giving and taking of space, of air. I tried to think of something else, something good, something nice, and all that came to mind was the day Ryan tried to explain *ampacity* and I decided he was probably the worst teacher I'd ever had.

"Well, what is it?" Addie said.

"Not much," he said. "Not enough. But it was all we had at the moment. There wasn't time to make anything else." He pointed. "See the light?"

"Yes," Addie said.

"Ryan fixed the light to glow when the chips are together," he said. "If we were a little farther apart—"

"They'd flash?" Addie said.

He nodded. Addie brought the chips closer to our eyes, studying the light and the tiny screws in the back. "Was it hard? To make them?"

"Easier than hacking into your school files," he said.

Addie looked up sharply. Then, to my surprise, she cracked a smile. "I'd imagine so."

A moment passed, less tense now, but more awkward. The sink's sharp edge still dug into our back.

"I should go," Devon said. "He'll wonder why I'm taking so long."

"Mr. Conivent?" Addie said. "Is he sitting by you?"

Devon nodded. "And you?"

Addie gave a tiny jerk of our head. "Down that way. Thirty-four-something. I guess . . . I guess my ticket was sort of last-minute."

His eyes were steady, unblinking. "Did he say they were just going to do a few tests?"

Addie nodded, then finally broke eye contact. "He said I'd be back in two days."

Devon slipped his chip back into his pocket, but he didn't move to leave. The plane rumbled. Addie looked down at our fist, our elbow clamped against our side.

"They might not be able to tell," Devon said. "With how things are, with how weak Eva still is, she might not show up on the scans. You might still be able to go home."

"Yeah," Addie said quietly.

"I'll go out first since Conivent's waiting," Devon said. "Wait a few minutes before leaving." He and Addie shuffled awkwardly in the cramped space until he could reach and unlock the door. His eyes shifted back to our face. "Keep denying everything. And keep the chip with you, so we can find each other again."

"I will," Addie said. He nodded, opened the door, and shut it again before anyone in the nearby seats could realize there was more than one person inside. Addie relocked the door, sat on the toilet lid, and put our head in our hands. She trembled in the confinement.

Addie stared out the window for the rest of the flight. The lights multiplied below, popping up like fairy rings. A rumbling lay below every seat like an enormous slumbering cat. Once, a baby started screaming. Its mother hushed it with coos and a rattle.

The men sharing our row were both asleep by the time the captain announced our impending descent. We began dropping just as the sun came up, the plane plunging into the gold pool seeping from the horizon. Squinting, we watched the skyscrapers draw closer and closer. We hadn't seen such tall buildings since we'd moved. Already, my mind swam with memories of sterile waiting rooms, too-big hospital gowns, ticking clocks, and distant doctors.

Addie took deep breaths as the plane hit the runway, the purring engine intensifying to a growl, then a snarl, and then an all-out roar. The air screeched past. We barreled forward so fast I was afraid we'd take off again. But little by little, the plane slowed until we were just rolling along the runway. The lights came on. Beside us, the businessmen stirred.

The captain welcomed us to the city and state as the plane turned a corner, then told us the temperature and time.

<How will he bring Devon and us out at the same time?> Addie said.

<I don't know.>

We sat and waited. We sat and waited as the plane slowed and came to a stop. We sat and waited as everyone else stood, yawning and stretching.

"Time to get up," the man beside us said. He rolled his shoulders and rubbed the back of his neck.

"I'm waiting for someone," Addie said.

The aisle filled with people pulling luggage from overhead compartments. The man on our left joined them while the one on our right kept giving us meaningful looks. Addie was about to say something when we heard a commotion a little ways up the corridor.

"Sorry," someone repeated, threading through the people in the aisle. "Sorry. Excuse me."

An airline stewardess tumbled into the hollow by our seat. She smiled, a little unsteady on her black heels, and tried to brush her bangs from her eyes.

"Mr. Conivent sent me to get you," she said. "He's a little caught up over there and doesn't want you to wait too long—or get in anyone's way." The man stuck between us and the window gave her a grateful smile.

Addie stood, holding the seat in front of us for balance.

"Which bag is yours?" the flight attendant asked as she looked toward the overhead compartment.

"The red duffel," Addie said. She slid out into the corridor, squeezing in beside the woman. "Where are we going?"

The lady tugged our bag free and set it in our arms. "Just to the terminal. He'll come find you as soon as he gets out."

Addie checked the chip in our hand a few times as we edged toward the front of the plane. The light stayed steady. Devon and Ryan were here somewhere, close by.

A sliver of dawn peeked through the crack between the edge of the plane and the tunnel. As Addie stepped over it, hugging our duffel bag to our chest, the chip's light changed from a solid glow to a rapid blinking. Devon must have moved farther away.

"Coming, honey?" the flight attendant said.

Addie closed our hand and quickened our pace.

The terminal was bright and bustling. People scurried about, their suitcases bumping along behind them. A disembodied voice announced the name of a lost child. Electronic panels blared a list of flight times, delays, and cancellations.

I'd thought we'd just wait by the door, but the stewardess led us through the tiled corridors, her black heels clicking. There were windows everywhere. Outside, the sun had broken through the horizon. It hung in the golden air, half asleep but stretching yellow-tipped fingers across the sky. In our hand, the light on the chip pulsed slower and slower until it went out completely.

The flight attendant kept walking until we reached a noisy food court. Addie looked around, taking in the smell of coffee grinds, the early morning grease of biscuits and fried chicken, the overbright menu of the sandwich stand. The flight attendant steered us to a table but didn't sit.

And so we stood, two statues in a sea of tables and coffee drinkers and too-big muffins. One tall, thin statue in smart black heels. A shorter statue in a school uniform's patent-leather shoes. The silence was like an unwelcome child, pulling at our hair, running its fingers over our lips.

<*Eva*> Addie said.

What were our parents doing now? We'd flown west, so it was later in the day back in Lupside. They'd be up by now, probably. Had they even slept last night? Or had they stayed up the way they used to sometimes before our childhood appointments, emerging from their rooms the next morning looking like ghosts?

What had they told Lyle?

<*I . . . didn't really mean it*> Addie said. <*Last night. About this being your fault.*>

I started to speak, but she interrupted me, words bursting from her like bubbles—fragile, transparent. <*Were you happy, Eva?*>

It was a moment before I could reply.

The wall between us was crumbling down, down, down. Her emotions washed over me, a sea of worry and fear and . . . guilt.

<*Yes*> I said. <*Yes, I was.*>

Addie sighed. The last fragments of her wall swirled away in eddies of some emotion I could not name.

<*What are we going to do, Eva?*> she said.

<*We get through it as best we can*> I said. What else could I say?

"Ah, there he is," the flight attendant said, interrupting our conversation. Relief seeped into her voice, tucked itself into the corners of her smile.

Mr. Conivent parted the crowd with his brisk steps and stiff shoulders. Neither Devon nor Ryan was in sight.

"Thank you," he said to the flight attendant, then turned to us. "You're ready?" Addie nodded. "Wonderful. Let's go, then."

Addie slung the duffel bag over our shoulder and followed him out of the food court, walking in the shadow of his fine leather shoes.

<*Get through it as best we can*> Addie said.

<*As best we can.*>

FOURTEEN

A driver met us at the curb outside the airport, opening the door to a sleek black car much like the one Mr. Conivent had used in Lupside. Addie climbed into the backseat, holding our duffel bag tight against our chest. Other than a quick, murmured sentence or two, Mr. Conivent and the driver didn't speak to each other, and neither said a word to us.

We stared out the window as the foreign landscape flashed past. At first it was just highways, broader and busier than the ones at home. A city shone in the distance—a proper city, with skyscrapers gleaming silver and gold in the morning sunlight. But eventually, we left the city and the highway behind. By the time we reached the clinic, we hadn't seen another building in ages. The land here was untamed, and the sun had baked the life from all the plants, leaving the trees stunted and the grass barely green.

In contrast, Nornand Clinic of Psychiatric Health loomed over a wreath of shrubbery and trimmed green lawns, a silver-and-white oasis in the desert. Three stories tall, the building was full of strange angles and enormous panes of glass, all reflecting the light. Addie and I stared as our car pulled into a parking space up front. Other than two men doing some sort of maintenance work on the roof, the building looked deserted.

The air here was dry, no trace of the humidity that had plagued us back home. But it was just as hot, and Addie squinted as we got out of the car.

All traces of the sweltering summer day disappeared as soon as we entered Nornand's lobby. Here, the air was cool enough to make us shiver. Mr. Conivent headed for the front desk, and Addie glanced at the security guard standing nearby before following after him.

The receptionist checked Mr. Conivent's ID, then nodded and motioned for us to continue to the elevators. I wanted to ask Addie to check the coin in our pocket, but didn't dare. There were too many eyes here, too many windows, too many shiny, mirrored surfaces reflecting our every move.

Flat green and yellow flowers carpeted the elevator. There was a mirror in here, too; instead of one man and one girl, there were double of each. But the mirror helped. It made the already good-sized elevator seem even more spacious. Our heartbeat quickened anyway.

Mr. Conivent pressed the button for the third floor, and our stomach dropped as the elevator lurched up. As kids, we'd jumped whenever the elevator at the shopping mall started or stopped, feeling the split second of weightlessness and its parallel moment of double gravity. It had distracted us from the fact that we were stuck in a small metal box.

A bell dinged. The elevator slowed to a stop. I didn't whisper to Addie, *Hey, let's jump.* Instead, we stood very still and very straight until the great silver doors slid open and Mr. Conivent stepped out.

The long, white corridor stretched to infinity on both ends, lit by row upon row of fluorescent lights. A faint scent of disinfectant clung to every surface like death to gravestones.

A nurse in a gray-striped dress bustled toward us. "Speak of the devil," she said, smiling, and waved forward a delivery boy standing behind her. "I was afraid I'd have to make him wait."

The delivery boy couldn't have been more than two or three years older than we were, with an impressive but lanky height. He carried a small brown package in one hand and held out a clipboard for Mr. Conivent with the other. He also kept staring at us. Just quick looks at first, then more brazenly when Mr. Conivent bent down to sign the papers on the clipboard.

"Perhaps next time, I could just ask Dr. Wendle to sign," the nurse said. "Or even Dr. Lyanne—"

"I'd rather you didn't," Mr. Conivent said.

The nurse nodded, but we saw that only in the periphery of our vision. Addie was too busy staring back at the delivery boy. His eyes were a cold, clear blue, like a doll's eyes.

<Stop it> I said. *<He's going to think you're crazy.>*

<He already thinks we're crazy> Addie said. *<Might as well give him something to talk about.>*

But she was looking away even as she spoke. She'd spent too many years fighting to avoid attention. Old habits are hard to break.

"Oh, hello," the nurse said, as if noticing us for the first time.

She was pale and thin. The corners of her mouth crinkled with a smile. "How are you?"

"Good," Addie said.

Mr. Conivent had taken his package from the delivery boy and was already turning away. "Put her in a room for tonight, please, but bring her to Dr. Wendle first."

"Certainly," the nurse said. "Come on, dear. What's your name?"

"Addie," Addie said.

"Well, come along, Addie." She moved down the hall in the opposite direction, away from Mr. Conivent.

Addie followed her, our bag thumping against our thigh with each step, a shock of red in the midst of Nornand's silver and white. What would the delivery boy tell his friends, I wondered, about the pale-faced girl in the rumpled school uniform?

What would he say about us, locked in here, when he'd long since gone home?

We walked and walked and walked through the long halls. Nornand wasn't as busy, it seemed, as the hospitals we'd visited as a kid. There were a few nurses chatting in doorways, and once we saw a man in a white doctor's coat swish past, but that was it. No people in plain clothes waiting anxiously outside examination rooms, no mothers or fathers or adults of any kind other than the nurses and the doctor. No patients. Except for us. Once, Addie dared a peek at the chip in our pocket, but it was cold and dead.

Finally, the nurse stopped in front of a door labeled 347 in small black letters.

"Dr. Wendle?" she said, knocking.

There was a shuffling sound before a voice called back. "Yes? Come in."

She opened the door and hustled us inside. "This is Addie, Dr. Wendle. Mr. Conivent just brought her in."

Dr. Wendle was a short, sturdy man with a dark-brown comb-over that Addie might have snorted at any other day. He squinted at us through thick-framed glasses before jumping up from his desk. His lab coat flapped behind him.

"Oh, yes, yes," he said, shaking our hand. His eyes flitted over us: our face, our hands, our legs—like we were some new archaeological find. "Mr. Conivent told me to expect you."

I wished someone would tell *us* what to expect.

The nurse tried to take our bag, and when Addie resisted, smiled indulgently. "I'll put it in your room for you, dear. It'll be safe. Don't worry."

She gave one last hard tug and the bag slipped from our hands. We teetered, off balance. Without the bag, I felt small and exposed.

"Come," Dr. Wendle said as the nurse left. "Pull up a chair."

We looked around and saw nothing but a tall metal stool that squealed as Addie dragged it over. Dr. Wendle settled into his own seat, smiling. The tall-backed chair dwarfed him. "I wanted to ask you a few things before we began our testing." He adjusted his glasses and leaned forward. No preamble. No *How was your flight? You must be tired. Where are you from?* Just an eagerness in his eyes that made me feel like the moth the second before the pin goes in. "First, how have you been dealing with Eva?"

Addie jerked backward. "What?"

"Eva," he repeated, his smile dimming a little. He tapped one of the dozen sheets of paper sprawled across his desk. "It says here you had a lot of trouble settling—didn't until after your twelfth birthday, am I correct?"

Addie didn't nod, didn't speak, didn't even move, but the doctor seemed to take her silence as agreement.

"So, it's been about three years. Honestly, I can't believe things have gone on this long. But what can I say? People get lazy, officials get lax, or . . . well, anyway." He steepled his hands. The smile grew again. "So, here's your chance. Tell me. How have you been dealing with Eva?"

I should have been ready for this. The scene with Mr. Conivent last night should have prepared me for anything. But my name on Dr. Wendle's tongue still sent waves of nausea swirling through me.

"No need to be shy," he said. "This is all strictly confidential." His thick lips strained now, fighting to keep their curve beneath his mustache.

Our stomach lurched.

"I—I don't know what you're talking about," Addie said. Our face was hot, our hands slick.

Dr. Wendle raised an eyebrow. "You don't?"

"No," Addie said.

His mustache seemed to emphasize his frown. "You do realize, Addie, that once we test you, we're going to know the truth. So there's no point in lying now."

"I'm not lying." Somehow, Addie kept our voice steady. "I think there's been a mistake."

We sat in silence for a long while, our eyes intent on our lap, the doctor just as quiet as we were. Finally, he sighed and stood, as sullen as a boy promised games and given coal. "All right, then; if you insist." He motioned for us to follow him out of the office. "I'm going to run a test or two," he said without looking at us. "A brain scan, a cog-phy . . ."

Addie hurried after him through the corridors, struggling to keep up with his breakneck pace. We ended up in a laboratory, where Dr. Wendle started fiddling with a large, rectangular machine, squinting at the attached screen. It was the only thing in the room. Addie stood by the door, as far from the yellow-gray contraption and Dr. Wendle as she could be.

Finally, he turned and said, "Come on. Don't be nervous."

Our shoes hardly made a sound against the gleaming white tiles. Our hand was in our pocket, Ryan's coin pressed against our palm.

"Stand there and don't touch anything," Dr. Wendle said. "I just need a second to set things up."

The machine was longer than he was tall and stood almost five feet high. One of the narrow ends was open, revealing a hollow interior. Addie fidgeted beside it. She didn't touch anything. Dr. Wendle seemed to take much, much longer than a second. An hour, at least. How else could we explain the hot, acid sickness burning through our stomach? The buzzing in our ears?

A low whirring started. Dr. Wendle pressed a few buttons, studied the jumble of information on the screen, and then finally looked up.

"All right. It's just about done. I—you haven't changed." He blinked as if he'd expected us to magically know to do this, then scurried to the back of the room. "You can't wear that while you're being scanned." He dug through a drawer and pulled out a long, white hospital gown. "Here, put this on."

Addie took a step back. "What's it for?"

"For being scanned," he said, and pushed us to an adjacent room. The far corner was hidden by a thin blue curtain. "Now change. Quickly, please."

Bronze rings scraped against a metal rod, zipping us up into the dim, phone-booth-sized compartment. For a moment, we didn't dare move.

<*Close our eyes*> I said.

Addie obeyed. It helped a little, but we still undressed as quickly as we could. The hospital gown laced up in the back. We had to bend our arms at awkward angles to reach the strings.

"Almost done?" Dr. Wendle called.

Addie pulled aside the curtain, then bent to fold our clothes and set them on a metal stool nearby.

"Good," Dr. Wendle said, pressing a button on the machine. "Just leave your clothes there. You'll be changing back in a few minutes."

The top of the yellow-gray machine eased open with a hum.

Addie froze halfway across the room.

"What is it?" Dr. Wendle said.

"Tell me—" She swallowed. "Tell me what's going to happen."

He gave us a strange look. "Nothing, really. You're going to just lie down here"—he pointed to the machine—"and—"

"But the top," Addie said. "The top will be open?"

"Well . . ." he said. "It'll only be for a minute."

She was already shaking our head and backing away. "No. No, sorry. I can't."

His hand shot out faster than we'd thought possible, thick fingers locking around our wrist. Our muscles hardened to stone.

"What—what's it for?" Addie said, fighting for time. "The scan." Our chest was so tight she could barely speak. "What're you looking for in the scans?"

Dr. Wendle's frown deepened. But he didn't look angry. If anything, he looked slightly confused. "Brain activity, Addie, of course. You must have done something similar as a child. Less advanced technology, most likely, but the same idea." He gestured at the yellow-gray machine. "This will let me know how bad the problem is." His explanation continued, veering into terminology we didn't understand and studies we'd never heard of.

<*Addie*> I said. <*Addie, we have to do it.*>

<No. *No, I'm not getting in that thing, Eva. I can't.*>

Dr. Wendle had released our arm, and Addie wrapped it around our body. We could hardly register what he was saying.

Fear made our heartbeat rabbit-fast, our throat dry. Fear polluted each breath, thickening them until it was impossible to swallow.

"In the end," Dr. Wendle said, "the more we know, the better we'll be able to fix you right up."

He smiled, like he thought it might be reassuring. Addie didn't smile back. I felt the scream bubbling in our chest even as our lungs seemed to collapse, our airways crumbling shut. Dr. Wendle took our shoulder and started forcing us toward the machine, grunting with the effort. "It'll only take a moment, Addie. Don't be silly."

"No," Addie said. "I can't. I—"

"You can," he said.

"I *can't*—"

I hesitated. The machine winked wicked black eyes at us.

<We have to> I said.

<We can't. We—>

"Addie," Dr. Wendle said.

<Look at it> she cried, small and white in the corner of our mind. *<It's tiny, Eva. It's tiny, and he wants to lock us inside.>*

She didn't need to tell me. But I begged Addie to listen anyway, hoping against hope that if I said it enough times, I'd believe it, too.

<If we don't do it, they'll just drag it on longer. They're not going to let us go home until they're satisfied, Addie. Devon said—Devon said they wouldn't be able to tell, right?>

Dr. Wendle's lips moved, but neither of us was listening.

<*We have to do it*> I said. <*Two days, remember? We tough it out two days. Then we go home.*>

Addie hesitated, then echoed my words.

The mouth of the machine yawned gray and silver. A white tongue lolled down the middle, crinkling slightly as Addie sat down.

<*Slowly*> I said as she lowered us onto our back. <*Carefully. Breathe. Breathe.*>

The last bit was imperative. She'd stopped several times already.

Dr. Wendle leaned over us and adjusted some kind of white arch thing until it curved a few inches above our forehead.

"You're good?" he said. "Comfortable? Lie very still. You won't feel anything at all. I promise."

Just hurry, I thought. Just please, please, please hurry and get it over with.

<*Eva*> Addie said. Tiny, trembling. <*Eva?*>

The top closed, slowly sealing off the light. Soon, all that remained came from the opening by our feet. There was a click, then a louder click. The lid was shut. We were trapped.

Darkness. Our rough breaths. Our drunken heartbeat. I tried to curl myself up as small as possible, tried to hide from whatever this machine was using to probe our body, our mind. I wasn't here. I wasn't here. I didn't exist.

<*Eva*> Addie screamed <*Eva, I can't breathe—*>

Our arm smacked against the side of the box. Panic surged up our throat, bubbled into our mouth. "Let me out—"

<Shh!> I said. <Shh, Addie . . .>

"Please don't move," Dr. Wendle called, his voice muffled. "I can't take a good reading if you move."

Our fist pounded against the horrible, crinkly paper bed. Whispers of fear escaped our lips. I gave up on trying to disappear, on trying to hide. I couldn't, not with Addie so terrified, not when she needed me.

Her fear clashed with mine. But mine was smaller. I was used to being paralyzed.

<We're not trapped> I said, holding her, hugging her, hiding her from our terror's long talons. *<Look, there's light. We could slip out if we wanted to. But we won't. We're going to hold still, okay? Just for a little while.>*

Our hands trembled. I kept talking, wrapping Addie in the warmth of my words.

<Distract me> Addie said. *<Distract me, Eva. Tell me—>*

<A memory?>

<Please.>

So I did. I told her about the time we climbed our old apartment building's fire escape and pretended we were chimney sweepers. I reminded her of the summer we went fishing and fell in the lake. I picked out all the happy memories, the ones shining through the tangled weeds of all our years in and out of hospitals. The free weekends. The days our parents were happy. The time we spent with our brothers, before Mom and Dad started worrying what effect an unsettled child might have on them. Before Lyle's own illness set in.

Slowly, shakily, our fists stilled. Tales from our shared life wove around us, their edges softened and worn by frequent use, their taste mellowed by the passage of the years. I spun them one after another until, an eternity later, there came a pop—a click—and Dr. Wendle's voice: "There. Now that wasn't so bad, was it?"

A hand touched our arm. We jerked upright, our eyes flying open, squinting from the sudden assault of light.

Mr. Wendle smiled at us. "All done," he said. If he noticed how hard we shook, he made no comment, only waved us up and said, "Out you go. The results will take a little while. In the meantime, go ahead and change back."

We stumbled to our pile of clothes. Pulled the curtain half closed before sinking down, our shoulders hunched, our head bowed, our cheek against our knees. It was a long time before we stopped shaking. Blind fingers fumbled with too-tight knots. There was no one to help, and our shoulders ached by the time all the laces were undone.

Addie massaged our neck with one hand and reached for our clothes with the other. She couldn't quite grab everything at once, and the skirt almost slipped from our grasp. Something clattered to the floor. She looked around our feet, but there was nothing there. Had we imagined it?

A red flash in the corner of our eyes.

Ryan.

A wave of longing surged over us. We needed to see a familiar face. I wanted to see *him*.

Addie scrambled into our clothes, jammed our feet into our shoes, and tumbled from behind the curtain. Dr. Wendle was typing something into the computer with one hand and pushing at his glasses with the other.

"I need to use the restroom," Addie said.

"Out the door, turn left, then left again," he said without looking up. "Actually, I should take you—"

"I'll be fine," Addie said, and darted out the door. The chip in our hand blinked on, off, on off on-off onoff.

But Ryan was nowhere to be seen.

A pair of nurses chatting in the hall glanced at us before returning to their conversation. They wore the same gray-striped uniforms and had their hair pulled back in identical buns.

<Which way?> Addie said, looking right, then left, then right again.

<I don't know. Left. Go left.>

She ran down the hall, our eyes flying between our palm and the people around us, searching for a familiar face.

Red white red white red white red white red.

<Where is he?>

Shoes squeaked against tile. We careened around the corner and nearly slammed into someone coming the opposite way. He cried out, dropping a pile of folders. Papers scattered across the floor. White on white.

"Sorry—" Addie said. She kneeled and snatched up a sheet of paper before it slid too far away.

"No problem." The man laughed and bent down, too. "What's the hurry?"

"I was looking for the restroom," Addie said.

He laughed again. "Go on, then. I'll be fine."

"No, I'm okay," Addie said. We didn't meet his eyes.

"Whose kid are you?" he said as we gathered the remaining manila folders and sheets of paper. Our eyes caught a glimpse of a black-and-white brain scan on one of them, then a name. There was another scan and a different name on the sheet under it.

"What?" Addie said.

"Aren't you someone's kid?" the man said. "Someone's daughter, I mean?"

She shook our head.

He frowned. "No?"

CORTAE, JAIME read the paper beneath our fingers. *HYBRID*. Two scans were pasted side by side, looking almost identical except for a black patch marring the one on the right. Each scan had a date scribbled below it. One was from about a week ago. The other was today's. Below the dates was some text—*Age: 13, Height: 5', Weight*—

The man jerked the sheet of paper away before we could read any more.

"You're not a patient, are you?" His voice had lost all traces of laughter.

Addie hesitated. The man snatched up the remaining papers and stuffed them back into his folders.

"I'm just here for a checkup," Addie said. "Mr. Conivent, he—"

"Why are you in street clothes?" he said. "Aren't you supposed to be somewhere?"

<Dr. Wendle> I said. *<Tell him we're with Dr. Wendle.>*

"We were just with Dr. Wendle," Addie said quickly. "He—he did a scan thing on us."

"On us?" the man said.

Addie blanched. "Me and another kid," she said. "He's going to be worried if I'm gone too long. I—I've got to go." We jerked around and hurried back in the direction we'd come, ignoring the man when he called after us, praying no one would make us stop. No one did. Addie darted around the corner and pressed our back against the wall, our eyes closing for a moment before snapping open again.

I trembled.

Us.

Addie had said *us*.

The last time Addie had referred to ourself as *us* aloud, we'd been in single digits. We'd still promised each other nothing could ever, ever come between us. It had been me and her against the world.

<*We should go back before Dr. Wendle comes looking for us*> I said softly.

<*Yeah*> Addie said. <*Yeah, I know, Eva.*>

But I heard the waver in her voice.

FIFTEEN

It wasn't hard to find Dr. Wendle's lab again. All the doors were clearly labeled; we just had to follow the numbers back. *What if we don't go back?* I wanted to say. What if we found that elevator again and rode it back down to the first floor? What if we just walked right past the receptionist, the guard at the door . . . But I didn't say anything, because then what?

Better to stay. Stay and do as they asked and wait, because Dad was going to bring us home. He'd promised.

Besides, we needed to find Hally and Ryan. We couldn't leave unless we knew they were safe.

Addie was just about to open the door to Dr. Wendle's lab when we heard the voices.

". . . she had her vaccinations . . . shouldn't be a problem . . ."

"There have been . . . before . . . when doctors get the prescription wrong or the kid is just . . ."

Addie stilled. Then, slowly, she pressed our ear against the door. One voice belonged to Dr. Wendle. The other to a woman. Both spoke too quietly for us to pick out more than a few words.

". . . still the cog-phy test . . . more effective sometimes . . ."

" . . . es, but only in the latter stages. When . . . can't tell . . . there's al . . . chan . . . at . . ."

The woman's voice dropped even more in volume until we could barely hear it at all.

<Turn the knob. Open the door a crack> I said, even as a part of me warned that this was too much of a risk. We shouldn't be trying to eavesdrop—we should be trying to be the perfect patient.

Gingerly, Addie pressed down on the handle and pushed inward an inch.

"There isn't much we can do until we have all the test results," Dr. Wendle said.

"No," the woman said. "We'll have to wait."

A pause.

"You weren't able to make it to this one, right?" Dr. Wendle said. "Have you heard anything yet? About how it went?"

There was no reply for a long moment. Then: "Better than the others."

Dr. Wendle laughed, then trailed off when the woman didn't join in. He cleared his throat. "Well, of course. But that doesn't mean much. It won't be enough for the review board, surely."

"No."

"There's still time. And there are plenty of other avenues we're still exploring. Eli's doing much better now, isn't he? I was thinking of putting him on Zalitene starting this week. It might help with his episodes, and—"

"He was a sweet boy," the woman murmured.

"What?" Dr. Wendle said. "Eli?"

"No," she said. "No, I meant . . ." Heels clicked across the floor. "I better go. Send me the girl's file when the results are final."

<*Move*> I said. <*Hurry. She's coming.*>

But Addie didn't budge. Our hand was clamped to the door handle, our ears straining to catch every word.

<*Move*> I shouted. <*Go in! Go in! Now!*>

Addie lurched into the room, clutching the door to keep from falling. The woman cried out and stumbled backward. We stared up at her, matching her face with her voice. She was younger than we'd expected, perhaps in her late twenties or early thirties. A pale woman with ash-brown hair and wide hazel eyes.

"Are you all right?" she said, tugging at her lab coat to smooth it out. The surprise disappeared from her face as neatly as the wrinkles from her coat. Without it, she looked suddenly older.

Addie nodded. "Yeah. Sorry. I—um, fell, and—"

The woman pulled her lips into a polite smile.

"I got lost," Addie said. "I was searching for the bathroom, and I must have taken a wrong turn because I kept looking for this room and—"

"Well, you're very smart to have found your way back," the woman said. The detachment in her voice knocked Addie from her babbling. Our face smoothed over, our expression becoming nearly as distant as hers.

". . . I just knew the room number, that's all."

"Addie, right?" the woman said. She held out her hand, and after a second, Addie placed ours in hers. Her grasp was dry and cool, her smile closed-lipped and brief. "I'm Dr. Lyanne."

"Nice to meet you," Addie said automatically.

"Where are you supposed to be headed?" said Dr. Lyanne.

"I don't know," Addie said. She looked at Dr. Wendle, who hadn't said a word this entire time. Dr. Lyanne followed our gaze.

"Ah, well," Dr. Wendle said, clearing his throat, "I'll need a little longer with these results, and we won't be ready for the cog-phy until after lunch. Until then, she . . . well . . ." He paused, and our stomach growled in the bubble of silence.

All eyes turned to us. Our face heated.

Dr. Lyanne frowned. "Have you had breakfast yet?"

Breakfast? We'd forgotten all about breakfast.

"No."

If I hadn't known better, if it hadn't been such a preposterous idea, I would have sworn the woman just barely kept from rolling her eyes. But Dr. Lyanne was the picture of professionalism in her black A-line skirt and dark blue blouse.

She muttered something under her breath, so low and so fast we couldn't catch it. Then she took our arm and guided us toward the door. "Come on, let's get you something to eat."

"You aren't taking her to the other children, are you?" Dr. Wendle called as Addie followed Dr. Lyanne into the hall, trying to match our feet to the woman's brisk steps.

Dr. Lyanne spared a glance behind her as the door swung shut. "Why not? She'll end up with them anyway."

"When can I call my parents?" Addie said as we hurried after Dr. Lyanne. Unlike the nurse, she didn't check to make sure we were keeping up.

"Later, I'm sure," Dr. Lyanne said. "It'll be taken care of."

We turned down a hall that looked much like the last. Nornand was a maze of white corridors. Our black skirt and shoes were like splotches of ink on a clean canvas.

"This is the way to the Ward," Dr. Lyanne said. "You'll always be accompanied in the hallways, so it's unlikely you'll ever get lost, but it's good to have a general sense of the layout just in case." She pointed down another hallway without even looking. "Over there's the locker rooms, where the kids shower and get ready for bed. The Study room is in the opposite direction, but I'm sure someone will take you there later."

"I was—I was told I'm only supposed to be here two days," Addie said. "So I don't really need to . . . I mean, I'm going home soon, anyway."

Dr. Lyanne slowed, like she was ready to turn and face us. But at the last moment, she quickened her pace again. "Well, no harm in knowing. This whole wing of the clinic is dedicated to hybrids, but—"

She stopped walking. Addie almost slammed into her.

"What—" Addie said, then snapped our mouth shut as she saw the gurney round the corner.

We'd seen plenty of gurneys before, nameless people

sliding past us in crisp, white beds, IVs drip, drip, dripping into their veins. Mostly frail old men and women—papier-mâché people who trembled with every breath.

The boy in this gurney was not papier-mâché. He was small and young and brown-eyed, staring upward at the ceiling as the nurse wheeled him across our path.

Dr. Lyanne made a soft, strangled noise. It lasted only a second before she muffled it. But it was enough to draw everyone's attention—ours, the nurse's, and that of the boy on the gurney with the bandages around his head. And it was enough for me to pick out the name buried in the cry.

<*Jaime.*>

Jaime Cortae?

Everyone else turned to Dr. Lyanne, but Addie couldn't stop staring at the boy. He didn't move, but his eyes met Dr. Lyanne's for just one moment, and then he looked away. Jaime Cortae. Thirteen. Two scans. Two dates.

Two dates. Two scans of the same thing, but different. Jaime Cortae and a bandage around his head and the two scans of his brain—

Two scans.

A *before* and *after* shot.

And just like that, the world fell away.

SIXTEEN

The nurse quickened her pace, and soon she and the gurney were out of sight. But neither Addie nor Dr. Lyanne started walking again.

Surgery. I flashed back to all the doctors we'd seen before. All the treatments they'd proposed when Addie and I were children. There had been pills—so many pills. There had been the guidance counselor and the psychiatrists and the chilly white examination rooms. But there had never been talk of surgery.

"Breakfast," Dr. Lyanne said, more to herself than to us. Her voice echoed. "Down this way." And she threw herself forward again, walking even faster than before. She didn't bother pointing out any more places. She didn't speak at all until we reached a pair of double doors just as a nurse stepped out, pulling a large steel cart behind her.

"Oh, hello, Dr. Lyanne," the nurse said with a smile. "The children haven't finished eating yet."

Dr. Lyanne touched our shoulder lightly but firmly, making us take a step forward. Her eyes were even more distant than before. "I'm just here to drop Addie off."

"Of course," the nurse said. She turned her smile to Addie and held the door open. "Go on and sit down. I'll bring you a plate."

Addie didn't move. Surgery. *Surgery.*

Dr. Lyanne pushed us through the doorway, Addie twisting around just in time to see the door click shut. Dr. Lyanne and the nurse had remained on the other side. Our heart sat like a jagged rock in our chest.

The room looked like a miniature version of our school cafeteria. One long table stretched across the middle of the floor, surrounded by matching stools. The group seated on those stools was less uniform. All the boys wore light blue shirts and dark pants, all the girls a similar shirt and navy skirts—but the older kids looked about our age while the littlest boy, copper-haired and pale, was barely taller than Lucy Woodard. If he was ten, he was awfully small.

We didn't focus on him for long. Because there, near the end of the table—half hidden by all the other kids—were Devon and Hally.

Devon was still in his regular clothes, but Hally wore the same blue uniform as the others. Our hands fisted, fingers curling inward, biting into our palms. Addie almost, *almost* cried out.

Devon's mouth opened—

"Who're you?" the youngest boy said.

Conversation ceased. All eyes shifted to us. Thirteen, I counted. Thirteen kids. Fourteen including Addie and me. . . .

Twenty-eight, if they were really all hybrid, and we were being truthful. They filled the table almost to capacity. There were, however, a few empty seats, hiccups of space unshaded by blue.

"Shush, Eli," said the blond girl sitting beside him. He did, but he didn't stop staring. There was something unsettling in the way he watched us, something wary like a cornered animal. He shouldn't have been here. Now that we looked closely, there was no way he was ten yet. He should have had at least another year or two with his family.

"It's because Jaime's gone home," said another girl. She was probably two or three years Eli's senior and built like a fairy, her long dark hair coming nearly to her waist. It looked heavier than she did. "They've brought somebody to replace Jaime."

Silence wound around everyone's necks, flicking scaly tails in troubled faces. Most of the children averted their eyes. Plastic forks sat abandoned on industrial yellow trays.

They thought Jaime had gone home.

"Well, don't just stand there," the blond girl said to us. She was among the oldest in the room, and her glare darkened an otherwise pale face.

Slowly, Addie walked over and sat in the empty chair diagonal from Devon. He nodded at us, a movement so slight it was barely noticeable. Next to him, Hally pressed her lips together and kept her expression more or less under control.

"What *is* your name?" someone said. It was disconcerting to be the center of so much attention after a lifetime of avoidance.

"Addie," Addie said. Though the room wasn't large, our voice echoed in the silence. Everything was so bright it was like being under interrogation.

"And?"

"*Shh!*" someone said. Nervous eyes darted about. I caught snatches of whispered sentences, arguing and denying and hushing—the nurse wasn't here, so it was okay—but that didn't mean anything, because they had *cameras*—they don't have cameras in *here*—and even if they *did*—well, *I* thought—

"*Shh!*" everybody seemed to say at once.

And just in time, because the door opened and a nurse entered. She smiled at the silence and rows of round, staring eyes. "So quiet this morning. Are we not awake yet?" A special little smile was allowed to Eli, who didn't smile back. "Well," she said. "I see Addie already found a seat. Sorry for the wait, dear. I had to go back to the kitchen to get you a plate."

Our tray looked exactly like the others. Each partition had its little scoop of breakfast food: sodden scrambled eggs; burned, brittle bacon; a pair of pasty pancakes.

"Thank you," Addie said quietly.

"You're welcome," the nurse said. "I'll be right over here if you need anything." She settled into a folding chair by the door, crossing her legs and retrieving a magazine from the ground.

The stillness lasted a moment longer. Then, like a movie winding into action, a murmur of conversation started up again. Silverware clacked as people stabbed at their hospital-brand breakfast. No one spoke above a whisper. Heads stayed bent, shoulders forward. Only Eli let his gaze roam to Addie and me, then across the room to the nurse.

"Addie . . . *Addie.*"

Our eyes flickered toward Hally, who gave us a tiny smile. Then her face crumpled. "I'm sorry," she whispered. "I'm so, so sorry. I didn't mean—I just—I had to see him. I couldn't just—"

"Shh," Devon said, tilting his head toward the nurse.

Hally swallowed the rest of her words. And I remembered what Ryan had told me about Hally, about how much she'd longed to meet other hybrids, to be with people like herself. Like us.

Addie hesitated. "It's okay."

"None of that matters now," Devon said, working at a pancake with his fork and butter knife. His face was carefully expressionless, without even his customary frown of concentration or mild annoyance. "They're here. We all need to get out."

"How?" Addie said.

"Keep a low profile, for one," Devon said. "Eat something, Addie—she's watching. No, don't look now. Just eat."

Our hunger had dulled to an ache. The food did nothing to revive it, but Addie ate anyway, tasting the eggs first. They were rubbery on top, spongy in the middle, and salty all the way through. She chewed mechanically as Devon continued speaking, his lips barely moving. None of the other kids seemed to be listening to us, but it was hard to tell. The ones who weren't talking to anyone stared at their trays. "Keep your head down. Deny everything. You've still got hopes of your tests coming back negative. Or shady, at the very least."

I'd be lying if I said I didn't feel a cold rush of relief. Just hearing him say it made us both feel better, however slightly. But it was quickly overcome by another source of fear. "What about you two?"

"We'll figure something out," Lissa said; it was Lissa now—I knew it without thinking. Her voice almost broke a whisper. "You worry about yourself, okay? There's something going on in this place, and—" She took a deep breath. "We don't think Jaime went home, Addie. We—"

"Stop it," someone said before Addie could shout the truth, before she could describe the boy we'd seen on the gurney, the *before* and *after* scans, the bandages wrapped around his skull.

Our head jerked up, a mirage of the nurse's face already dancing before our eyes. But no, it had been a girl's voice that had spoken. The blond girl with the neat, thin braids. She met our eyes unflinchingly, then glared at Lissa and Devon. "Don't talk like that."

Addie snuck a look at the nurse, but she was reading her magazine and didn't seem to notice a thing.

The blond girl's mouth tightened until, slowly, Lissa nodded.

Surgery rang inside us, louder and louder, but if the other kids thought Jaime had gone home, then we weren't meant to know. Or we were supposed to pretend we didn't know. Addie clenched our teeth.

<We'll tell them later> I said. *<As soon as we get a moment alone.>*

The rest of the meal was eaten in silence.

Fifteen minutes later, the nurse stood, clapped her hands, and announced that breakfast was over. She led us from the room and through the halls, keeping us on the right-hand side. We made a messy line, many of the younger kids walking side by side.

It wasn't long before we stopped in front of another door. Door, hallway, door. Door, hallway, door. Nornand, it seemed, was nothing but a series of hallways and doors and whatever horrors might lie within.

The room inside this particular door was carpeted in somber gray and blue. It was much larger than the room we'd just left, but narrower, like it had once been a conference room. Now, instead of one long table, there were six round ones staggered throughout and a large desk at the very end, farthest from the door. A man in a white button-down shirt nodded at the nurse, who smiled and turned to go. I recognized him immediately: Mr. Conivent.

"All right," he said. "You guys know what to do. Eli, Dr. Lyanne is going to meet with you today instead of Dr. Sius."

Eli turned at the sound of his name, but he looked away again without any sign of comprehension. The rest of the kids started drifting to the far side of the room, where a low bookshelf was pushed against the wall, and a couple of clear plastic drawers sat stacked on top of one another. We could see notebooks and a box of pencils.

Addie and Devon were about to follow Lissa when Mr. Conivent stopped us with a hand on the shoulder. "Hello again," he said with a smile. He'd grabbed Devon, too, who shrugged off his touch, his face impassive.

"Hi," Addie said softly.

"So," he said, ushering us and Devon across the room, toward the bookshelves and the desk. "How are you two getting along so far? Had a good morning?" He grabbed a binder from a shelf. "Have you taken geometry yet? I have a few work sheets here."

"Sorry?" Addie said, thrown by the sudden change in topic. Devon said nothing at all, watching Mr. Conivent as one might watch a particularly dull child who thought he was clever. "Geometry?"

Mr. Conivent smiled at us. "I'm sure your parents wouldn't want you to lag behind in your schooling while you're here."

Of all the things to be worrying about right now. School. Geometry!

"It's Saturday," Addie said coldly.

"Yes," Mr. Conivent said. "We don't pay attention to things like that here." His smile had gone hard, like cake left out too long. "Now, have you or haven't you taken geometry?"

Addie wrestled the disgust from our face. "Yes, last year. And Devon's two grades higher, so I'm sure he has, too." Devon's eyes shifted to us, but he remained silent, accepting Addie's answer for him.

"Wonderful. Then this shouldn't be too hard for either

of you." Mr. Conivent pushed a few sheets of paper into our hands. "There are pencils and calculators in the second drawer by the bookshelf. I'll come check on you in a little while."

"But—"

"Yes?" he said, still smiling. His expression was smooth, composed. Understanding.

Frightening.

<*Just take it*> I said. <*We can't argue with him, Addie. Just take it.*>

The rest of her protest slid bitterly down our throat. "Okay," she said.

Mr. Conivent's teeth were very white and very straight. Perfect, just like his perfectly pressed shirt and perfect white collar. "Good girl," he said, and extended the same work sheets to Devon. "Devon, you will be seeing Dr. Wendle at ten, so try to get your work done before then."

No one looked up as we sat down, not even the kids to our left and right. The silence was oppressive. We bent over our papers and got to work, not knowing why or what for.

The math was even easier than we'd expected. We zipped through the first page in a few minutes. But instead of turning to the next work sheet, Addie glanced around the room. Each person sat focused on his or her own work—a book, a packet, a pile of work sheets. They all *looked* normal. If we'd met any one of them outside of Nornand—at school, maybe, or on the street—we'd never have known the secret in their heads. We'd never have known they were like us.

<Look> Addie said. She moved our eyes a fraction to the right, to what she wanted me to see.

Eli.

<Look at his face> she whispered.

It started with a twitching near his eyes—a blinking, winking, trembling motion. Then his forehead creased, his eyebrows jerking in and out of a frown. Soon it spread to his whole face, from his wide brown eyes to his mouth. Two different expressions battling for supremacy.

Our heart throbbed, *thump, thump, thump* against our ribs.

<Should we—>

Eli groaned softly, covering his face with his small hands. The girl sitting next to him didn't look up, but she stared a little too hard at her workbook, and the pencil in her hand shook. No one else seemed to have noticed.

<Eva? Eva, should we—>

"No!" someone whispered and grabbed our arm. Addie jerked around, coming face-to-face with the small, dark-haired girl. The fairy child. Her blunted nails dug into our skin. "No," she repeated. "You can't."

"But—"

"No," she said.

Eli cried out, burying his head in his arms. His entire body spasmed. Once, when Addie and I were very young, during one of our first trips to the local hospital, we'd seen a boy tumble from his bed in the frenzied grip of a seizure. The nurse didn't make it into his room until he hit the ground, his head snapping back and forth so violently I feared his neck would break. Eli was approaching that now, but it wasn't his head that moved. It was his fingers, his legs, his shoulders, his arms. Everything, as if he and the other soul sharing their body were trying to tear it apart.

But this wasn't right—this wasn't right. Addie and I had never been like this. Never, no matter how hard we'd fought for control as children.

Then Mr. Conivent was there, yanking the boy from his chair with one hand while reaching for a walkie-talkie with the other. "Dr. Lyanne, you're needed. It's Eli. Do you hear me? Dr. Lyanne, *answer.*"

A burst of static. Then: "Coming now."

Eli writhed in the man's grasp, his arms flailing—a jumble of pale skin and red hair and blue Nornand uniform. "Stop it," he kept crying, the words half garbled. But to who? "Stop it. *Stop it.*" One of his sneakers smashed against Mr. Conivent's shin. He grunted, nearly letting go. Eli jerked one arm free. But his movements were too muddled, his coordination too haphazard for him to make it far. The man half dragged, half carried him all the way from the room.

The door slammed. Silence reigned, iron-fisted. But only for a moment.

The whispers started like a rustling in a field. All work was abandoned in a heartbeat. Heads bent together, shoulders hunched, eyes glued on the door. The watcher was gone. Everyone came alive. Across the room, Devon and Lissa were speaking quietly to each other, and both looked over at Addie and me.

The hand on our arm—we'd forgotten it was even there—tightened. "You've got to pretend he's not there when he does that," the dark-haired girl said. "Unless he gets violent. Then you can run away. But we're not allowed to talk to him whenever he gets like that."

"Why not?" Addie said.

The girl frowned. "Because he's sick," she said. "And the doctors are working on making him better. We might mess him up again."

"This is *better*?" Addie said. "What was he like before?"

The girl didn't have time to respond. Because just then, Eli screamed.

Footsteps came pounding from all directions. Muffled calls and commands filtered through the door. The boy screamed again, and this time, the tenor was different. Off.

"He's Eli now," the girl said. She tugged at her hair, nervously winding long, dark strands around her fingers.

Addie frowned. "What do you mean? Wasn't he Eli before?"

The fairy girl pressed her lips together.

"They say it's Eli," said a boy from the table on our right. "They pretend, because it was always Eli who was dominant before." He looked around at the other kids. No one met his eyes, and he shrank a little.

"Shut *up*," said the blond girl. The one with her hair in long, thin plaits tied off with black ribbons. *Bridget*, Lissa had whispered in our ear as we trekked through the hall after breakfast. "Shut up. Now."

The door opened before anyone could speak further. Dr. Lyanne scanned the room, meeting every eye that didn't look away.

"Everything's fine," she said. Her ash-brown hair was slipping from its ponytail, but she ignored it. Her voice was calm, modulated. "Go back to work."

Mr. Conivent slipped in after her, and the two exchanged a few quiet words before sliding past each other. We heard only the very end of their conversation: *Take care of it before they come.*

"All right," Mr. Conivent said to us. "You heard what Dr. Lyanne said. Back to work."

We worked in absolute silence until ten, when a nurse came to retrieve Devon. Lissa's fingers twitched. She seemed to check herself from grabbing on to her brother's arm. Instead, the two of them met eyes before Devon set down his pencil, rose, and left.

No muss. No fuss. Just a quiet exit.

While we watched, terrified.

SEVENTEEN

Lunch was at twelve thirty exactly. At twelve fifteen, Mr. Conivent told us to put away our things and line up by the door. The nurse led us back to the breakfast room, and we ended up sitting across from the dark-haired fairy girl, who had her head bowed. Lissa grabbed the seat to our left, and I felt a pang of relief when Bridget chose one near the other end of the table.

The nurse set down our trays one by one, sliding them from her silver cart. Mashed potatoes. A pool of thin, yellow-brown gravy. Something that was probably a fried chicken cutlet, but who could tell under all that soggy breading?

Like at breakfast, a murmur of conversation started up when the nurse retreated to her corner.

"Jaime didn't go home," Addie whispered in Lissa's ear, our voice so low I wasn't sure Lissa would understand. But she went still. "I saw him. In a gurney. With a bandage around his head."

"Devon," Lissa said too loudly, and people turned to stare. She hardly seemed to notice, looking at us with wild eyes.

"Devon. They took Devon—"

"They only took him for a test," the fairy girl said. She was poking at her cutlet, her eyes flickering to the nurse before settling back on us and Lissa. "They do a lot of those when you first get here. He'll be back."

Lissa looked too stricken to speak, and Addie said quickly, "Are you sure—?" She hesitated.

"Kitty," the girl said.

The name didn't fit her. It was too ordinary, too sweet. This girl deserved a name from a fairy tale. Kitty stopped chewing and stared at us. She flushed, glancing at the kids on either side of her before mumbling, "Yes. I think so." She tugged on a lock of hair, which was held away from her face by two wedge-shaped clips. They still bore traces of color, a deep red, but most of the paint had been chipped off to reveal the metal skeleton.

"Is that what they do here?" Addie said. "Tests and things? All the time?"

The little girl swirled her gravy into her mashed potatoes. "Not all the time. We do school. And we play board games. Sometimes they let us watch a movie."

"They ask us questions," the blond boy on our right said quietly, looking at the nurse while he spoke. Addie jumped, but he kept talking as if he'd been a part of our conversation the entire time. "They make us talk to them about the things we did that day, or that week or whatever. We have to tell them about things that happened when we were little."

Kitty nodded. "Sometimes they make you take pills, too,

like Cal—" She blanched, her voice faltering, then continued so quickly her words were garbled. "Like Eli. Like Jaime did."

"What kind of pills?" Lissa said. "What do they do?"

"They make us better," Kitty said.

Lissa's face twisted, and Addie interjected before she could speak. "What did that boy mean this morning? In the Study room. He said . . . he said the doctors *said* it was Eli, that they *pretend*, because Eli was dominant . . . before?"

Kitty bit her fork. The blond boy's mouth twisted downward.

"Hanson's just messed up in the head," he said finally, gruffly. "Eli's dominant. Always has been."

"Well, of course," Addie said, "But—"

The boy looked away from us.

Our eyes met with Lissa's. Addie tried another question: "Isn't Eli too young to be here, anyway? He can't be ten yet, can he?"

Eli sat five or six seats farther down from Lissa. No one spoke to him. Because he was so young? Or because of what had happened earlier in the Study room? Dr. Lyanne had returned him to the group at the beginning of lunch, leading him in by the hand. The animal wariness was gone, replaced by a vapidness in his eyes and a stumble in his step.

"He's eight," Kitty said, just as the blond boy said, "His parents got rid of him."

"Why?" Addie said. "He's got two more years."

Kitty shrugged, her thin shoulders barely tenting up her

short sky-blue sleeves. "They didn't want him. Didn't want him hybrid, anyway. Maybe if they cure him, they'll take him back." She pushed a forkful of mashed potatoes into her mouth, swallowed, and looked at us. "They should, if he's cured." But there was a tremor in her voice that matched the tremor in the blond boy's eyes and the tremor in Lissa's chin and the tremor in every movement of every child at this table. The undercurrent of fear.

A whole tableful of children, pretending we knew nothing, pretending we trusted our guardians. Pretending we weren't afraid.

Today turned out to be a board game day. Everyone split into small groups, each with their own box or deck of cards. Kitty's eyes trailed after us, so Addie motioned for her to follow us and Lissa into a corner of the room.

We chose our pieces and rolled to see who would go first. The door opened just as Addie reached for the dice. First a nurse walked in. Then came Devon. A little shaky, a little pale, but Devon.

Lissa jumped, her hand shooting out to grab our wrist. To keep us from going anywhere? Or to keep herself?

The nurse who'd come in with Devon spoke quietly with the one already in the room. Then they turned and looked in our direction. No, not just in our direction. At *us*. At Addie and me.

One of them nudged Devon, who stumbled forward.

<*What's wrong with him?*> Addie said. Caught up in

her swirl of fear was an unexpected splotch of anger, dark red. *<They did something to him.>*

"Addie?" one of the nurses called. Our eyes didn't leave Devon. "Addie, come here, please."

Addie didn't move. Her voice was tight. *<What did they do to him?>*

<I don't think—>

And then Devon seemed to see us for the first time. His eyes focused. His steps quickened. "Addie—" he said.

"Addie!" the nurse said, sharper this time. "Come here."

"Go," Kitty whispered. But Lissa didn't loosen her grip on our wrist, and Devon was still calling us.

Except it wasn't Devon. I recognized Ryan only when he was less than two feet away, but I recognized him, even if Addie didn't.

"Addie," he said, dropping down beside us. "Addie. Don't—when, when they . . ." He frowned as if he couldn't find the right words to put on his tongue. "It's a lie, Addie—"

A hand pulled us up—tore us from Lissa's grasp and Ryan's muttered, cluttered sentences.

"Didn't you hear me?" the nurse said.

Addie strained to look behind us, trying to catch Ryan's last words. "No, I—"

"Well, Dr. Wendle is waiting for you. Come along." To Lissa, who stared after us with frightened eyes, she said, "You look after your brother. He's a little woozy from the medicine, but he'll be fine in a bit. Don't worry."

"*What* medicine?" Lissa said.

But the nurse didn't—or pretended not to—hear. She pulled us away from the others, away from Kitty's wide brown eyes and the black-and-white dice and the colorful, forgotten board game.

The last thing we heard before the door shut was Ryan's voice, finally having found what he'd wanted to say.

"Don't believe them, Addie. Don't—"

And that was all.

Dr. Wendle smiled when we walked in. I'd thought we were going back to his office, but we were in a much smaller room instead. Here, the walls were a dull gray-blue, the floor shining from the luminous overhead lights. Dr. Wendle stood beside something vaguely resembling a dentistry chair.

"There you are, Addie," he said, as if we were a lost penny. He reached toward us, and Addie flinched. "What's wrong? Oh, it won't be anything like this morning. I promise." He pointed at the chair. "All out in the open, see?"

"Devon," Addie said. "Devon, he—"

"Was a little woozy? Don't worry, it's just a sedative. He'll be back to normal soon."

Addie dodged another attempt to grab our arm. "Why'd you give him sedatives?"

Why did Eli—or Cal, or whoever he was—quake in his own skin until I was afraid he'd shatter or tear apart? What did you do to Jaime Cortae?

And why did you tell the other children he'd gone home?

Dr. Wendle had a laugh like a wheeze. He readjusted his

glasses, setting them higher on his short nose. "It was to help him calm down a little. You know, like how they give you laughing gas at the dentist's?"

Calm him down for what? I wanted to ask, but Dr. Wendle allowed us no more time for speech. He patted the chair. "Sit. It will only take a moment, and then you can rejoin your friends."

A metal tray sat on the counter, a syringe glinting inside.

"Addie? Hurry, please."

Addie walked step by laborious step to the dark blue chair and climbed on, leaning back against the headrest. What else could we do?

"I was looking through your records," Dr. Wendle said. "You're missing a vaccination you should have gotten a few years ago."

"For what?" Addie said. Our nails dug into the padded chair arms.

"Tetanus. I'm surprised your school didn't make you get it."

<Tetanus?> Addie said.

<I don't know. I don't remember.>

We'd had all the required vaccinations before, of course. Measles. Mumps. That sort of thing. Failure to have a child vaccinated was punishable by hefty fines. But most of the shots had been when we were a baby or toddler, far too many years ago to recall. The tetanus shot must not have been compulsory.

Addie eyed the needle in Dr. Wendle's hand. "Are you sure?" she said. "Can't I—can't I call my parents first?"

"It says it right here in your file," he said, though he wasn't looking at the file at all. "It's no big deal, Addie. It'll just be a pinch."

It wasn't the needle we were afraid of.

"But I—"

"Hold still," Dr. Wendle said. "It's only a shot, and an important one at that. Do you know what tetanus does?"

We didn't. And before we could protest further, he'd somehow positioned the needle and slid it into the crook of our elbow.

Addie cried out, but Dr. Wendle's free hand gripped our arm and held us still as he pressed the plunger. We fell silent as he matter-of-factly pulled the needle out and briefly pressed a cotton swab against our skin.

"There," he said. "No need for a fuss, see?"

We couldn't speak. Our eyes were glued to the tiny red dot on our inner elbow. Then Dr. Wendle covered it with a Band-Aid, and that was that.

"All finished," Dr. Wendle said with a smile.

We just sat there for a second, staring at him. He was so short that we hardly had to look up. The tender skin of our inner elbow throbbed.

He coughed and gestured toward the door. "I'll call a nurse, and she'll take you back to the group."

"What?" Addie said. "What about—about the test?"

"Afraid that's not quite ready for you yet," he said. "You might have to come back before dinner." He'd already turned back to his instruments. "Now go stand by the door, please.

The nurse will be here soon."

We stared at him a moment longer. Then, slowly, Addie did as he bid, walking to the door and stepping outside. As he'd promised, a nurse showed up a few seconds later.

We walked in a daze, all our built-up adrenaline crashing down around us. Just a vaccination. Come back later for the real test.

"Come on, dear," the nurse said. She was farther ahead of us than we'd thought. Addie quickened our pace, but it didn't help. The woman walked too quickly. In fact, everyone seemed to be walking too quickly. A blur was stuck in the corner of our vision, moving when we moved, stopping when we stopped.

"Don't lag, now," the nurse said, doubling back. She reached out, frowning, as if—as if ready to . . . catch us. "The others are waiting, and we wouldn't want—"

We never heard what it was we wouldn't want.

There was a muffled cry.

A weakening . . .

A fall.

Darkness.

EIGHTEEN

<Addie?>

Her name was the first thing that entered my mind as I woke. When we'd been children—before the doctors, before the fear—we'd almost always called to each other as we emerged from shared dreams. It had happened less and less as the years passed, until the habit faded away completely.

<Addie?>

We lay very still. I stretched in the fog of our mind, reaching for Addie. She couldn't still be asleep, but sometimes she got up slower than I did.

<. . . Addie?>

She didn't answer. I searched harder, fear's sharp, cold blade peeling away my slumber.

<Addie, where are you?>

Memory and awareness hit me all at once. Hospital. We were at the hospital—the clinic. We'd been in the hallway. There had been a nurse. And now? Now what?

<Addie!>

My voice rang out and echoed back with the tremor of

déjà vu. This was the second time I'd called Addie's name like this—scrabbling through our mind for a shred of her existence.

The first had been more than a month ago, when we'd drunk the drug-laced tea. Refcon, Ryan had called it.

What's it usually for? I'd managed to say. It had been one of the later sessions, when I had better control of our tongue and lips. Ryan had said something about specialty care and psychiatric wards.

Psychiatric wards. Psychiatric hospitals.

Nornand Clinic of Psychiatric Health.

Here.

<Addie> I screamed.

No reply. I was alone. This was not Hally's home. No Ryan sat beside us, talking to pass the time.

I forced our eyes open.

Wherever we were, it was dim. There were no windows. A yellow glow lined the bottom of the door, but that was all. I closed our eyes again. *<. . . Addie?>*

But I didn't hope for an answer, and none came. She was gone. For how long? At Hally's house, it had never been more than an hour. But at Hally's house, I'd never fallen unconscious along with Addie, either.

I couldn't think about it. The more I thought about it, the more nauseated I felt.

It was okay. Maybe we'd already been unconscious a long time. Maybe Addie would be back soon. I'd just lie here on this bed and wait.

I didn't let myself think about what I'd do if I kept waiting and waiting and nothing happened.

Our chest moved gently up . . . down . . . up . . . down. Our eyes stayed closed. I kept my distance from the hazy darkness that had swallowed Addie. Usually when she came back, I'd feel her pressing at the edges of it, folding away the emptiness like a blanket, flowing into the space next to mine. All I had to do was wait until the drug wore off and she woke up.

I wouldn't think about anything else. I wouldn't think about why we were here, why they had done this to us, why they had lied. What we would do once Addie was awake.

No. I'd wait until she came back. Until we were whole again. Then we could worry about things like that together.

Our breathing was calm, smooth. The breathing of a girl asleep. For all our body knew, we *were* asleep. Addie was, anyway, and that was all that mattered. How long had it been since my anger could quicken our breaths, my fear make our heart pound, my embarrassment make us blush? Of course, usually when I was angry, frightened, or embarrassed, Addie was, too, so it wasn't such a big deal.

Or so I—

A siren sliced through my thoughts. Our eyes snapped open.

A light on the ceiling flashed red—red—red—

My mind went blank, then overloaded.

A fire? A gas leak?

Our breathing caught.

Something was wrong.

<Addie. Addie, wake up—!>

Nothing. Nothing but that wild, keening siren and the flashing red light.

<Addie!>

Maybe someone would come. Yes—yes, definitely. Someone had brought us here. They would know. They would come. They would save us.

Because Addie was asleep, and I could not move.

Our eyes flickered frantically to the door, but the crack of light stayed clear and uninterrupted. No one stood in the doorway. No one was here.

But they would come. They had to.

<Oh, please. Addie!>

I thought I heard a stampede of feet—distant voices calling, yelling. People evacuating. People running. Running away from us. It was the Bessimir museum all over again; the day of the raid all over again.

<Addie, you have to wake up. You have to call for help—>

But she didn't wake. And we just lay there.

More voices, right by our door this time. Murmurs, then footsteps moving quickly on.

<No> I cried. *<No, no, no. Please. Come back. Come back.>*

I'd spoken before. I could do it now. If only I could concentrate.

<Please! In here. In here!>

Our mouth stayed shut, our tongue still. Not a sound.

On and on the siren wailed. On and on the light flashed. Red-white-red-white-red-white-red—

A noise gurgled from our throat, followed by a word—a weak, whispered word:

. . . *Help.*

"*Please. Please*—help!"

Our body trembled. I sucked in breath after noisy breath, crying as loudly as I could, "Somebody! In here! I can't get out!"

Someone should have heard. Someone should have come. But nobody did.

Only a few minutes had passed since the alarm started. Not long enough for everyone to leave. Not long enough for us to be here alone.

Right?

I screamed, forgetting words. Our throat stretched at the unfamiliar sound—Addie never screamed like this. No one was coming. No one was going to come.

<Addie!> I shouted one last time.

She wasn't there. She wasn't going to move us. And I couldn't.

But I would have to.

I focused as hard as I could on our fingers. On curling them. On bending our elbows to prop up our body. In the darkness, with our head immobile, I couldn't tell if I was really moving or just imagining it.

I didn't realize what was happening until our nail snagged in the bedcovers.

No time to think about it. No time to stop. Our heart pounded so hard it couldn't possibly stay in our chest for long. Either it would burst or I would burst—and neither option was promising.

I flexed our fingers, searching for a way to push ourself up. Our arms wouldn't work properly. They twitched on either side of us, bent like chicken wings, jerking as my control waxed and waned. With a silent scream, I lurched forward and sat up.

The world spun. I wanted to shout or laugh or cry. There wasn't time for any of it. The siren wailed; the light flashed.

I had to get out.

Standing was no less awkward. Our muscles were strong—I just couldn't control them. I swayed, then fell back onto the bed and had to start over again. The second time was a bit easier than the first.

Finally, sweat running down the back of our neck, I took my first step.

My first step in almost three years.

No time to celebrate.

Second step.

Third.

Fourth.

I wobbled. Cried out. Fell.

I grabbed the side of the bed and pulled ourself back up. Balancing was the worst part. How far apart was I supposed to put our feet?

I fell twice more before reaching the door.

Our hand gripped the doorknob. I pressed our cheek against the cool wood and closed our eyes. The door. I'd made it to the door.

Now what?

Would someone find me in the hallway? Or would I have to walk all the way outside?

I shuddered. Actually shuddered, our body reacting to my disbelief.

No way I could make it outside.

Just go into the hall. Just go into the hall and call for help again. Someone will hear you. Someone will come.

Our hand slipped slightly, then tightened again around the doorknob. I twisted it. For a second, the door didn't move. Fear weakened already shaky legs. Was it locked? But no, no—I twisted the knob a little farther, and the door swung open. We swung with it, riding the momentum outward into the hall, clinging on for dear life.

And then someone was there. Someone was holding us up. Someone was pushing us, pulling us, dragging us back to the bed. Back to the bed? No, no—that was the wrong direction!

"We have to leave," I said. "The siren. The fire—the—"

"Shh," he said. "Shh . . ."

"Ryan," I cried. I almost smiled, though he obviously didn't understand. "Ryan, it's me! Me! Eva."

"Shh," he urged, over and over again. We were back by the bed now. He half pushed, half set us onto the mattress. His movements were stiff, his jaw tight.

"I moved, Ryan," I said, laughing. Laughing. Gasping. "But we have to go. The alarm—"

"There's no fire." He held me down when I tried to stand.

"Then the gas leak, or whatever—we have to go. The alarm—"

"Is a trick," he said. "They tricked you."

Tricked me?

I laughed again, louder. "What?"

"To make you move. To bring you out."

A rubber stopper slammed into our windpipe, stopping my breathing so sharply I saw starbursts.

To make me move? To bring me out?

The laughter started up again, a weak, incessant giggling. I couldn't hold it back. "Well, it worked, didn't it?"

Ryan looked at me, the light still flashing above his head, casting red and white shadows on his face. He wasn't laughing. He didn't even smile.

I laughed for him, laughed until I could barely breathe. "I moved, Ryan. I walked. I *walked*!"

"Yes," he said, and he sounded so grim.

A strange, giggling headiness clouded up my mind. If Ryan hadn't been gripping our shoulders, I might have fallen down.

"I moved," I said again, just to make sure he'd heard correctly. I laughed and laughed. I felt full of bubbles, full of clouds.

And then I grabbed the collar of Ryan's shirt—grabbed him and pulled him closer and felt his arms tighten around me. The laughter went putrid in my throat. *"I won't let them cut me out,"* I said breathlessly. *"I won't. I won't."*

Addie and I sat with the light on.

The brightness was enough to alert someone in the hall, but neither of us suggested turning it off. We'd had enough darkness for one day.

They'd let us call our parents, but only for a few minutes, and a nurse watched us the entire time. She'd pretended to dust and tidy the already impeccably clean room, but we knew she was listening. Even if the nurse hadn't been there, we couldn't have told them about the forced drugging, about how they'd tricked us. If we told them, we'd have to explain how I'd moved. We'd have to say that yes, their fears were true, that Mr. Conivent had been right. That we were still defective.

Not that they wouldn't learn soon enough anyway. The doctors would tell them. They would have to if they wanted to keep us here.

But they didn't seem to have said anything yet. First Mom, then Dad had come on the phone. How are you? How was the flight? Was it exciting? Is the food okay? Did they find you a nice room?

Just before the nurse began coughing meaningfully and looking at us, Dad said, "I suppose it doesn't matter so much, right? It's only one night."

"Yeah," Addie whispered. She'd been whispering since she woke up. "That's right."

The nurse came over and murmured that the hospital had

rather busy lines. They couldn't afford to have one taken up so long. Which seemed silly, but what could we say?

"We'll call again tomorrow," Dad promised.

They didn't let us go back to the other kids, claiming we were Overstrung and Exhausted and Too Nervous.

You need rest, they told us, walking us through the halls. *Your room's all ready for you now. We'll bring you dinner.*

And they'd all but locked us in our room.

Silently, Addie unlaced our shoes and climbed into bed. There was a wall around her half of our mind, a shield that had started forming as soon as she'd woken hours earlier and felt Ryan's arms wrapped warm around us. A nurse had dashed in the door a second later, her face livid, her dark eyes huge. She'd pulled Ryan away, yelling about staying with the group and listening to directions. He hadn't fought her. But his eyes had never left our face.

<*Eva?*> Addie said now, staring at the ceiling. It looked nearly identical to the walls, a plane of white interrupted only by the harsh overhead light. This room was tiny and Spartan, containing only a bed and a nightstand. The bed nearly stretched from one wall to the other, and there were no windows. At least our duffel bag had been waiting for us, like the nurse had promised this morning.

I stirred. <*Yes?*>

A pause. Then: <. . . *What's it like?*>

At first I thought I'd somehow missed part of her sentence. <*What's what like?*>

It took her another moment to answer.

<*Being alone.*>

Being alone?

<*What do you mean?*>

She sighed softly, our eyes still tracing the bumps in the ceiling. <*When I woke up, you were sitting with Devon, and—*>

<*Ryan*> I said. <*It was Ryan, not Devon.*>

She fell quiet, then said <*You were sitting with Ryan, and he was—*> She stopped again. <*You were alone. Without me.*>

<*They tricked us*> I said, not quite sure where she was going. <*They set off the alarm. I thought there was a fire or something. I didn't know they were watching—*>

<*That's not what I'm talking about*>

I stopped. <*Well, what are you talking about?*>

She squeezed our eyes shut. Our fingers clenched the edge of a pillow. <*I don't know. . . . You. Ryan.*> She took a long, deep breath. <*What's it like to talk without me listening, Eva?*>

When I didn't immediately answer, she rushed on. <*For more than a month now—every day. Every day you get to talk to people by yourself. You get to . . . to be here when I'm not.*>

I didn't say the obvious—that for most of that time I hadn't been able to string together enough words to make a sentence.

<*I've never gotten to do that*> she said.

For one wild, ridiculous moment, I thought she sounded jealous.

Addie. Jealous of me!

Laughter bubbled up and spilled over, too bright and sickly sweet. Silent laughter, because without the medicine, Addie was in firm control of our lips, our tongue, our lungs. But she heard the laughter just as she heard my silent voice.

<*What? What's so funny?*>

What's so funny? Did she really have to ask?

<*You've never gotten to do that, Addie? Oh, I'm so sorry. Life's just so, so unfair, isn't it?*>

She flinched. Our eyes popped open. <*Eva, I—*>

<*Maybe we should change places, then. Would that be more fair, Addie? Would you like that better?*>

She flipped onto our side. <*Eva—*>

<*I got five minutes today, Addie. Five minutes out of the last three years, and you're jealous of that?*>

<*I'm not!*> she said. <*That's not what I meant.*>

<*Then what did you mean, Addie?*> I said. <*Tell me.*>

She was quiet.

A storm cloud rolled between us, boiling with thunder, icy with rain.

We stared at the wall. Slowly, Addie turned so our face was flat against the pillow.

<*You think it's so easy, don't you?*> she said.

<*I have no idea what you're talking about.*>

Our breathing grew tight. <*Go ahead, throw yourself a pity party, Eva. You deserve it. I'm the lucky one, right? I'm the fortunate one. Addie's dominant, so anything bad that happens is all her fault, anyway. It's not like you're ever to blame.*>

<*You're not even making sense*> I said.

A wall slammed down between us. White. Trembling. A cry pushed through our lips. Addie buried our face into the pillow, muffling the sobs until there was no sound. Just tears.

<We've gone and screwed it all up again> she said. *<We were going to be normal this time, Eva. I just want to be* normal *for once.>*

I shrank into myself, folding up as small as I could. I tucked myself away in the corner of our mind, hiding from Addie's tears. But I couldn't hide from what she'd said.

I wanted to disappear, to slip into that nothingness I'd found the winter of our thirteenth year, where there was nothing sharp, nothing that hurt, just a stream of dreams that swirled me around and around until I was a part of them.

But I couldn't. I had too much, now, to lose.

NINETEEN

The next morning, they dressed us in blue. Sky-blue button-up blouse. Navy-blue skirt that fell to our knees. They were starched stiffer than Mom had ever managed to do, the collar crisp and snow white. Unlike our school uniform, this one had no emblem or decoration. We were allowed no pockets.

"Come along," the nurse said once Addie tied our shoes. They'd let us keep those, at the very least, along with our long, black school socks. I wished I knew what would happen to the rest of our clothes.

Addie had snuck Ryan's chip from our pocket. Now it pressed snugly into the hollow beneath our ankle bone, our sock tucking it against our skin.

"Where are we going?" Addie said, our voice dull.

We'd both woken silently this morning. My name had not formed on her tongue as the last veils of sleep slipped away. Or perhaps it had, but she'd swallowed it bitterly down, as I had hers.

The nurse smiled. "To meet your new roommate. All the

other children live in their own special little ward. You'll be moving in today."

"Moving in?" Addie said. The nurse didn't reply, just continued giving us that small, bland smile.

Addie reached for our duffel bag, but the nurse touched our hand. "Someone will bring it to you later."

It couldn't have been past eight in the morning. Without a watch, we couldn't tell exactly, but once we entered the hall, we could see the sun hanging golden in the sky through Nornand's great windows. We seemed to be the only one looking beyond the glass. The woman leading us through the halls stared only straight ahead of her, and the other nurses or doctors who passed by all seemed to have more important things to do than gaze out past Nornand's walls.

Finally, the nurse stopped before a plain-looking door. She produced a ring of keys from her pocket, selected one, and stuck it into the lock.

"Welcome to the Ward, Addie," she said.

Inside, it was still dark. A nightlight cast a fuzzy glow in the far corner of the room, but it wasn't enough to see by, especially not after the brilliance of Nornand's halls. Addie blinked, trying to acclimate our eyes.

It was wasted effort, though, since the nurse flicked on the lights a second later. Now we could see everything.

The Ward and the Study room were similar in many ways. The carpet was made of the same tightly woven fiber, the walls painted a pale blue, interrupted only twice—once by a gray door and once by a small alcove that seemed to lead to a pair of bathrooms. A broad-leafed plant stood in one corner, fairly bursting from its tiny pot. There were two round, medium-sized tables, a few chairs, and one small cabinet. But no kids.

"Everyone's still in their rooms," the nurse said, as if she'd read my mind. She gestured at the gray door. "Let's get you to yours, shall we?"

The door led to another hallway, this one narrower and shorter than any of the others we'd seen. A faint glow lit the far end, but the nurse quickly overwhelmed it by turning on the overhead lights.

I managed to count eight doors before the nurse opened one and hustled us inside.

"Kitty?" she said as she stepped in behind us and flicked on the lights. "Wake up and shine, sweetheart. You're finally getting a new roommate."

The girl in bed flew upright so fast she kicked her blankets onto the floor. The fairy girl. Her long dark hair was tangled and frizzy from sleep, making it seem even larger in comparison to the rest of her body. Her eyes were huge, her lips parted.

"This is Addie," the nurse said. Her voice was relentlessly cheerful, like that of a kindergarten teacher on the first day of class.

Kitty stared at us but said nothing. The long silence hung heavily on our shoulders. Finally, the nurse clapped her hands. "All right, then, girls. I'll go wake up the other kids. You get dressed, Kitty, and tell Addie about our morning routine."

Kitty climbed out of bed, stealing a glance at our face as she hurried for her clothes. They were already waiting for her on her nightstand, stacked in a small blue pile. The nurse closed the door on her way out.

Addie stood absolutely still, our hands clasped in front of us.

"Hi," Kitty said quietly, and didn't speak again as she dressed.

She'd barely finished when a voice rang out in the corridor: "Everybody into the hallway, please."

Kitty hurried to the door. Addie took one last look at the room—the white walls, the tiled floor, the metal-framed beds and thin pillows. The solitary window was obviously not meant to be opened, ever. I tried to imagine sleeping here. Waking here. How long would it take to grow accustomed to cool white hospital sheets?

No, the nurse was wrong. We hadn't spoken with our parents properly yet. Dad had promised to come for us.

This wasn't our room.

"Aren't you coming, Addie?" Kitty said, lingering in the doorway.

For a second—just a split second—I felt a crack in the wall between Addie and me. Then it was gone. But brief as the lapse had been, it was enough for me to catch a whisper of Addie's emotions.

A hint of fear.

"Yeah," Addie said. "I'm coming."

The main room was full of quiet chaos. Some of the kids were still half asleep, slumped into the wooden chairs, their heads resting on the tabletops. Eli had curled up in a corner, scrunched down so low his knees practically shielded his face from view. A few of the older kids talked quietly near the far door.

Hally was just coming out of the alcove. She held her glasses in one hand and rubbed her eyes with the other, her mouth open in the wide O of a yawn. A second later, Ryan stepped into view. He gave a quick glance about the room, and our eyes met. Addie looked away. But in another moment, he was by our side.

"You all right?" He kept his voice buried under the Ward's sleepy murmur of noise.

"Fine," said Addie.

He hesitated.

"She's fine, too," Addie said, and pushed away from the wall, moving toward a corner of the room. She'd just passed the nurse when the woman clapped her hands.

"Listen up," she said. "Eli? Shelly? I've got your meds, if you'll come over, please."

Addie had stopped moving at the clap. When she started walking again, the movement must have caught the nurse's eye; she looked down, frowned a moment, and then smiled again. "I almost forgot, Addie. Someone just came to tell me that your parents are on the line."

Our parents. They'd have told them our results by now. All else flew from my mind. Our parents were on the phone and that was all that mattered in the world.

"Can I talk to them?" Addie said. Our voice came out louder than I'd expected. "Please? I need to—"

"One moment, Addie." The nurse held up her hand and turned to a little girl who'd just walked up. "Here you go, Shelly—where's your cup? You need water with this, remember, dear?"

The girl moved off again, and Addie tried to recapture the nurse's attention. "Please, can't I talk to them now?"

The woman hesitated. She looked around the room, then at the bottles of pills in her hand. Finally, she sighed. "You can't wait five minutes?" Addie shook our head, eyes pleading. "Well, all right, then. I'll find someone to take you to a phone."

"Thank you," Addie whispered.

Ryan raised his head as we passed, but said nothing.

It was early, and the hall was relatively empty—just a delivery boy and a pair of doctors bent over a clipboard, talking quietly. But before long, another woman in a gray-and-white nurse's uniform showed up, and the nurse flagged her down.

"Addie here needs to use a phone," the first woman said. "I'm bringing the other children to breakfast. Would you take her to an office? It's line four."

"Sure." The other nurse smiled at us. "Right this way."

We hadn't walked more than a few minutes before she let us into a small office. A desk, littered with papers and manila folders, took up most of the room. The nurse gestured toward a swivel chair behind the desk. "You can sit there."

Addie did as she bid, watching as she lifted the phone from its cradle and pushed one of the glowing orange buttons.

"Hello?" she said. A pause. "Your daughter, sir? Her

name?" Another pause. "Okay, then. Yes, she's right here. One second, please."

She placed the phone in our outstretched hands. Addie smashed it to our ear. *"Hello?"*

"Hey there, Addie," Dad said. False cheer strained each word. "How're you doing?"

"Okay," Addie said. She twisted the telephone cord around our wrist, swallowed, and curled away from the nurse, who hovered near the desk. "I miss you. And Mom. And . . ."

And Lyle, but our voice gave out before we could say it.

There was the tiniest of hesitations. Then Dad spoke again, and the cheer was gone. "We miss you, too, Addie. We love you. You know that, right, sweetheart?"

Addie nodded. Gripped the phone. Whispered, "Yeah. I know." When Dad didn't speak, she said, "How's Lyle?"

What did you tell him?

"Oh, he's great, Addie," Dad said. Then, as if realizing how this might come across, he added, "He's really upset about you being gone."

Addie said nothing.

"But we . . . got a call last night," Dad said. "From his doctor."

Our muscles stiffened.

"Addie, they're going to move Lyle up the transplant list. They said . . . they said they'd give him top priority. Even if they've got to transport it from another area."

At first, nothing. Then coldness. Dizziness. Fire in the backs of our eyes. And finally, a gasp from clenched lungs. We knew what this meant, not only for Lyle but for us.

A transplant meant no more hours of dialysis every week for Lyle, no more meaningless bruising and days when he didn't want to open his eyes.

A transplant meant our parents' personal miracle.

A transplant meant a trade.

"You said it would only be two days, Dad. You said . . . you said you'd come get me if . . ." Our throat was closing up. We squeezed the receiver so tightly our fingers cramped. Addie couldn't finish her sentence.

"I know," came Dad's voice. "I know, Addie. I know. But—"

"You said," she cried. A sob punched through our chest. She squeezed our eyes shut, but the tears escaped anyway, hot down our cheeks. "You *promised*."

Our brother. Our wonderful, terrible, annoying little brother, fixed up nearly good as new.

And we would never see him again.

"Addie," our father said. "Please, Addie—"

The roaring in our ears drowned out his words. What did it matter what he wanted to say? He wasn't coming.

He wasn't coming.

He *wasn't coming*. Not to take us away.

"They say they can make you better, Addie," he said. "They're a good hospital—and they're the only place in this part of the country that specializes in this . . . this sort of thing. We want you to get better. *You* want to get better, Addie, don't you?"

There was no mention of what Addie "getting better"

would mean for me, for his other daughter, who he claimed to love. He'd said he loved me. I'd *heard* him.

Addie didn't respond. She held the phone to our ear and cried, knowing the nurse was watching us and hating her for seeing.

"Addie?" our father said quietly. "I love you."

But what about me?

"We—" Addie gasped. "I mean, I—"

It was too late. The silence seeping through the phone said it all.

"I want to go home," Addie said. "Dad, take me home. Please—"

"You're sick, Addie," he said. "And I can't make you better. But they—they say they've got all these ways. They can . . ."

"Dad—"

"I know this is hard, Addie." His voice was tight. "God help me, I know, but it's the best thing for you right now, okay? They're going to help you get well, Addie."

How much of that did he truly believe, and how much was he just saying it so he could feel better about abandoning us?

"But I'm not sick," Addie said. "I—"

"You are," he said. The words were so heavy with defeat they knocked our breath away.

"I'm not," Addie said, but so softly only I heard.

"We'll call again tonight, and we're going to fly up as soon as we possibly can," Dad said. "Addie, listen to what they tell you, okay? They only want the best for you. Mom and I only want the best for you. Do you understand, Addie?"

For a long moment, she said nothing. He said nothing. The phone line buzzed with silence.

"Addie?" our father said again.

We gave no reply.

TWENTY

We were numb for the rest of the day. There were too many people, too many pairs of eyes. The other kids. The nurses. Mr. Conivent. We were never alone, and we wanted nothing more than to be left alone. Instead, they shoved us from one room to another, one meal, one activity, to another, always under surveillance, always watched. Everything was background noise, like static on a radio. Again and again, Ryan or Hally tried to speak to us. Addie fled whenever either came too close, turning our face and threading through the crowd of kids until we were as far away as possible. I didn't try to persuade her otherwise.

Finally, night fell and a nurse lined everyone up, leading us through the now quiet halls to the Ward. Beyond Nornand's windows, a yolk-colored sun dropped slowly below the horizon. Some of the kids took their medication while the rest of us milled around. We sat in one of the stiff-backed chairs, staring at the carpet.

"Addie?" Kitty said, breaking us from our reverie. "We've got to go back to our room now."

Addie followed her silently. Hally walked beside us, too, her hands twisting one in the other, her eyes darting between us and her brother, who kept a greater distance. She seemed ready to say something just as Addie reached our door, but she didn't, just looked at the ground and disappeared into the room next to ours.

Kitty shut the door after we entered. Our duffel bag now sat beside the second bed, a folded white nightgown laying on top. Addie didn't bother changing, just crawled beneath the covers without even kicking off our shoes.

After a few minutes, the lights clicked off. Finally, there was darkness and no more watching, no more meaningless noise. Addie gritted our teeth, but the tears strained past our eyelids anyway.

Silence. Then a whisper in the night.

"Addie?" Kitty had slipped from her own bed and padded over to ours. Darkness shielded her expression; we saw nothing but the soft shape of her nose, the roundness of her cheeks and chin. Her voice was reedy, like a sad lullaby. "Addie, are you crying?" Addie turned our face toward the wall, but a hand brushed against our cheek. "Addie?"

"Yes?" Addie whispered.

For a moment, Kitty didn't reply. I almost thought she'd returned to her bed. But Addie looked up, and Kitty was still standing there, more fairylike than ever in her white nightgown.

"Sometimes . . ." She hesitated, then went on. "Sometimes it helps if I think about what they're doing at home." When

Addie didn't break eye contact, Kitty swallowed and said, "I used to talk with Sallie about home. About my brothers and sister."

"Sallie?" Addie said.

Kitty nodded. "She was my old roommate. But she hasn't been here for months."

"Where did she go?" Addie said, pushing ourself slowly up. She leaned backward until our shoulder blades pressed against the wall. Our eyes had adjusted to the darkness well enough to make out Kitty's trembling mouth.

"They told us she went home," she said. "Like Jaime."

Jaime again. Should we tell her? Would it do any good?

"Addie?"

Something in her voice made us bite back our weariness and the stabbing in our gut. It was the same voice Lyle used when it was just him and us and he was too tired to worry about sounding tough.

Thinking about Lyle made our chest clench again. If there was anything good coming out of this hell, it was the chance that our little brother might get the chance we'd all been aching for.

Addie patted the bed next to us. Kitty hesitated, then sank onto our mattress, tucking her legs up beneath her.

"Tell me about home," Addie said.

"Home?"

Addie nodded. "Home. Family. Tell me about your brothers."

"I've got three," Kitty said. "And a sister. But Ty's the nicest. He takes care of us since Mom. . . . He's twenty-one."

"Oh?" Addie said. Gingerly, she reached over and ran our fingers through the girl's long hair. It was tangled, and we had no brush, so she began working the knots out by hand. Kitty stiffened, then relaxed.

"He plays the guitar, and he's really good."

Addie continued smoothing the knots from Kitty's hair.

"He said he'd teach me to play, too," Kitty said. "But that . . . But he's in trouble now. Because he tried to keep them from taking me away—"

Our fingers stilled.

"Let's talk about your sister," Addie said. "How old is she?"

"Seventeen—no, I think she's eighteen now."

"I have a little brother," Addie said quickly, ignoring the pain as it intensified in our chest. "His name's Lyle. He's ten."

Kitty nodded, but I could feel the conversation ending, as tangible as the curtain fall at the close of a play. Addie brushed a strand of hair away from the little girl's face.

"Think you can fall asleep now?" she said. Kitty nodded without meeting our eyes. But she didn't move. "You can stay here if you'd like," Addie said. The air was cold, and her nightgown looked thin. "I can go over to your bed."

Another faint nod.

"Good night, Kitty," she said.

Addie slipped off the bed, but hadn't taken a single step when a hand shot out and grabbed our wrist.

"Yes, Ki—"

She pulled herself to our side, her mouth so close to our ear that when she spoke, we felt more than heard the word.

Nina.

And then her eyes were huge and bright and intent on ours. Waiting.

"Good night, Nina," Addie whispered.

The small hand on our wrist squeezed, nails biting into the hollow between our bones. We heard a sigh like the release of a dream. Then the hand was gone. Nina turned and slipped beneath our blanket without another word.

Hours later, we were still awake. A nurse had just come by and opened our door, casting a quick glance over our beds before stepping back into the hall.

We could hear Nina breathing softly, her dark hair pooled across her—our—pillow. If the nurse had noticed the change in beds, she hadn't tried to do anything about it. Maybe someone would reprimand us in the morning. Or maybe who slept in which bed was one bit of control we were allowed to keep.

Our head ached from lack of rest. We hadn't slept more than four hours a night since we'd left home. I hadn't spoken since last night. The wall between Addie and me stood sturdy and seamless, letting nothing through.

I told myself I was still angry with her. Angry at what she had said. Angry at what she had implied. But our parents were not coming. Our father was not going to whisk us away in his arms like he had when we were a child. We were alone. We had no one else.

We should have had each other.

Yet here was the wall and the silence and the anger getting in the way. Here were Addie and I, not speaking to each other. I could wait for her to make the first move, as I had for years.

But I was so sick and tired of the loneliness.

<*Addie.*>

She flinched. For a second, I was terrified she would ignore me. I'd never ignored her when she reached out after a fight.

<*Addie, I—*>

<*I'm sorry*> she said. The words brushed against me like tattered butterfly wings.

<*What?*> I said.

<*For everything. For—for everything turning out like this.*>

I fell silent. I knew she didn't mean coming to Nornand, wasn't talking about the doctors and the tests and the fear of never going home.

<*You remember how we used to dream about never settling?*> Addie said. <*Back when we were tiny. Before we even started school. We used to think we could stay even and equal. Always.*>

<*I remember*> I said.

Addie climbed from Kitty's bed, shivering as our feet pressed against the cold tiles. She crept to the window, staring out at the darkness and the pinprick stars.

<*Eva?*> she said.

<*Yes?*>

<*Sometimes I wonder what that would have been like. If we'd never settled.*>

If we'd never learned to hate ourself. Never allowed the world to drive a wedge between us, forcing us to become Addie-or-Eva, not Addie-and-Eva. We'd been born with our souls' fingers interlocked. What if we'd never let go?

<*Yeah*> I said. <*Me too.*>

Addie rested our forehead against the icy glass. <*I'm sorry*> she said again.

Her apology should have made me feel better. Instead, it only made the pain worse. How was I supposed to reply? Yes, I accept your apology? No, it's not your fault?

It wasn't Addie's fault. I'd never thought it Addie's fault. If anything, it was mine. I was the one who hadn't faded when I was supposed to. I was the one who'd ruined Addie's life forever. A recessive soul was marked for death before birth. I should have disappeared. Instead, I'd dragged Addie into this half life, this dangerous existence, forever afraid.

I reached for her, across the blank space between our souls. I said <*I'm sorry, too.*>

We looked out at the world on the other side of the window. There was some sort of shadowy courtyard below, an irregular-shaped space bound by a chain-link fence. We could just barely make it out in the darkness. Nornand curved around part of the courtyard, half obscuring our vision. But there was a stretch of the enclosure blocked only by the fence, and beyond that—beyond that was just blackness. Not a single light.

<*We're going to get out of here*> I said.

Addie pressed our fingers against the windowpane, and if

I imagined hard enough, I could almost see it giving way, see us landing unharmed in the courtyard below, scaling the fence like it was nothing, and running, running away until the darkness enfolded us and hid us from view.

TWENTY-ONE

We felt the change in the air as soon as we awoke the next morning. The nurse corralling everyone in the Ward didn't smile like she had the day before, and when Eli stumbled rising from his chair, she yanked him back to his feet so hard he cried out. Kitty must have seen Addie staring; she sidled up next to us and whispered, "It's because *they're* here."

"Who?" Addie said, but the nurse demanded silence and Kitty refused to speak again, no matter how quietly, until we reached the small cafeteria where we ate our meals.

Even then, Kitty waited until the nurse retreated to her chair in the corner of the room. "The review board," she said, leaning toward us over her breakfast tray. A strand of her dark hair trailed through her oatmeal, and she squeaked in dismay.

<*And what's that?*> Addie muttered, but there wasn't time to say it aloud.

Because at that moment, the door opened, the nurse froze, and Mr. Conivent walked in. Immediately, the atmosphere in the room twisted. Mr. Conivent didn't fit in here. Despite the cold tile floor, the blinding fluorescent lights, and the observing nurse, something about all fourteen of us eating at one table created a sense of intimacy that mixed about as well with Mr. Conivent as water did with oil.

No one spoke as he surveyed the room. He nodded at the nurse, who gave a twitchy nod back, like a bird. Many of the kids weren't actually eating, just pushing their food around. Hally looked just as confused as we felt. Devon's head tilted down toward his tray, but we could see his eyes fixed on Mr. Conivent.

The three of us sat on the side of the table opposite the door, so we all had a perfect view of the men and woman who entered next. They were only four altogether, but they moved with a power that gripped the room, made them seem to take up more space than they should have. The men were dressed sharply in ties and creased pants, the woman in a dark pencil skirt, a small diamond winking from each ear. They stared at us openly, like the lanky delivery boy had our first morning. As if they were taking a tour of the zoo and we were the next animals on the itinerary.

Mr. Conivent spoke softly to one of the men, who nodded without looking at him. They stayed perhaps two minutes, just watching us pretend we didn't notice them. Then they and Mr. Conivent were gone and the whole room resumed breathing again as one, as if we shared common lungs.

"Who was that?" Hally said as a hum of conversation sprang up around the table. The nurse had wilted slightly by her chair and didn't seem to be listening.

"The review board," Kitty repeated. "They're from the government."

"This *is* the government," Devon said, and she shrugged.

"They're from the *government* government. They're important."

"How often do they come?" Hally said.

Kitty shook her head and scooped up some oatmeal. She held her spoon the same way Lyle did when he was playing with his food, as if it were a shovel. "I've only seen them once before, about a year ago. After I first got here."

The nurse had regained her color—too much of it, in fact. Her cheeks were flushed. She rubbed at her forehead, then clambered back onto her feet and clapped her hands like the nurses always seemed to do. "Come on, children. Eat quickly."

No one spoke again. The silence left me to digest, slowly, just how long Kitty had already been at Nornand.

Study time and lunch passed without the review board's intrusion, as did dinner. But we didn't head for the Study room after our last meal, as we had the previous day. Instead, we ended up in a sort of waiting room.

Addie and I had been in countless waiting rooms over the years. Ones with coffee tables covered with glossy health magazines. Ones with wallpaper in cool, calming blue. Ones with those silly blocks-on-rails play tables for little kids. This room had none of those things. There was a row of chairs pressed against one wall, facing the two doors cut into the opposite wall. We could just see what looked to be bright white examination rooms beyond the doorways. And that was it. But the entire setup screamed *waiting room* anyway.

Dr. Lyanne, Dr. Wendle, and Mr. Conivent stood inside, a strange trio in the corner of the room. Dr. Wendle was flushed, Dr. Lyanne pale but speaking quickly and passionately, Mr. Conivent cold, his words colder. Their argument, never loud, stopped immediately when the nurse cleared her throat. The three looked up. Dr. Wendle blanched. Dr. Lyanne faltered. Mr. Conivent's expression didn't change.

"Good, the children are here," he said, and though his tone was polite and his face smooth, it sounded like a dismissal. "Would you two get started, then? The board will arrive in a moment."

He left, and all the kids parted for him at the door, no one touching even the edge of his shirt. For a moment afterward, no one spoke. Dr. Lyanne stared at the wall.

It was the nurse who finally broke the silence, drawing on the endless reservoir of smiles she seemed to possess and pasting one onto her face. "Right, then," she said. "Children, find a seat and sit quietly. The doctors will call you when they're ready."

Slowly, everyone settled down. Addie sat in a chair close to the door, and Kitty grabbed a seat next to us. Lissa took the one on our other side, Ryan the one beside her. He glanced at us, but only for a moment. We hadn't spoken much the whole day. All the nurses were too tense, cracking down on the slightest whisper during study time, patrolling the table during meals.

Ryan had touched our shoulder as we left lunch, and when Addie hadn't immediately jerked away, he'd asked, softly, if we were okay. Addie had nodded. He'd squeezed gently before letting us go. And that had been all.

We had to tell them what we suspected about Sallie. This wasn't just one boy anymore. This procedure, this *surgery*, had happened more than once. And neither Jaime nor Sallie seemed like they were coming back. Not if the doctors had told everyone they'd gone home.

Dr. Wendle disappeared into one of the examination rooms. Dr. Lyanne stood in the adjacent doorway—not even leaning against the wall or the doorframe—just standing there, holding up her own weight.

Eli whimpered. A ripple ran through the room, but no one spoke and only a few heads turned to stare.

<Is he—> Addie said.

"Cal's just scared of needles," Kitty said, catching our expression. "He always cries when they take blood."

"Cal?" Addie said.

Kitty wavered, then said, "I—I meant Eli."

"You mean you made a mistake?" Addie frowned. "You thought it was Cal, but it's Eli?"

Kitty looked at the little boy. He had his hands fisted, his short legs drawn up onto the chair. "It's Eli," she said, and her voice was deadened but sure. "It's always Eli."

The boy's crying had caught Dr. Lyanne's attention. She looked at him out of the corner of her eye, then away again. Her gaze moved across the room, studying each of us in turn.

Something in her seemed to slacken.

"Kitty," she said, glancing down at her clipboard. "You're up first."

Kitty slipped from her chair and followed Dr. Lyanne into the examination room. Addie waited until Dr. Wendle had called someone in with him, too, until both doors had shut. Then she turned to Hally and Ryan and murmured, "It's not just Jaime."

"We know," Lissa said.

"*What?*" Addie said. Ryan raised his eyebrows in warning, and she dropped our voice to a whisper. "How?"

"I've talked to some of the others," Ryan said. He tilted his head toward one of the older boys at the far end of the room. "Some of the kids have been here a really long time. Years. And they've seen other kids disappear. Gone home. Except . . ."

"No one really goes home," Addie said.

Eli was whimpering again. The blond boy next to him put an awkward hand on his shoulder, but everyone else pretended not to notice. Everyone seemed to spend a lot of time pretending not to notice Eli. He'd been oddly fumbling all morning, his steps uncertain, his words few and half slurred, but no one had commented.

"We've got to get out of here," Ryan said under his breath. "Now." There were no more questions of where we would go. What we would do. Anywhere was better than here. Anything was better than here. "This place has got to have cracks in the system. There are always cracks. We've just got to find them."

<*We can't like this*> I said. <*Not with them all on*

high alert. Maybe things will be looser once the review board—>

Said board members appeared at the door just then, as if summoned by my thoughts. The nurse on duty let them in. Mr. Conivent didn't lead this time. Instead, he followed after the others, whispering something to the same man he'd spoken to at breakfast.

All the kids hunched down a little. What little conversation had existed withered away. Like this morning, the review board stayed a certain distance from us, hushed and watching. Our eyes darted toward them from time to time, and we caught a few of the other kids sneaking glances, too. But no one stared at them as they stared at us.

The minutes ticked past.

When one of the examination room doors finally opened, the rattle of the doorknob shot through the silence. Kitty walked out first and started at the sight of the men and woman in their dark clothes. Behind her, Dr. Lyanne was still filling out something on her clipboard.

"Eli?" she called without looking up. Then she did.

She froze, just as Kitty had. The little girl recovered first, hurrying back to her seat beside us. Dr. Lyanne couldn't seem to make herself move again for the longest time, but then she cleared her throat and said, again, "Eli?"

Eli shook his head.

"Come on, Eli," Dr. Lyanne said. She held out her hand but didn't leave the doorway. Her jaw was tight, her voice almost hoarse.

"No," Eli said, panic in his voice. He'd regained a little of the wildcat wariness I'd noted the first day. "No, no, *no*."

Kitty's hand slipped into ours. She didn't look at us, didn't look at Eli or Dr. Lyanne or the review board, just stared down at her knees. But her grip was so strong it hurt. There was a Band-Aid on the inside of her elbow, and for some reason, Addie couldn't stop staring at it.

"Eli," said Mr. Conivent, and Kitty flinched.

The entire review board was watching him now, this eight-year-old boy who refused to leave his chair, refused to do what the grown-ups asked.

"Is there a problem?" Dr. Wendle said, opening the other examination room door.

"Will someone just get the boy into a room?" Mr. Conivent said. He didn't sound angry. Didn't even sound upset or annoyed or frustrated. But his right hand was pressed in a fist against his side, and we saw the tension in his neck. "Dr. Lyanne? If you would?"

Dr. Lyanne came at Eli, who jumped out of his chair. He'd been wobbly all morning, his steps teetering. But we'd been distracted, and we hadn't looked too closely, hadn't seen the haze over his eyes. It fought with his wariness, opposing forces battling over his body.

Take care of it, Mr. Conivent had said that first day. Was this it? Was this *taking care of it*?

Eli lurched forward, stumbled, fell. Dr. Lyanne grabbed at him—whether to drag him into the examination room or just to keep him from hitting the ground, I didn't know—but whatever the reason, Eli screamed like she'd sliced him open. She jerked away. He scrambled to his feet and ran.

Addie gripped our chair to keep from jumping up, from tearing out of Kitty's grasp so we could dart over and scoop Eli up. He'd pressed into a corner of the room, trapped between the members of the review board and Dr. Wendle, who'd abandoned his own room to come chasing after him, and all I could think about was Lyle during his first dialysis sessions. He'd cried and cried and cried and the nurses had comforted him; our parents had been there to distract him; Addie had been there to read to him. And now this boy, screaming and kicking, was being *manhandled* by Dr. Wendle, and everyone was just *watching*—

"Let him go," Addie cried.

We froze. Ryan's eyes darted toward us. But the words had been spoken, and Addie couldn't take them back. Mr. Conivent turned and stared, but Dr. Wendle didn't stop—he didn't let Eli go—and before I knew what was happening, we were out of our seat and across the room, because couldn't they see how upset he was? Couldn't they be kinder in this tiny way?

Someone grabbed us before we could reach him. One of the review board members—the man always speaking with Mr. Conivent—and his grip *hurt*. He yanked us, pinning us against him, and the first words we heard from his mouth were *You will stop this. You will calm down. Right now.*

His nails dug into our skin so hard it brought tears to our eyes, and we couldn't see his face; we could only hear his voice in our ear. He spun us around, our back still against his torso but our face toward the other kids. Every single one of them stared back at us. Every single one of them wore a different expression. But in every one of them, the same current of fear. Ryan was half out of his chair, but he'd frozen.

Slowly, silently, the man brought Addie and me back to the row of seats. We were a doll in his hands, crafted of plastic and artificial coloring, every joint stiff. He shoved us down into a chair, and we did not rise again as Eli, cornered and captured by Dr. Wendle and a pair of nurses, was carried flailing and screeching into one of the examination rooms.

TWENTY-TWO

Kitty was quiet that night after the lights clicked off. She curled up facing the wall, her knees almost pressing against her chest, her hair spilling like ink across her pillow. In less than half an hour, her breaths had slowed and evened.

We couldn't shut our eyes, let alone sleep. I heard echoes of voices that weren't there. Eli screaming. The board official's words in our ear. They'd ended up not even finishing the testing. Instead, the doctors and the board members had disappeared somewhere with Eli, leaving the rest of us with a disgruntled nurse who shoved us in our bedrooms, muttering that her shift was supposed to be over.

No one had dared venture back out. Even if the nurse had left and wasn't sitting in the main Ward, someone else was sure to hear a door open . . . and who knew if they would tell?

<What do you think they're doing to them?> Addie said. She grasped Ryan's chip in our hand, our eyes fixed on the slow pulse. Maybe it comforted her the same way it comforted me.

I didn't need to ask who she was talking about. *<Same*

thing they're trying to do to the rest of us.>

<*No*> She flipped onto our back. <*There's something more about Eli and Cal. They're not just trying to get them to settle. . . . He's here so young, and—*>

<*He's here so young because his parents didn't want him*> I said.

Addie's frustration buffeted against me, and I knew she wasn't going to just let the matter drop. But before she could speak again, the chip in our hand began to pulse faster.

For a moment, we just stared at it. Then, without a word, Addie pushed back our covers and swung our legs over the side of the bed. The icy floor raised goose bumps on our skin.

Kitty didn't stir. Addie crossed the room, our nightgown gleaming white under the moonlight, our bare feet whispering against the ground. By the time we reached the door, our chip was solid red. She twisted the door open, took a step—and almost crashed into Ryan.

Addie crushed our knuckles against our lips to hold back a yelp of surprise. Ryan wasn't quite fast enough. He managed the first startled syllable of Addie's name before she shoved our other hand against his mouth, dropping our chip in the process. Luckily, the corridor was carpeted, and it didn't clatter.

We stood absolutely still for several seconds, trying not to breathe, trying to come up with valid excuses if someone had heard and came to check. But no one did.

Ryan stared at us. His hair stuck up in random directions, some of the curls crushed, others seeming to defy gravity. I could feel his breath against our skin, the curve of his lips fitting in the creases between our fingers.

Slowly, Addie lowered our hand from his mouth. She reached behind us and eased our bedroom door shut while Ryan bent to retrieve our chip.

Then, without a word, without even some sort of unspoken signal, Addie and Ryan turned and headed for the main Ward.

It seemed smaller in the darkness. There were no windows here, so the only source of light came from the glowing red chips in our hands. We sat at one of the tables, and still, neither Addie nor Ryan spoke.

I had a hundred things I wanted to say. A hundred little things I could imagine doing, that I wanted to do, if I could. If I just *could*. But Addie was in control, and she squandered her time sitting still and unsmiling in the darkness.

"The nurse will come and check on us soon, probably," she finally murmured.

"Not for another hour," Ryan said, looking at his watch. He seemed a bit relieved to have something to say. "Lissa said the nurses come about the same time every night."

Addie nodded. Then, before things could lapse right back into an awkward silence, she said, "Well, what did you want?"

"Sorry?" Ryan said.

Addie spoke even more quickly. "You came by our room. You must have a reason. If you've got something to say, then say it."

Ryan's chip clicked against the table. "I don't have a reason," he said, "because I wasn't coming to your room. I was passing by." He jerked his head toward the alcove on the far side of the Ward. "There's only one bathroom in this place."

Our face heated. "Right." She rose. "Well, then—"

"Addie—" Ryan said before she could slip away down the hall. He stood, too, more slowly. "Addie, I'm lying. I wanted to ask if you were okay."

"You keep asking me if I'm okay," Addie snapped. "I'm *fine.* You're okay. Hally and Lissa are okay—"

"I'm *not* okay," Ryan said. Even in the dim light, I could see, almost feel, the tension in his shoulders. His eyebrows knit. His fingers curled around the back of his chair. "I don't have a plan to get us out of here. I don't know where we'd go if I did." He sighed and pushed at his bangs, making them stick up even more. "The more I see of this place, the worse it gets. And today, when that guy grabbed you and Eva . . . So, no, I'm not okay. And if you are, Addie, then you're doing a lot better than I am, all right?"

If I'd been in control, I'd have told him it wasn't his responsibility to free us. I'd have promised him we'd figure it out together. I would have sworn we'd all be safe, soon. I would have said anything to ease some of the worry lining his forehead.

Addie looked away, our eyes tracing the carpet.

"You don't need to worry about Eva and me," she said. "We've got each other."

"Not if the doctors can help it," Ryan said.

This brought our head back up so fast it was dizzying. "You think I don't know?"

"Then maybe . . ." Ryan hesitated. "Maybe you shouldn't do things like what you did today."

Addie bristled. "They were practically torturing him."

"You couldn't have helped," he said. He flipped his chip over and over in his hand, his shoulders still squared and tight. "And now they're going to pay more attention to you."

Addie said nothing, but I could feel her seething, feel her emotions boiling helplessly inside us.

"Just be careful, okay?" Ryan said. "Please."

He looked us in the eye until Addie nodded.

Eli still hadn't returned to the group by lunch the next day. The nurse served one fewer yellow trays than usual and didn't offer any sort of explanation. When Hally wondered aloud where he might be, no one replied—or even looked at her for the remainder of the meal.

As the hours passed and Eli didn't show up, my mind kept returning to another boy. The one we'd seen stretched out on the gurney. The one with the stark white bandages and the staring, vacant eyes and the *before* and *after* pictures.

At least no one told us that Eli had gone home. I took what comfort I could in that.

"Is this how it started?" Addie whispered to Lissa as we left our evening study session. Over the past three and a half days, I'd gotten a general sense of this wing of Nornand; we were definitely heading back to the waiting room we'd been in yesterday. "For Jaime. When they took him—was it all sudden like this? He just disappeared?"

Addie and I were last in line, Lissa just ahead of us. She had to turn slightly to answer, and even then she spoke so quietly we all but read her answer from her lips. "With Jaime, they called him . . ." The nurse looked over her shoulder, and though there was no way she could hear us back here, Lissa paused until the woman turned back around. "They called him out of the Study room one morning . . . and he never came back."

The line stopped moving as we reached the waiting room. But the door was shut, and the nurse didn't try to enter, just sighed and checked her watch. Devon had been sitting with Kitty near the door in the Study room, and now both of them were stuck up front, right next to the nurse.

We all stood in the corridor, a straight blue line on a sheet of paper. The tag on the back of our uniform's blouse scratched against our neck. There were goose bumps on our arms, a testament to Nornand's permanent chill.

If we were home right now, we would be getting dinner ready with Mom and Lyle. The microwave would be humming with last night's leftovers. We'd all be sweating from the heat of the stove and the smallness of the kitchen. Lyle would be telling us every last thing that had happened to him that day and, if he ran out of things, throwing in a couple things that had happened the day before, or the day before that.

I could almost see him at the counter, standing on a three-legged stool as he cut carrots with surgical precision, his fingers bent under as Addie had taught him.

We'd—

Addie started as the door we stood in front of swung open.

Dr. Lyanne stepped out, a pile of manila folders under one arm, a chipped red mug in the opposite hand. She just barely seemed to notice us and Lissa in her way.

"Excuse me," she muttered and moved to close the door behind her, then paused and looked at the mug in her hand as if just realizing it was there. She sighed and turned, disappearing back into her office. When she reappeared, the folders and mug were both gone and her eyes looked somewhat clearer.

"Excuse me, girls," she said louder, and this time Lissa and Addie moved out of the way.

"Dr. Lyanne," the nurse called, prompting a twitch in the doctor's jaw. "Could you come here, please? It's already half past seven. Mr. Conivent said—"

"I'll see if they're almost done," Dr. Lyanne said. She tugged at her lab coat and moved toward the nurse, every step a sharp click of heels against the tiled floor. Addie, along with almost everyone else in the line, watched her go. She disappeared into the waiting room.

<Quick> I said. *<She didn't lock the door—>*

I was afraid I'd have to waste precious time explaining, but Addie didn't ask any questions, just cast a swift look around, met eyes with Lissa, and slipped into Dr. Lyanne's office. We'd recognized those folders, the tabs marked with blue labels.

The office was small and trapezoidal, with a slightly slanting ceiling and a large window at one end. The last rays of sunlight filtered in, bouncing off the tiles on the roof outside. Dr. Lyanne's desk was pushed against the far wall, next to a filing cabinet and a low bookshelf. The pile of files sat at the edge of her desk.

"*Addie*," Lissa hissed. She'd followed us into the office, her eyes wide. "What are you *doing*?"

"Figuring out what they're doing to Eli and Cal," Addie said.

Would he be the next child on the operating table? The next body on the gurney, moved in haste while the others sat penned in the Study room or eating quietly from their yellow trays?

And perhaps—perhaps, if we could find Jaime Cortae's folder, or Sallie's folder—we'd figure out where they were now. What was happening to them now that Nornand claimed they'd gone home.

Addie crossed the office. "Let me know if anyone's coming."

"But—" Lissa said.

<*Hurry, Addie*> I said.

<*This was your idea*> she snapped. <*And I am hurrying.*>

Our hands shook as she flipped through the manila folders. *Bridget Conrade*—the blond girl with the long, neat braids. *Hanson Drummond*—the boy who'd spoken up about Eli that first day. *Katherine Holynd*—Kitty? *Arnold Renk* . . .

Addie Tamsyn.

Addie hesitated, but I reeled her back on task. <*No time. Keep looking. It's got to be here.*>

She glanced up. Lissa stood just beyond the doorway, facing away from us. She'd eased the door almost all the way closed; we could just see her hands fidgeting behind her back through the remaining inches of space.

Addie pawed through the rest of the files. <*It's not here,*

Eva. And neither are the files for Jaime or Sallie. There're only nine files. We're missing five.>

<Check the filing cabinet> I said.

Addie bent down and jerked it open. She leafed through the files, pulling them out to check the labels. Our hands trembled so hard she could barely stuff the files back in.

<This'll take forever> Addie said. *<We haven't got time—>*

<Calm down> I said. *<Keep looking.>*

Her aggravation spiked, pressing daggers against me, but she did as I said, glancing at each folder before cramming it back into its slot.

<Wait!> I said. *<Wait, that one—we've heard of that one before.>*

Addie froze. We reread the label.

Refcon.

The night we were taken. The scene in the dining room, Dad's helpless gaze, Mom's knuckles white on the back of our chair. Mr. Conivent's words rang through our mind: *It's what we call a suppression drug, a highly controlled substance. It affects the neural system. Suppresses the dominant mind.*

Addie rocked back on our heels and pulled the file all the way out of the cabinet. Checking the doorway had become a nervous twitch. But Lissa hadn't moved from her spot or said a word, and our eyes jerked back to the file. It was worn, the edges soft and rolled from handling. Addie flipped it open.

<It's all just . . . drug information> she said, skimming the first page. *<This is what Mr. Conivent was talking*

about, isn't it? What Hally . . . what Hally stole from her mom's hospital. That suppression drug.>

So why did the sheet of paper also say *Vaccinations*?

Addie leafed through the file. The papers inside were stacked a good half-inch thick, some printed on official-looking paper with fancy letterheads, others scribbled handwritten notes on notebook paper, one edge tattered. Addie shifted, then cursed as the movement caused half the papers to slip off our lap and onto the ground. She continued swearing under our breath as she grabbed the sheets and stuffed them back into the folder. I prayed Dr. Lyanne didn't have some special order we were breaking.

It was with a sense of déjà vu that our hand landed on a sheet of paper with a small picture clipped to the top corner.

BRONS, ELI

HYBRID

We skipped his basic information for the longer report below. Someone had scrawled notes in the margins and above the printed text. There was already a sourness in our stomach—it had been there since we'd stepped foot in Dr. Lyanne's office. But now a new revulsion crept through me—half nausea and half pain. Our hand pressed against our lips, then against our teeth. We bit down. I didn't know if our tears came from that or the pain inked into Eli's report. The secret connecting Refcon and the vaccinations and all the children here, at Nornand. All the children in the country.

<God> Addie whispered. *<Eva—>*

A sound cut her off. A stifled cry. Then the squeak of

shoes against tile. Our head jerked up.

The crack of space between the door and the doorway was empty.

Lissa was gone.

Every nerve—every nerve and muscle and sinew in our body—slacked and then snapped rubber-band tight.

We threw the file back into the cabinet and slid it shut. Scoured the room for somewhere, *anywhere*, to hide. There was none. We didn't need more than one glance to know that—we'd known that since the moment we entered the office. The desk wasn't solid but built like a table, with no backing. The window lacked curtains. The best we could do was crouch on the other side of the filing cabinet, and we didn't even have time to do that.

The door opened.

The board officer—the man who'd grabbed us in the waiting room, whose fingerprint bruises still bloomed on our wrist—stepped inside.

TWENTY-THREE

For a fraction of a second, a millisecond, we didn't move. The man didn't move. He didn't leave the doorway. We didn't scream.

Scream. A laugh bubbled at the back of our throat. As if that could do anything. As if that could help.

The man beckoned behind him without taking his eyes off us. "Bring the other girl in here and get the rest of the patients out of the hall, along with that nurse." He spoke in the same low, even tone we'd heard yesterday.

There was a rush of footsteps against tile. Devon shouting. Then Lissa was in the room with us, yanked in by the female board official. We could see her nails digging into Lissa's shoulder. The door slammed behind them.

"Get Conivent," the man said. The woman nodded, released Lissa, and left. Then it was just us and Lissa and that man in Dr. Lyanne's office.

He watched us, his eyes shifting from Addie and me to Lissa. He wasn't any taller than Mr. Conivent. Wasn't any broader in the shoulders, any bigger. He wore clothes like he was going to the symphony—shirt with cuff links, a dark waistcoat, pants with pressed creases, black shoes. Our wrist throbbed from the memory of his touch. And our chest hurt from the look on his face, the look that said, quite plainly, that whatever this situation was, whatever it was we'd done, whatever it was we *thought* we could do, we'd never, ever, ever win against him. We could fight until we were bloody, and he'd still win.

And he'd come out of the fight looking as perfectly put-together as he did now.

"Jenson?" Mr. Conivent said, opening the door. It allowed us a glimpse of the now empty hall.

The man, Mr. Jenson, didn't turn to look at him. "You said this building was secure, Conivent—that the *patients* were secure, that no one could ever go missing from *this* hospital." Even when he inflected his words, his tone hardly changed. His expression never so much as flickered. "But apparently, this one was unaccounted for long enough to get in here." Jenson didn't wait for a response. "Whose office is this?"

There was the briefest of pauses before Mr. Conivent opened his mouth to answer, but another voice spoke for him.

"It's mine."

Dr. Lyanne came to the doorway. She looked at Mr. Conivent. He looked at her. Then, with a jerk of his arm, he gestured her inside. The office, never large, now seemed crushed to the brim though no one so much as touched.

"Close the door," Jenson said, and it was done. Mr. Conivent stayed on the other side.

We pulled each breath like a saw from our lungs.

"It's not policy here to lock your office when you leave?" Jenson said.

"I was only gone a moment," Dr. Lyanne said. Her voice was quiet but cool. "I'd planned on returning immediately."

"The nurse on duty does share a portion of the blame," Jenson said. And finally, his gaze flickered from us to Dr. Lyanne. It was like being released from some crushing weight, like surfacing from the bottom of the ocean. "What I'd like to know is why these patients wanted to access your office."

Dr. Lyanne studied us. "Perhaps we should ask them."

"They would lie," said Jenson. "And it would waste time."

Now Dr. Lyanne's eyes moved toward the pile of manila folders on her desk. I realized with a flip of the stomach that we'd left them in a messy pile instead of stacked. She scrutinized us next, and by extension, the filing cabinet. Wordlessly, she walked over and began pulling the drawers open. There were only two. When she got to the bottom one, she saw the file lying on top, the one we hadn't had time to shove back.

I was still trying to come up with something to say. Or someplace to run—we could just push Dr. Lyanne aside, grab Lissa's hand, and *run*.

Dr. Lyanne looked up at us.

"Give it here," Jenson said. She picked the file up and handed it over. He flipped it open, and we had to stand there, Addie and I and Lissa, as he read through the pages, and every moment I just wished for death because the fear and the unknowing were making us so sick we couldn't breathe.

Finally, the man looked up again and examined our face. Eli's report had been on top, and he held it up now, watching us carefully, and we tried, *tried* to keep our expression neutral, but we couldn't. The room blurred slightly. Our skin pricked with heat.

"Interesting case," he said.

"It's in the *vaccinations,*" Addie blurted, and the room blurred more. We struggled to keep from blinking, because if we blinked, we might cry—really start crying—and that would just be another sign of weakness before this man, who showed absolutely none.

Dr. Lyanne straightened. Lissa was still by the door, so still and quiet she might have been furniture. But her gaze was pinned on us. Not the board official. Not Dr. Lyanne. Us.

We released the edge of the filing cabinet. "Those vaccinations everybody has to get as babies . . . you put something in it to—" Our breaths stuck in our throat. We had to pause for air. A tear fell. "To kill off one of the souls. To keep people from being hybrid—"

Hybridity was genetic. Everybody knew that.

But the rest of the world—the rest of the world was so predominantly hybrid, and there were so, so few hybrids here, and we'd always thought—we'd always thought it was just a matter of genetics, a matter of *like begets like,* the way they'd taught us in biology, but it wasn't that way at *all*—

"It's not like that," Dr. Lyanne said. "Most people in this country would lose their recessive soul anyway. The vaccines just . . . they help it along—"

"They're *sick*," Addie cried. "They're poison. You're poisoning us. All of us." We stared at Jenson through blurry but steady eyes. "And when it doesn't work—when there's someone like Eli, or Cal, or us—then you go and round us up and you try again. And sometimes, you even get to choose who you'd like to die."

There were dominant souls and there were recessive souls. Chosen before birth. Written into our DNA. A *natural process*, our guidance counselor had stressed during all those sessions. Unchangeable. Irrefutable.

Certainly not something to be decided by doctors, here in the cold halls, under the blinding white lights.

"Who was the one who decided Eli wasn't fit for society?" Addie asked Dr. Lyanne. "Who decided he wasn't good enough? Who told Cal he'd have to take his place and answer to a false name for the rest of his life? You?"

I thought I saw Dr. Lyanne flinch. Addie must have seen it too, because she straightened a little.

"Was there anything else you wanted to say?" Jenson asked, and his expression was so carefully composed it was almost bored.

"Who knows about this?" Addie said softly. "My parents didn't—I know they didn't. Nobody but you kind of people know, do they?"

We stared at Jenson, and he stared back at us.

He called for security guards after that.

They locked us in our room first, so we didn't see what happened farther down the hall. We just heard Lissa scream and a door slam—and Lissa never stopped screaming.

"Lissa?" Addie said. We pounded against the door, then the wall that separated us from her. "Lissa? *Lissa?*"

She didn't reply. She sobbed and we could hear her through the wall, but she *didn't reply* and we didn't know what had happened, we didn't know what was wrong.

"Lissa?"

The doorknob rattled in our hands but didn't turn.

"Open the door," Addie screamed. *"What did you do? What did you do to her?"*

No one came. Lissa kept crying. We stalked from one end of the room to the other and back again and back again and there was *nothing*, there was no way out. No way to get to her.

<*Except the window*> I said.

Addie didn't hesitate. She didn't pause. She picked up the small, wooden nightstand beside our bed and smashed the window to pieces. Glass flew everywhere, clattering to the courtyard below. We stretched out, and we could just reach Lissa's window, so we smashed that one, too, with a wild swing that almost jolted the nightstand right out of our hand. There were no bug screens. These windows were not meant to be opened.

There were no alarms, either, though I didn't think of that until we were already climbing out the window. The wind whipped at our hair. We'd gotten rid of most of the glass on the sides and bottom, but our legs and hands were bleeding by the time we found a place to put our foot on the outside of the building.

The sky was all peaches and cream, marred only by a giant, lazy swirl of bloody raspberry right through the center.

We didn't look down. We were three stories up, and a part of me laughed hysterically. This was ripped right out of Lyle's adventure books. But in adventure books, no one ever died falling off a window ledge trying to sneak into a room three feet away. We had no such security.

We held our breath and let go of the sill with one hand to grab the edge of Lissa's window. We hadn't cleared the glass enough, and a shard bit into our skin, but we didn't let go. We swung one foot up to the edge of the window and pushed hard, hard with the other and tumbled into Lissa's room, cut up and bleeding but more or less intact.

Lissa gasped. She had tears on her cheeks and a mouth falling open and her glasses askew. She stared as we said, hoarsely, "Are you okay? Are you okay? Did he hurt you?"

TWENTY-FOUR

Lissa had red marks on her arms from where the security guard had grabbed her and a cut on her hand from I didn't know what, but otherwise she seemed okay, and we couldn't imagine what had happened to make her struggle like that, to make her scream like that, until she flew into our arms and cried, "*They're going to do it to me next. They're going to cut into me next.*"

"What?" Addie grabbed her shoulders.

Lissa was shaking. "The man from the review board. He said—Oh my God, Addie, you're *bleeding*. The *window*."

"Forget the window," Addie said. I'd never heard our voice sound so hard and fierce and cold. Never in our life. "What did he say? Exactly."

"He said we would be a good candidate for surgery," Lissa said.

Our hands and legs throbbed where the glass had cut, but other than the gash on our hand, nothing seemed too deep. Addie collapsed onto one of the beds, staining the sheets with our blood. "They can't," she said, two words on a breath. "Why you? Why not us? We were—I was the one who actually—"

Lissa hadn't sat down. Her tears were disappearing now, replaced by a sort of heat that burned through her eyes and her voice as she said, "Addie, Addie, *look* at me."

We did. We looked at her and saw her wide-framed black glasses with the artsy white rhinestones, her thick, curly hair, her long hands and small feet and sharp nose.

"Addie," Lissa said, and now she sounded tired, so tired. "My father can't find a decent job because no one will hire him. My mother's parents send money because they've got enough of it to throw around, and their conscience is at least that strong, but I've never met anyone on that side of the family. They've never wanted to meet us." She came and sat beside us on the edge of the bed, bunching up the sheet and pressing it against our hand to stanch the bleeding. Addie flinched but didn't draw away. "Addie," Lissa said. "Don't you see? They think our lives are all worthless because we're hybrids, but for us, it's worse than that. If they operated on you, someone might still care. If your parents complained and kicked up a fuss, there's a tiny chance someone might listen." She took a shuddery breath. "But us? Or Devon and Ryan? No one would care about us."

No one would care about a half-foreign, hybrid child. The government could do whatever it wanted, and no one would say a thing. They could destroy the Mullans, rip them out of their house, take away every last cent, throw them into jail on a technicality, and no one would blink, no one would question it. It would almost be expected. I could hear the whispers that would arise, the relief. *I'd always known they were up to something,* they'd say. *Didn't I keep telling you? A family like that . . . They had to be up to something.*

"Well, it's wrong," Addie said. "It's all wrong."

I couldn't remember the last time Addie had hugged someone other than our parents or Lyle. Not willingly. Not on purpose. But she put our arms around Lissa now. "I shouldn't have gotten you involved," she said into her shoulder.

"Hey," Lissa said softly. "I'm the one who got *you* involved."

It was at that moment, our chin resting on Lissa's shoulder, that we looked through the ruined window and saw a nurse on the other side of the building, across the courtyard. Staring back at us. We couldn't see her clearly enough to make out her expression, but there was no mistaking the flash of her wrist, the black walkie-talkie. The obvious call for help.

Addie jerked backward.

Lissa started, then spun around, following our gaze. "You've got to get back to your room," she said, then laughed at the ridiculousness of her own suggestion. As if that would help, considering the state of the windows, the state of our hands and legs.

<*Put the bed against the door*> I said, and Addie jumped to our feet, pulling Lissa up after us. We winced. Our hand was still bleeding. But there wasn't time to worry about that.

"Help me move this." Addie grabbed one end of the bed and attempted to ignore the new stab of pain. "Hurry."

The steel frame was heavier than it looked and screeched

every foot of the way across the floor. We were barely strong enough to shove the bed against the door, and by the time it was jammed against the wood, Addie was breathing hard. She let go of the bed frame to brush our hair out of our face, and I tried not to pay attention to the bloody handprint we left on the metal.

"Now the other," Addie said, and soon the second bed was jammed against the first.

"What now?" Lissa said.

What now? The beds were against the door, but that only kept *them* from getting in—and only for so long. Addie ran to the window. Going back to our room wouldn't do any good. That door was locked, too. Below us was a three-story drop and hot, hard concrete. We could maybe break the window on the *other* side of Lissa's room and try getting out through there, but just as Addie went to grab one of the nightstands, we heard the unmistakable sound of someone starting to unlock Lissa's door.

Down was impossible. Sideways was useless.

A half-formed memory swam in my mind, something I'd seen—we'd seen—that I had to remember. Something important.

"Addie—" Lissa said as the pounding started, the shouting, *Open up! Get away from the door!* "Addie!"

Then it came to me. The first day. Before we'd ever stepped foot in Nornand's sanitized halls. We'd seen someone on the roof.

<Up> I said. *<Can we go up?>*

Addie stuck our head out the window and craned our neck. Yes—yes, we could, maybe. There was a small overhang not far above the window, and if we were careful, if we were very, very careful, we could reach it and, from there, get onto the roof.

This was ten times crazier than what we'd just done getting to Lissa's room from ours, but now that we knew what they were planning to do to Lissa, how could we stay and wait for them to take her away?

"Come on." Addie darted over and grabbed Lissa's hand. "We're going up."

"Up?" she cried.

"To the roof," Addie said grimly as the pounding got louder, more rhythmic, like some sort of battering ram. The beds screeched toward us, bit by bit.

"And what do we do once we're on the roof?" Lissa said, staring at us. "We'll just be stuck there."

Addie explained about the men we'd seen our first day, speaking as quickly as she could. "They got up there somehow, and it certainly wasn't through breaking windows. So there's got to be another way down to the ground."

"What if they had a ladder?" Lissa said. "What if they block all the ways down? And we can't just leave my brother—"

The door was open half a foot now.

<*We don't have time to argue*> I said.

"There's no other way," Addie said. "I'll go first. Then I'll pull you up. Lissa—*Lissa*, listen to me."

"But Devon and Ryan—"

"Lissa," Addie shouted. "Lissa, they would want you to go. You can only help them if you go."

Lissa threw one last look toward the door, her lips thin, then nodded. Addie took a deep breath.

We prayed that the last thing we saw on this green earth wouldn't be the side of the Nornand Clinic of Psychiatric Health as we plummeted to the ground.

"Careful," Lissa whispered as Addie eased out of the window. We'd never been athletic. We'd never played sports or run track or even danced. What we had done a lot, as a kid, was climb trees. I'd loved it, loved the shade of the leaves, the feel of the bark, the smell of sap and dirt and sunlight in the park.

I pretended we were climbing a tree as Addie grabbed hold of the overhang far above our head and gritted our teeth as our wounded palm scraped against the concrete. We'd have to rely mostly on arm strength to pull ourself up. Us, who'd never been able to do a single pull-up in gym. But we'd never had a team of security guards breaking down a door to motivate us, and as I whispered encouragement and prayed and hoped, Addie reached up with our other hand, held on as tightly as we could, and then launched upward with our feet.

There was a terrible moment of weightlessness. Of hanging in the air. Of not knowing, of scrambling with our arms, our elbows, our fingers, for purchase against tiles. Of blind panic and the thought that this was it; it was all over. And then we stopped sliding. Addie grabbed on. And with a wrench that made our muscles scream, she hauled us up and over and onto the overhang.

The sky was awash with color. Violet. Red. There wasn't time to drink it in. There wasn't even time to catch our breath.

"Lissa!" Addie shouted and reached down. "Grab my hand!"

We yanked Lissa up beside us just as the bedroom door shattered.

The wind battered our faces as we tore across the roof, whisking the sweat from our forehead, our brow, our neck. Every step clanged. Every breath hurt. But we couldn't stop. We had to find a way down. Any way down.

The roof seemed enormous, and it wasn't all flat. Nornand was a building of odd angles, of strange protrusions that hid parts of the roof from sight. We didn't like looking over the edge of the building, but we had to, searching for some kind of fire escape or built-in ladder or *something.* Something.

<*There*> I said. <*There, on the left. What's that?*>

Something flashed in the dwindling sunlight. Something metal. Addie darted toward it, but Lissa was faster. It was a hatch. A metal hatch that led back into the building.

And just as Lissa reached down to grab the handle, the hatch flew open and a security guard climbed out.

Lissa lurched away, spinning around and running full tilt back toward us, but she wasn't fast enough. The guard grabbed her around the waist. She screamed. We launched forward and smashed into the security guard's side. The man grunted but didn't seem particularly hurt.

"Let go!" Lissa said. Her legs flailed—kicking, thrashing.

"Some help?" the guard shouted. The roof rang with flying footsteps. Another second and two more men surrounded us. Black-clothed. Hard-faced.

"*Stop*," Lissa said. "Let *go*!"

"Calm down," one of the new men said. "No one wants to hurt you."

He eyed Addie and me as he spoke, moving closer and closer. We backed away. One step. Two.

"Let her go," I said, our eyes flickering to Lissa. "He's hurting her."

"He's not," the man said. Another inch forward. Another. Another.

Lissa screamed. I flinched, scrambling back two or three feet.

And discovered with a sudden weightless, breathless shock that there was nothing there.

Our head jerked around. I flailed for balance.

"Addie!" Lissa shouted.

The sky was deep, deep purple.

I swallowed one last breath.

And felt the security guard's fingers just slip through ours as we tumbled backward off the roof.

TWENTY-FIVE

Hey. Hey, remember?

Remember when we were seven and those kids locked us in that trunk?

We were playing hide-and-seek, remember? And that kid—what was his name? He told us to hide in the trunk because no one would ever look in there.

He was right, wasn't he?

No one found us.

Not for hours.

Waking up. Pressure. Pressure and pain in our head. Dizziness. Nausea. We tried to move—Lissa and Hally. The man had Lissa and Hally. I tried to move. Everything was blurry. "*Lissa?*" I said. Hands pushed us down, held us still. A new prick of pain. Something pulled us back under, burying us in the darkness. *Shh. Shh . . .*

I woke, pulled from one kind of darkness to another. It took a moment to remember what had happened. Memories of today mixed with those of yesterday and the days before, slippery silver fish in a murky pond. It was a little hard to think—thoughts dissipated, half formed. But one thought lingered through it all.

Lissa. The men in black uniforms closing in on the rooftop, one of them clutching her as she screamed and twisted.

I jerked upright—and nearly cried out as the nausea hit, stone-fisted against our skull. Our breathing was shallow. Our head pounded, each heartbeat sending another burst of pain shuddering through us.

We weren't in our room. Something crinkled under us. Paper.

I clutched our head and fumbled off the examination table, nearly crashing onto the cold ground. Our fingers pressed against something cottony and soft on our right temple. A bandage. I winced. There were more bandages on our legs and one wrapped around our left hand and—

And *I* was the one moving.

Addie . . .

Oh, God, no—

<*Addie*> I screamed. <*Addie!*>

She answered.

<*I'm—I'm here.*>

We crouched there on the floor, assuring each other that we were still okay, both of us, still alive and present and *here*. The bandage tore against our skin as we peeled it off, and we almost cried when our fingers brushed against the open wound beneath, but it was just that—a wound. No stitches, even. No surgery. I went weak with relief.

"Lissa?" Addie whispered.

No answer. The pain was receding enough for us to stand and keep our balance. We looked around and saw the big light on a swiveling arm, the monitors, the abandoned silver trays. The examination table.

A surgery room.

<Get out> I said. *<Get out, Addie—get out. Now.>*

She stumbled toward the door and ripped it open.

The hallway was dim, lit only by emergency lights. Addie looked right, then left, using our shoulder to prop open the door. The sickly, pallid light didn't reach very far. Darkness loomed on either end of the hall. Other than a faint buzzing, all was quiet and still.

Addie edged out into the corridor and eased the door shut. We didn't recognize this hall. *<Which way?>*

I didn't see a difference, and I told her so. It was hard to think straight. Our head still pounded. The nausea came in howling waves. Our hand throbbed.

Addie hesitated, then turned right. The silence amplified our breathing, the rustle of our clothes, the sound of our footsteps on the tiled floor. Doors flanked us on either side. Like people. Like soldiers.

Was Lissa inside one of those rooms? What about Ryan? Had they taken him, too? Addie checked the chip still tucked inside our sock, but it sat cold and blank. Wherever he was, he wasn't nearby.

If this was the third floor, it was a wing we'd never seen

before. The walls looked different—somehow starker. Maybe it was just the sallow light. The doors, though, were clearly metal, not wood like the ones near the Ward, and there were no windows at all.

Addie kept staring at one of the doors, as if looking at it long enough could make Lissa appear beyond it. On the left, there was what looked like a small speaker and two black buttons. Another button, red and shaped like a triangle, sat a little on the side. The door itself was plain but for the *B42* stamped high on the frame and a small, rectangular panel at eye level. A keypad was installed above the doorknob, taking the place of a normal lock.

<*I think the panel's a window*> I said.

Addie nodded. She grabbed hold of the panel's metal handle. It was cold in our palm. We'd check every room if we had to, if that was what it took to find Lissa and Hally.

But there were so many rooms. What else might we find first?

We swallowed.

<*Ready?*> Addie said.

<*Ready.*>

She pulled. The panel slid smoothly aside, revealing a glass pane underneath.

At first, we saw nothing but a pinpoint of light shrouded in darkness. When we squinted, we realized it was a night-light—a little kid's night-light in the shape of a sailboat. It illuminated the corner of the room farthest from the door, but the room wasn't big; soon our eyes adjusted enough to see the bed.

And the boy sitting on it.

His head was bent, his shoulders slightly hunched. Thin legs hung over the edge of the mattress. We couldn't see his face clearly, only enough to tell that—

<*He's saying something*> Addie whispered. <*See? His lips are moving.*>

But whatever the boy was muttering didn't stand a chance of making it past the thick door.

<*The speaker*> Addie said. She reached over to the small, circular grate and its accompanying buttons. Neither was labeled. She jabbed the one on the left before I could protest.

Immediately, a boy's voice filtered out of the speaker: ". . . and . . . uh. And, uh, they, on—on the day before. Before yesterday. We . . . we, uh . . . again. Again, and, uh . . . when they . . ."

Addie pushed the button again. His voice cut off.

For a moment, neither of us spoke.

Our eyes flickered back to the window and the boy still muttering inside.

<*Does the other button let us talk?*> I said.

It did. There was a popping, crackling sound when Addie first pressed the button, then quiet.

"Hello?" she whispered.

Inside the little room, the boy looked up.

And immediately, immediately, we recognized the boy from the gurney. Jaime Cortae. Age, thirteen. Jaime. Before and after.

Surgery.

Jaime, who stood and limped toward the door. Every step rocked so badly he listed from side to side like a sinking ship. But his eyes were bright, and there was a grin on his face when he stepped up onto something and pressed his forehead against the glass.

And oh, God—oh God, the long, curved incision line. The half-shaved head. The staples in his skull, holding it together.

Our stomach rebelled, acid rising in our throat.

Jaime's mouth worked even more furiously now, opening and closing. When he saw us staring at him, he flapped his right arm and jerked his head to the side.

<The speaker> Addie managed to say. *<He wants us to hear him.>*

But when she pressed the *receive* button, there was nothing but more gibberish: "I—always, I—and, um—uh . . . please . . . I, I need—"

His feverish words reverberated in the corridor.

Jaime started laughing—or crying—or both. He turned his face away from the window and the speaker, so it was hard to tell. All we could see were his shoulders trembling. Jerking. He was always jerking.

Then he put his mouth against the speaker again. He whispered. "Gone . . . gone . . . they—they cut him out. Out. He . . ." He moaned. "He's gone."

Addie slammed the window shut.

A terrible, crippling nausea sucked the breath from our lungs. We pushed past it, gagging as we tore down the hallway.

Jaime's quiet, stuttering voice rang in our ears, pounded in our veins, vibrated in our bones.

We ran until we smashed into someone barreling down the hall in the opposite direction.

Dr. Lyanne cried out, but her arms wrapped around us—entangling us. I screamed.

Everything was cold sweat and hot fear and the inability to breathe.

He's gone.

He's gone. He's gone.

His fellow soul, born with ghost fingers clutching his. They'd cut him out. The surgery had succeeded—if this could be called success. *Success!*

Dr. Lyanne held our limbs still, yelling at us to *Calm down. Calm down. Calm down.*

Someone was crying, and it wasn't until the haze cleared a little, until the pain receded a little, until we could breathe, breathe, breathe again, that we realized it wasn't us.

We'd forgotten to switch off the speaker to Jaime's room.

Dr. Lyanne's hand was a shackle around our wrist as she led us back to Jaime. We didn't want to go, held back by fear and shame. Shame for being afraid. For having run. For having left this boy who was already more alone than he'd ever been in his life.

"Jaime," Dr. Lyanne said. "Jaime, shh. It's all right." She released us in her haste to enter a code into the keypad, unlocking Jaime's door. We hung back, pressing against the wall, trying to shove away the throbbing headache and the dizziness. *Run*, I thought, but it didn't transfer to our limbs. "Shh, Jaime. Sweetheart, it's all right. It's all right."

Slowly, we pushed ourself from the wall. We held the side of the doorway for support as we turned and looked into the room.

The little blue sailboat night-light shed a soft glow. Together with the yellow emergency lights, it was enough to show us Dr. Lyanne on the bed, her arms around Jaime, rocking softly, softly, softly.

"Shh, sweetheart. Shh . . ."

Dr. Lyanne shone a penlight in our eyes. Addie squinted and turned away, our fingers curling around the examination table. Jaime had quieted, and Dr. Lyanne had locked him in his room again before pulling Addie and me back to the surgery room where we'd woken up.

"Do you feel dizzy?" Dr. Lyanne said. Her voice was missing some of its normal authoritative edge, like a knife that had gone dull. "Nausea?"

Addie shrugged, though our head pounded and our stomach rebelled. "Where are we?"

"The basement," Dr. Lyanne said.

"Where's Li—Hally?"

Dr. Lyanne turned away from us, fiddling with a tray of medical equipment. She dropped something and had to bend down to pick it back up. Her movements were jerky, her usual mantle of composure ragged at the edges. "In bed, probably. It's late."

Was she lying?

Addie swallowed, then cleared our throat softly. "Is she okay?"

Dr. Lyanne didn't turn around. "She didn't fall off any roofs, so I'd have to say she's doing better than you are. You and she are both lucky not to have ground any glass shards into your skin."

"But she's okay?" Addie said. "She's in her room? They haven't cut into her? They haven't operated on her?"

The woman looked at us sharply. Maybe we shouldn't have revealed how much we knew, but at the moment, neither of us cared.

"She's fine," Dr. Lyanne said.

Addie looked down at our lap, at the smooth blue cloth of our skirt, the dull faux leather of our school shoes. The black socks. Our chip was still tucked against our right ankle. Ryan's chip. Our fingers slid down, tracing the outline of it. No light at all.

But the feel of it, the solidity of it, gave her the strength to say, "Jaime." Dr. Lyanne stilled. "That was Jaime. He didn't go home. He was the one we saw the first day. He—" Addie looked up. Caught Dr. Lyanne's eyes. Whispered, voice hoarse. "You cut into him. You—"

Dr. Lyanne grabbed our collar and jerked us toward her. "No." Her voice shook. "I never laid a finger on Jaime Cortae. Understand me? I never laid a finger on *any* of those children. I *didn't do this to any of you*—didn't prescribe the vaccinations, didn't hold the scalpel, didn't—"

Addie twisted away. "Then *help* us. Don't let them do it to Lissa—you *can't* let them do it to Lissa—"

The anger in Dr. Lyanne's eyes dimmed, replaced by something quieter. "I *am* helping. You know what they do to kids like you—throw them in some middle-of-nowhere holding bin and forget they exist. I work here because we're trying to make things better, Addie. We're figuring out ways to *fix* you. Why can't you see that?"

"Like how they fixed Jaime?" Addie said.

Dr. Lyanne's cheeks were splotches of red, stark against the rest of her pale skin. Her eyes were huge and dark and fierce. "We're getting better. We've come a long way already. Someday—"

"Someday," Addie spat. "What about *now?* What about Lissa?"

"It's not about Lissa or you or me," she said. "It's about what's best for everyone. For the country as a whole."

She stared at us and we stared at her, both of us breathing hard.

"What was she like?" we whispered. Dr. Lyanne stared at us silently, her face tightening into something bland and expressionless. "Your other soul. The one you lost. Do you even remember her name?"

She didn't answer.

"Help us," we said, grabbing her arm—squeezing tighter and tighter and tighter. "Please."

TWENTY-SIX

We spent the night down in that basement, lying curled in the room across from Jaime's, listening to our own breathing in the dark. Slowly, the sickness receded and we slept. But every time we started to dream, Dr. Lyanne would come and wake us back up. Something about a concussion. Something about making sure we hadn't suffered any brain damage.

Brain damage. We laughed, and she turned away.

We slept and woke and slept and woke, dreams weaving into reality and reality melting into dreams. I don't know if it was a dream or reality when we slipped out of bed and saw, through our door's tiny window, the door on the other side of the hall standing wide open. The sailboat night-light. The shadowed figure sitting at the edge of the bed, arms around a boy who murmured endlessly to himself about someone who no longer existed.

It might have been real. Or it might have been my wishes manifesting themselves into dreams. Our memories of Mom at Lyle's bed whenever he got sick. At our bed when we had a fever.

We were too confused to know.

The night passed, though there was no way of telling down so deep in the ground. No windows. No sun. Not even the rush of doctors and nurses that signaled the start of a Nornand day on the hospital's upper levels. No, down here the only way we knew it was time to get up for real was Dr. Lyanne's voice telling us so.

We were exhausted from the cycle of sleep, wake, sleep, wake, but she looked like she hadn't slept at all. She told us we seemed fine and would return to the other kids at breakfast.

<Ryan> I said when we finally caught sight of him in the cafeteria, and judging from the look that flashed across his face, he was just as relieved to see us. Our eyes scanned the table for Lissa, but she wasn't there. Cal was there—he was Cal, no matter what the doctors said—the haze in his eyes stronger than ever before. Kitty was there, staring at her food, moving like a doll. But no Lissa. No Hally.

The nurse stopped us when Addie tried to sit next to Ryan. "I've been asked to keep you two separated," she said without emotion. "Choose another seat, dear." Ryan's mouth thinned, but he didn't protest, just watched as Addie slowly walked to the opposite end of the table.

Even then, the nurse kept eagle eyes on us throughout breakfast. Addie kept our gaze on our industrial yellow food tray and our mouth shut. And when the nurse called us into line, Addie didn't even try to find a place next to Ryan. In the Study room, she joined one of the younger girls, across the table from Bridget. Neither met our eyes. We were like Cal now. A danger.

This morning marked our fifth day at Nornand. I had to count back the days to even remember which day of the week it was—Wednesday. All the days melded together. What did it matter if it was Monday or Tuesday or Sunday? There was no more walking to school, no more laughing in the halls between bells, no more running across the street to the café for lunch. Just a quiet, somber Study room and the fourteen of us in Nornand blue. The thirteen of us. Because Lissa and Hally were gone.

I found myself wondering all these stupid little things. What sort of clothes had Kitty worn before coming here? Had she liked dresses, or, with all those brothers, had she insisted on pants? Did Bridget only wear black hair ribbons because she liked them, or because that was the only color she'd thought to bring when she left home?

We stared at these kids bent over their meaningless work sheets and essays. I still didn't know most of their names, hadn't even spoken a word to some of them, and a guilt like a physical pain knotted inside me. Most of them weren't much older than Kitty. I tried to look at each and every one of them, picking out details in their faces, their hair, the way they sat or slumped in their chairs. One girl had a cloud of light brown curls. The boy next to her was covered in freckles and had bitten his nails to the quick. Many of the other kids wore sneakers, but a few wore school shoes, like we did. One girl was in white sandals, another in black dress-shoes, as if she'd been abducted from a party and taken straight here.

But with every tiny thing I noticed about the other hybrids around us, a nauseating thought grew and festered. How many of them would end up like Jaime? How many of them would submit to the knife, two souls whispering good-byes as anesthesia robbed the strength from their limbs?

<Lissa> I said, over and over again. A moan of fear. I couldn't stop. *<Lissa. Hally.>*

We broke our pencil point, and Mr. Conivent came to give us another pencil. He was dressed in the same crisp, white shirt he'd worn the day he'd come to steal us from our family. The shirt that was like snow and ice—cuffs folded back, collar stark against his skin. He walked up beside us, bending down so he could whisper, could say so, so quietly in our ear, "It's supposed to be a beautiful day today." The pencil jabbed, point first, into our hand. "Perfect day for a surgery."

It *was* a beautiful day. We got a look at it firsthand when a nurse led us down three flights of stairs and out the back door. A tremor had run through the kids as soon as we stepped foot in the stairwell after study time, an almost physical hum of excitement.

"She's taking us outside," Kitty whispered. It was the first thing she'd said to us since our return, and though she didn't look at us when she said it, she did say it, and that meant something.

What had the nurses told the other kids, if anything? Had

they told them to leave us alone, or had that come naturally? Avoid the ones that cause trouble, like Cal, like Eli, for fear of bringing that same trouble onto yourself.

The courtyard was much bigger than it had looked from the third-floor window. The chain-link fence stretched a good three or four feet above our head and didn't contain so much as a gate. We'd been released from one cage only to be caught in another. But while the hospital's insides were sanitized and cold, someone had at least attempted to make the courtyard homier. They'd filled it with random childhood objects, anyway: a basketball hoop on a rickety stand, a toddler's plastic play set that even Cal would have had trouble using. Half-erased hopscotch squares littered the ground. A garish pink-and-red playhouse sat nestled in one corner, plastic doors yawning open. And that was just what we could see from the stairwell; the building's irregular side made it so that certain parts of the courtyard were half blocked from view.

The nurse started distributing plastic-handled jump ropes and rubber balls. They were snatched from her hands as soon as she pulled them from her bag. Then, with screeches of laughter that sounded almost crazed, everybody scattered. Kitty threw a look at us over her shoulder, hesitated, then followed the others.

Our mind still rang with Mr. Conivent's words. Where were Lissa and Hally now? Dr. Lyanne had lied when she'd said they were okay—how could they be okay if they were hidden away like this? Taken away from the group like this?

We caught sight of Ryan at the far end of the courtyard, half hidden by the side of the building, pressed into a small space between the rough wall and the chain-link fence. The nurse was mediating a fight between two kids over a four-square ball. Addie took the opportunity to slip by her and head for the hidden enclave.

"Addie," Ryan said as we darted into the building's shadow. His back had been pressed against the wall, but he came toward us as he spoke. "Thank God—What happened? Are you okay? Where is she? Where's my sister?" His eyes kept catching on the bandage on our forehead, our hand, our legs. "What *happened*?"

"I don't know where Lissa is," Addie said.

He froze. The look on his face made the nausea come back, made something in me twist harder and harder until I thought I would break. "How can you not know? She was with you. Wasn't she?"

Addie told him about breaking our windows to reach Lissa's room. About fleeing to the roof. About falling and waking up in the darkness. About what—who—we'd seen there.

She told him about the horrible information that had set this all off. What we'd discovered in Dr. Lyanne's office—about the vaccinations, about Eli and Cal. What the man on the review board had said as they locked Lissa in her room.

Ryan didn't speak when Addie paused to breathe, just stared at us, unmoving. The day was blistering hot, even in Nornand's shadow. Sweat made our blouse stick to our skin. Addie repeated, just loudly enough to be heard, what Mr. Conivent had whispered in our ear that morning.

For a long moment—for a long, long, unbearable moment—no one said anything and the whole world was still.

Then Ryan spoke again. "Did you give her your chip?"

Automatically, Addie looked toward our sock. No, no we hadn't. We hadn't thought of it, and her silence was answer enough.

"Why didn't you give it to her?" Ryan said. Now he didn't seem able to keep still—he made little half movements with his hands, his feet, like he wanted to pace or rub his temples or *something* but cut each motion off before he could begin. He looked up, then down, his mouth pulled to the side, his lips pressed together. "That's what these things are *for*, Addie. So we can keep track of one another. So we don't lose anyone—"

Our jaw hurt from being clenched so tight. "I just didn't think of it, okay?"

Ryan pressed his fist to his mouth. "I thought she was with you. She could be anywhere. They could be—"

"I was falling off the roof," Addie snapped. "I was a little busy—"

He couldn't shout. He didn't shout—he had enough control to keep his voice low, but it shook. "Too busy to think about saving my sister?"

"Ryan, that's not fair," I said, and nearly bit our tongue.

Because I had said it.

There wasn't time to figure out what I was doing or how I

had done it or what this meant or anything at all because Ryan was being unfair and Addie was roiling beside me and I was just barely, just barely, able to hang on to my control.

I shook from the tension of keeping upright, of standing and speaking and thinking and watching and reacting and moving. I said, "You're not helping, Ryan. This isn't helping. We didn't give her our chip. I'm sorry. But what now? What *now*?"

He stared at us. He said, in a tone I didn't understand and couldn't try to understand because I was working too hard just to hold everything together—"Eva?"

There was a funny feeling, like swimming through molasses. Our limbs were heavy—thick. I couldn't move, but neither, it seemed, could Addie. We were stuck in between. Our heart thumped feverishly in our chest, the only part of us still moving. We were frozen, sweating in the heat, our uninjured hand pressed against the side of the building, the rough grain digging into our palm.

<Addie> I said.

Then Ryan took our bandaged hand in his. If someone—either of us—had been fully in control, we might have flinched as his fingers pressed just a little too hard against our wound. But Addie and I were stuck in this in-between, this terrible in-between—and the pain was muted by the struggle going on in our mind. Ryan's fingers were familiar against ours, the same grip I'd felt the first time I'd been alone in our body, blind and feeling like there was nothing else anchoring me to the world. I fought to hang on, to close my hand around his, because *he had to calm down*. He had to concentrate. We had to save Lissa and Hally.

But I couldn't—I couldn't squeeze his hand, because Addie was fighting to go in the opposite direction.

"Let her, Addie, please," Ryan said. His voice was low; everything we said had to be spoken in a whisper. But the words were clear. "Let her take control, Addie. Just for a moment—just give her one moment—"

Addie started to cry. But she no longer controlled enough of our body to produce actual tears. Her crying was silent and invisible. To everyone but me. Like mine had been to everyone but her all those days and weeks and months after we first settled. After I was shunted aside and locked up in my own body, my skin a straitjacket, my bones prison bars.

I let go.

"Let *go*," Addie hissed. Our face burned. Our whole body burned. She twisted away from Ryan, who released our hand before she could rip it away.

Addie turned toward the chain-link fence, our breathing rough, our arms tense at our sides. Her emotions grated against me, so entangled I couldn't begin to sort them out. She stared out at the parking lot. The warm metal pressed against our face. Our fingers clenched the fence so tightly the links bit into our skin.

The fire was dying, replaced by a deep, cold sickness. In the background, we could hear the other kids screeching and laughing all across the courtyard.

"Go away," Addie said. She closed our eyes, lost for a moment in the whirl of our own head.

When she opened them again, Ryan lingered a few feet away, watching us.

"I'm *not* her," Addie said. Our face crumpled. "I'm not Eva. So just—stop it. *Stop it—*"

Her tears were real now, tangible on our cheeks. Ryan hesitated, but Addie glared at him, and finally, he slipped around the corner.

I could feel Addie quarantining herself into an empty, barren place. A safe place, silent and unfeeling and cold. Our chest hurt. Our breathing was ragged. A rare wind kicked up the dust along the bottom of the fence, swirling it against our shoes and socks.

<Addie> I said softly. My words slipped through the cracks of Addie's self-imposed prison. I felt her shuddering inside, wrapped around herself, trying to shut me out. *<Addie, I get it. Really, Addie. I do.>*

If Addie lost control, I'd be her and she'd be me—stuck in our head. Watching, listening, paralyzed.

I understood.

<I'm not going to force anything> I said. *<Addie? Do you hear me? Not ever. Not ever, ever, ever.>*

Addie said nothing, just stared blankly through the fence. There were a few odd cars parked near the building and a black van a bit farther away, but that was all. Nornand's backyard was not the neat green jewel the front was. A delivery guy unloaded boxes from the back of a van, a cap jammed low on his head to protect him from the unforgiving sun. He rolled his shoulders, stretching out his arms and flexing his fingers before making his way to a side door with a bulky box cradled in his arms. His trip took him within a few feet of us. We watched him silently. Focusing on him meant we didn't need to focus so hard on each other, could speak without scrutinizing each other's souls.

<*We can wait, Addie*> I said. <*I don't mind.*>

<*Of course you do*> she said. Her words tore at our tenuous peace. Our heart clenched. She closed our eyes. <*You want to move. You want to be in control. You want—you want to be in control whenever he's around and—*> She took a deep breath, our muscles aching from the pure tension in our limbs. <*And I—*>

Something clattered against the fence, jarring us from the recesses of our mind. We snapped back to the world around us: the courtyard, the hot, dry air, the metal links beneath our fingers. The fence. Something was caught against the fence—a square of something—cardboard, blown by the wind. We bent and tried to grab it. Our hand was just small enough to fit through the fence. We winced as we pulled it back, the rough metal scratching our skin.

Addie's unfinished sentence still hung between us, gossamer and smoke: *And I—And I—*

But it would hang forever unfinished. We read the message scribbled in black felt-tip marker on the piece of cardboard in our hands.

Addie. Eva.

We want to help you get out.

Addie looked up, but there was nobody. Nothing. Nothing there but the cars and the pavement and the—the delivery boy, almost to the building by now.

He saw us staring at him, and he smiled.

TWENTY-SEVEN

Devon didn't sit next to us at lunch, and I wasn't sure if it was to appease the nurses or to appease us. No. Appease Addie. Because Addie wasn't me and I wasn't her, and that was good—but right now, we felt so separate I was afraid we'd rip right apart.

We no longer had the piece of cardboard. It was too dangerous. Addie had hidden it under our shirt until we got indoors, then stuffed it to the bottom of the trash can in the bathroom after smudging the writing with water. She would have flushed it, but it might have clogged up the pipes.

Addie. Eva.

We want to help you get out.

The nurse clapped her hands, calling everyone out of their seats to line up at the door. I saw Devon glance at us, just once, but his expression betrayed nothing. Then he looked away and there wasn't anything I could do to catch his attention again. We still felt dizzy from time to time, the world tilting when we stood up too quickly. Our limbs hurt. Bruises had materialized overnight, purple and red on our legs, our arms, around the bandage on our forehead.

Devon was near the front of the line, so we edged in toward the back. The other kids were still ignoring us. We must have looked such a mess—almost frighteningly so. In a way, I was glad to be left alone. We had too much to think about already.

The delivery boy. The one we'd seen our first day, our first few minutes in Nornand. He'd stared at us then, and we'd assumed it was because we were hybrid and he'd been morbidly interested. But what if it had been because we were hybrid and—

We want to help you get out.

But not just us, surely. He meant everyone. All the kids. So why contact us, and why now?

And what did he meant by *We*?

Did it matter? If they were going to help us get out, did it matter who they were?

We closed our eyes and I saw a flash of Jaime crying in the basement.

He's gone. They cut him out. He's gone. He's gone.

Mr. Conivent in the Study room, the pencil jabbing into our hand.

Perfect day for a surgery.

We would leave this place for anywhere. More importantly, we had to get Lissa and Hally away before it was too late.

We ran into the little girl in front of us when she stopped walking. She turned around just long enough to frown at us and gesture pointedly at the nurse, who'd paused to chat with one of the orderlies. The girl had the palest blond hair we'd ever seen and was perhaps eleven, Kitty's age. Pretty, I would have thought at any other time. Now I just fought to keep from imagining her locked down in the basement next to Jaime, sobbing and pounding on the door. Or laid out on the surgery table, her feather-light hair half shaved, baring her scalp to the knife.

Addie nearly cried out when someone grabbed our wrist. But thank God we swallowed it down, because when we twisted around to see who it was, we caught a glimpse of the delivery boy's face—pale blue eyes, a long nose, ragged bangs—as he put his finger to his lips and pulled us a couple of yards down the hall, then pushed us through a half-open door.

We stood in some sort of storage closet, surrounded by shelves of cleaning solutions, cramped between a mop in one corner and a broom in the other. Everything smelled funny.

"We don't have a lot of time," the delivery boy whispered. He leaned toward us and didn't seem to notice when Addie shifted away, nearly knocking over a bottle of window cleaner. The only light came from a penlight he'd clicked on after shutting the door. "Addie?"

"I'm listening," Addie said. She squinted in the light beaming toward our face; the boy jerked the penlight aside. "But I—who are you?"

Despite everything—the cramped quarters, the looming threat of getting caught—the boy grinned. We could just barely see his teeth in the dimness.

"Jackson," he said. "And I shouldn't be talking with you. I

really shouldn't—Peter would kill me if he knew. But Sabine agreed that you ought to know."

"Know what?" Addie said. It was so, so hot in the storage closet. It took everything in us to keep from pushing past the boy blocking the door to cooler air. He was skinny enough and the closet was big enough to keep us from touching, but his height made him loom. Addie had to tilt our head up to meet his eyes, and that only reminded us constantly of how low the ceiling was.

"To keep hope," he—Jackson—said. "You've got to keep hope."

Keep hope. Such a strange way of phrasing things.

Keep hope.

"*What?*" Addie said.

Jackson took a quick, sharp breath. This seemed to bolster him. "We've been watching Nornand. For a while now. And we're going to get you out."

"Who's *we*?" Addie said.

"Emalia calls us the *Underground*," Jackson said, and dared to smile, as if there was time for jokes. "I think—"

"I don't care about your group name," Addie said.

<Maybe we should try not to make him mad, Addie> I said, but Jackson didn't seem fazed at all. In fact, he was still grinning. He had a smile like a lit match, warm approaching hot.

"Hybrids," he said, and something jolted in our stomach. "Like you. Like us."

Us. *He* was hybrid? The boy who we'd imagined judging

us a freak was one of us?

"Peter—he's sort of the leader, you know. He's done this kind of thing before. Breaking kids out. He had a plan for Nornand, but it fell through. Someone he thought would help"—his expression darkened—"well, *she* fell through."

Breaking kids out. Plans. Peter.

Before we could digest even this much, Jackson was hitting us with more. "He's planning again. He's got to change the plan now, and he wants to keep a low profile until then, so I'm not supposed to talk with you at all. But I know—I know what it's like." He wasn't smiling anymore. Not a bit, and it made him seem much older. "So I'm telling you we're coming. You've just got to wait a little longer. And you've got to keep hope."

We were woozy again, whether from the tight quarters or yesterday's fall or the stream of information the delivery boy kept dumping over our head, I didn't know. Maybe all three.

"They're cutting kids open," Addie said finally. It was the most important thing we knew right now, and in the face of so much confusion, we had to get this piece of information out. She looked away. "And the vaccines they give everyone . . . those vaccines for babies—they make it so most people lose one of their souls. And . . . and with some of the kids, they're *deciding* who's dominant and who's not. They're choosing who lives—"

Jackson put his hand on our shoulder, and Addie met his eyes again. "I know," he said.

"Are you people going to stop those things?" Addie shifted

away from his touch. "Is this *Underground* going to make it all better?" She inflected the name as he had, mocking him.

"We're trying," Jackson said, and suddenly, it wasn't enough. It wasn't enough at all. "Addie," he said quietly. "Trust me, okay? I—"

"I don't even *know* you," Addie said, and he threw up his hands, urging her to keep our voice down, his eyes wide.

"You will," he said, as if that was any sort of legitimate argument.

<We have to trust him> I said. *<Anywhere is better than here, Addie. Anywhere.>*

Jackson smiled that exasperating smile again. "There's so much you don't know yet—but you will. You've just got to get out of here first."

Addie gave him a narrow look. We were sick and tired of learning things we didn't know. So far, none of it had been good. "Like what?"

"Like—" He hesitated, but Addie stared at him until he went on. "Like how the Americas isn't as isolated from the rest of the world as the government would like you to think." He hurried on before Addie could interrupt. "We don't have time to go into it now. But I swear, one day we'll talk as much as you want. You just have to wait a little longer."

I could feel Addie about to insist he explain himself, but Jackson was right—we didn't have time. *<Focus>* I said. *<He's telling us there's a way out.>*

Our lips thinned, but Addie bit back her questions. Instead, she said, "We don't have time to wait. This girl—my friend—she's scheduled to go into surgery. Maybe today. Maybe tomorrow. Why can't we leave now? Tonight?"

"All the side doors are alarmed and locked at night," Jackson said. "You can't even open them from the inside, so no one can get in or out. The only way is through the main door, and that's always guarded by a night shift."

There was a breath of silence. It might have stretched, but there wasn't time. Any moment now, the nurse would finish her conversation or one of the other kids would realize we were gone.

"What if we disabled the alarms?" Addie said. "Would that unlock the doors, too?"

Jackson grinned. "No, but it would give us time to break in without calling out the cavalry. Why? You an electrical genius?"

"No," Addie said. "But I know someone who is."

We stepped out from the closet slightly dizzy, Jackson behind us. The nurse was still a little ways down the hall, talking to the orderly. The other kids stood in a vague approximation of a line, some chatting quietly among themselves, some just leaning listlessly against the wall.

How long had we been hidden away? Three minutes? Four? Had no one—

No, someone had noticed. Devon had noticed us missing. He frowned at us, and it wasn't until Addie put our finger to our lips that he jerked his eyes away, pretending he hadn't seen.

We looked behind us, at Jackson. He grinned, and Addie stretched our lips in a shoddy semblance of a smile. What plans we'd made had been hastily stitched together, built from on-the-spot decisions and not a few guesses. But the basic structure was in place. We'd have to fill in the rest as we went. We didn't have time for anything else. Lissa and Hally didn't have time.

Addie turned and hurried back to the group.

TWENTY-EIGHT

Mr. Conivent quarantined Addie and me at a table close to his desk during study time. Every few minutes, he would look up and stare over at us, checking to make sure we were doing our assignment. Whenever more than a minute or two passed without us writing something down, he'd clear his throat. Maybe he assumed we were safer when doing math problems. Maybe he thought they were keeping us occupied, that if our head was a jumble of matrices and obtuse triangles and long division, we wouldn't have room for things like escape plans.

It might have been a safe assumption, if we weren't hybrid. Between the two of us, Addie and I solved math problems and had all the space in the world to figure out the important things.

Jackson had run through the plan during our last moments in the janitors' closet. The Underground had vans and plane tickets and fake identifications for fifteen kids. They had everything we'd need once we escaped the hospital. But we had to escape first.

We didn't steal a glance at Devon over our shoulder—Mr.

Conivent was sure to catch it—but we'd seen him sit down when we first entered, and I could feel his presence in the room as solidly as I could feel the coin-sized chip tucked below our ankle. It would be glowing an uninterrupted red right now, but it was pressed under the side of our shoe and our black sock. No one could see.

Mr. Conivent shifted at his desk, filling out some sort of paperwork. The review board hadn't shown up today, and I wondered if they'd left for good.

<They haven't> Addie said. *<That man. He chose Hally and Lissa. He'll stay.>*

The Study room door opened. Heels clicked, then quieted as they left the tiled hallways and sank into the carpeting. Our eyes rose and met Dr. Lyanne's. She stood framed by the doorway in her black pumps and her perfect, wrinkle-free skirt and blouse, her white doctor's coat. Pretty, almost beautiful. A woman full of angles. She headed for Mr. Conivent's desk.

Addie and I finished our work sheet as we watched them speak out of the corner of our eyes. They whispered, but Mr. Conivent sat only six or seven feet away, and though we couldn't pick out words, we could hear the tension in their voices, growing stronger and stronger and stronger until Mr. Conivent set down his pen with all the power of a judge pounding his gavel. He looked straight at us.

We forgot ourself and stared back.

"Addie," he said. His voice retained an echo of danger. "You missed getting your blood tested yesterday. Dr. Lyanne will take you to get it done now." Addie didn't immediately stand, and he said, "*Now*, Addie."

We stood, leaving behind our pencil and math problems. We followed Dr. Lyanne out the door. There was something we needed from her now, specific information she *had* to give us, and our mind whirled with plans.

"Hello," Addie said quietly as we sat down in the small examination room. It was our first word to Dr. Lyanne since this morning. Here in this room, almost everything was white. The walls. The floor. The small table that separated us from Dr. Lyanne. And we were a spot of blue, perched on a chair. The machine between us was gray, a contraption the size of a typewriter with glass vials contained inside, visible through some silver meshing. They were connected to plastic tubing that snaked out onto the table.

The room appeared even smaller once Dr. Lyanne closed the door. After being shut up in that closet with Jackson, it was nothing, of course, but both we and Dr. Lyanne seemed to take up so much space, though she was such a thin woman and we'd never been tall.

"Give me your arm," she said. Her voice was still authoritative for all the paleness of her cheeks. Addie complied.

We'd undergone so many blood tests when we were younger that needles no longer fazed us. Addie didn't flinch when the needle slid coldly in or when our blood spiraled out in the tube, dripping into one of the glass vials. For a long time, no one said anything. The needle under our skin barely hurt. We watched first one vial, then the other, fill up. Dr. Lyanne sat across from us, staring idly at the machine, too.

"What were you guys arguing about?" Addie said, and this brought Dr. Lyanne's attention back onto us faster than anything.

"Who?" she said. As if we could be referring to anybody else.

"You and Mr. Conivent," Addie said.

Dr. Lyanne pressed down on our arm with a cotton ball, then slid the needle out. "Nothing, Addie. And it's none of your business to begin with."

"Was it about Jaime?" Addie said.

"No," said Dr. Lyanne. "No, it wasn't about Jaime. Keep pressure on your arm."

Addie obeyed but didn't take our eyes off Dr. Lyanne as she grabbed a tangle of wires from behind her. They were connected to another gray machine—larger than the first—on one end and what looked like a skullcap on the other.

"Was it about Hally?" I said, and shuddered. My being in control wasn't part of the plan and I hadn't intended to take it. I'd meant to wait for Addie to ask. But she had taken too long, and I had to know. "Is Hally safe?" Then, because that was stupid—that was the most stupid question I could have asked; of course Hally wasn't safe—I said, "They haven't done it yet. They haven't—they haven't operated on her."

Dr. Lyanne's face was so bland. So bland and pale and cold. She was so *calm* and it grated against me. How could she be so calm?

"No," Dr. Lyanne said. Sweet, cold relief made our whole body limp.

I felt my control slipping, and I let it, but then Addie said *<Don't. Eva. Fight it. Fight it. Talk to her. You can do it better than I can, I know it.>*

<But—> I said.

<You can, Eva.>

"Where is she?" I said, punching back against the weariness. Dr. Lyanne was staring at us now, and I had to swallow, to take a breath, to reorient myself in our shared body, before I could speak again. "Where are they keeping her? In the basement? With Jaime? When are they planning the operation?"

"That isn't for you to know," Dr. Lyanne said.

"Why not?" Our voice shook. Dr. Lyanne had a bottle of clear liquid in her hands. She clutched it so tightly her knuckles shone white. "If things turn out anything like they did with Jaime, one of my friends is going to *die* and the other one's going to lose her mind—I deserve to know *when*."

"Most likely, it won't," she whispered. The plastic bottle collapsed in her grip. "Jaime was lucky."

Something icy slipped through me. Head to foot. Fingertip to fingertip. "What do you mean?"

She didn't speak, didn't look at us, didn't even seem to breathe. Still, like a rock, like a crystal.

"Dr. Lyanne—"

"All the other children they've operated on . . ." she said. "They never left the table. Jaime . . . Jaime was the only one to survive."

Methodically, Dr. Lyanne started unscrewing the bottle in her hands. They shook, and she fumbled the cap.

I swept the bottle off the table.

It clattered onto the tiled floor, spilling the clear liquid in a wide arc as it spun into a corner. The sting of alcohol pierced the air, acrid and pungent.

"Help us," I said, and it was no longer a plea.

Dr. Lyanne remained motionless, her eyes still on her hands. I tried to remember the woman in the basement, sitting in Jaime's room, the look on her face when he was in her arms, the way she'd held him.

"You could get Jaime out," I said, and, when she didn't respond, I took a deep breath. "There are people . . . people who would get us away. They'd take him, too. He'd be safe." It was the only thing I could think of—the only big, shocking thing I could think of to say to make her *look* at us, *acknowledge* us.

It worked. Dr. Lyanne's head shot up, her mouth opening slightly, a spot of color rising in her cheeks. A strange shift in expression—not confusion, but fear.

Then she spoke, and it was as if from a dream. "You spoke with Peter?"

Our limbs weakened. "You know Peter."

We could almost see Dr. Lyanne break apart, piece by piece. We'd entered the room feeling like it was too small, that we and Dr. Lyanne took up too much space. Now the woman seemed to take up no space at all. She was as insubstantial as a figment of the imagination. See-through.

"He's my brother," she said.

I couldn't do this. I couldn't hold ourself together like this—take in all this and manage to keep our heart beating and our lungs expanding and—

But I had to. I had to, because I was in control of our body.

"He's your *brother*? Your brother's a hybrid, and you work *here*?"

"I told you," she said. There was a touch of resolve in her voice again. "I wanted to *help*—"

"Then *help*," I cried. "Help. Now. Help us get out." The alcohol fumes stung our eyes. "If you're not helping us get out, Dr. Lyanne," I said vehemently, "then you're helping them kill us." I stared at her, and when she looked away I grabbed her hand. "Is Hally in the basement?"

Finally, finally, she nodded. Just once.

"The doors are keypadded." I forced our voice to be strong and demanding and powerful when I could barely breathe, could barely keep our body upright and our words clear. "I need the code."

Quiet. Breathing, hers and ours. Quick, quick, quick. Shallow. The hard wooden desk. The uncomfortable chairs. The angles of Dr. Lyanne's face. Her thin lips, the weary lines on her forehead, between her green-brown-green-brown eyes.

She told us the code.

TWENTY-NINE

I tried to hold on to my control. I did. I fought for it, struggled for it, and I knew Addie wasn't fighting back. But it slipped away like water through grasping fingers. I was so exhausted. And as much as I would never admit it, maybe I was just a little relieved to let Addie take back over, let her hold the reins so I didn't have to.

So it was Addie who got us through the rest of the day, Addie who caught Devon's eyes during what should have been game time but had been converted, instead, to solitary reading time—most likely because of us. Addie who whispered to Devon as we slipped by him in the hall: *Watch your chip after lights-out.*

Devon just nodded. And when Addie sneaked from our room that night, we didn't need to wait long for him to show up in the hallway.

There, seated at one of the small tables in the main Ward, Addie recounted everything. So much had happened; it felt like we'd never be able to relay it all. But Addie did, hesitating sometimes, answering questions as Devon came up with them, trying her hardest to stay calm and precise and reliable. She and Devon didn't look at each other when they spoke. They both had their chips out—the outer Ward was completely dark otherwise—and everything glowed softly red.

"So could you do it?" Addie asked finally, glancing at Devon. He sat perfectly still, staring off into the blackness. "Could you and Ryan disable the alarm system?"

He frowned. "Would we need to do it neatly? Subtly?"

"Just destroy it," Addie said.

"Then yes," he said. "If we got to the wiring box, we could shut off everything. Lights. Alarms. Maybe security cameras." He looked toward the door at the far end of the room, swathed in shadow. "We still have to get out of here first."

"I've asked Jackson to get us a screwdriver," Addie said simply. "The doorknob comes off, same as the one in Lissa's door."

And then it was Ryan sitting across from us, not Devon, and he smiled, just a little bit. That sideways smile I missed.

"We do it tomorrow night," Addie said. That made Ryan's smile disappear, because we *had* to do it tomorrow night. There was no more time to wait.

We'd demanded to know, and Dr. Lyanne had answered: Hally and Lissa's surgery was scheduled for the day after tomorrow.

"Should we tell the others?" Addie said.

"Not yet," Ryan said. He fiddled with his chip, pushing it around the tabletop with what might have been absentmindedness except for the deliberate pressure of his fingers. "Not until we have to. We don't know how good they are at keeping quiet."

Addie nodded. It didn't feel right to keep such a big secret from the other kids. But maybe it was best to hold off for a while. With eleven kids, someone might let something slip.

Bridget—Bridget was sure to. Would she even leave with us when the time came? Bridget with her hard gray eyes and sharp tongue and forever folded arms. So angry, but so certain she would be saved. That she'd be cured. Who else was hiding in her body? When it came time for us to escape, would this recessive soul be strong enough to take over? Would she want to?

"Then good night, I guess," Addie said, closing our hand around our chip. The red glow seeped between our fingers, lighting our hand from within. "I'll see you—"

Ryan stopped fiddling with his chip and looked up from the table. "Thanks, Addie," he said. He had a way of looking at people like they were all that mattered, like they were important. I'd felt it before, dozens of times, and I thought Addie felt a bit of it now. She fell still, anyway, staying in our seat. "Thanks for checking on Lissa when you were both locked up. If you hadn't, we wouldn't have known about the operation at all."

Addie looked down, rubbing our nightgown's hem between our fingers. "Wasn't just me. It was Eva, too."

<It was mostly you> I said.

"I know," Ryan said. "But that means it was also you." He smiled, and it was a little sad. "So thanks. And sorry. About before."

Our hands fidgeted in our lap. Addie shifted in our chair.

"We'll save her," she said finally. "We're saving everybody. And we're getting out of here."

The next morning, we got up before the nurse came for her usual wake-up call. Kitty hadn't so much as shifted in her sleep when we slipped in and out of bed last night, and she didn't wake now. Addie didn't do much, just sat on the edge of the bed. A few days ago, we'd been awake at this time, too. We'd moved to the window and watched the sunlight creep in. There, right up against the glass, we could feel heat through the window before Nornand's air-conditioning whisked it away. We could see a little of the world beyond the hospital.

But now the window was boarded up with planks of wood driven right into the hospital walls. Not a sliver of light made it inside.

By tomorrow morning, it wouldn't matter.

We were leaving tonight.

Jackson had told us he had another package to bring Mr. Conivent today. He'd make up some excuse so the delivery happened late in the day instead of during the morning and slip us the screwdriver then. We'd still have to find a way to hide it until we returned to our room, but at least we wouldn't have it on us all day. It would be hard enough already since we had no pockets to speak of. We could maybe stow it somewhere in the Study room while we were there, but when we showered, brushed our teeth, changed for bed—all that was done in a locker room with the other girls and a nurse by the door.

We'd manage it, though. We had to.

The review board was back today, but they no longer watched us as they had before. I guess we warranted only one day of observation. There's only so long you can be at the zoo before it gets old. Now we passed them in the hall and caught glimpses of them in examination rooms, mostly with Mr. Conivent, sometimes with Dr. Wendle as well. They seemed to be showing the board members the machines Nornand used. Once, we saw one of the men ushering a nurse into a room and shutting the door behind them. An interview? An interrogation?

Whatever they were doing, it kept the nurses high-strung and Mr. Conivent busy. When Jackson came that evening just before dinner, he stopped the nurse leading us through the halls and told her he'd dropped by Mr. Conivent's office but couldn't find him. He distracted her long enough for Addie to slip from our spot near the beginning of the line—where the nurse could keep an eye on us—to the very end.

Jackson, we learned, was a stupendous talker. By the time the nurse finally convinced him he simply could *not* disrupt Mr. Conivent at this moment—he would have to wait or come back—we were late to dinner and the nurse, flustered and irritated, hurried toward the cafeteria without checking the line behind her.

Jackson met eyes with Ryan as he passed, just a glance that both boys quickly broke. Addie lagged as the rest of the kids started walking again, and when Jackson passed, she held our hand just a little away from our body. Jackson was much taller than we were. He had to tilt down, just slightly, to slip his hand around ours. We felt the cold, sharp metal of the screwdriver, the crisp edges of the map he'd drawn us to the maintenance room, where Ryan would go to disarm the alarms. Our fingers tightened around them both.

It all took less than three seconds. Addie didn't look over our shoulder to watch Jackson continue down the hall, though we could hear the slight squeak of his shoes against the polished tiles. She picked up our pace until we were back at the end of the line, slipping the screwdriver into the waistband of our skirt. The paper, though, would fall through. She bent down to tuck it into our sock, next to our chip.

When she straightened back up, one of the other girls in line had stopped walking, too. She stared at us, her blond, plaited hair snaking over her shoulders.

Bridget.

Had she seen?

"What?" Addie said. "My sock was falling down."

Bridget's eyes were inscrutable. "You're supposed to be at the front of the line."

"Girls?" the nurse called, finally noticing two of her flock had stopped. "Hurry it up. And Addie, get back up here. You know you're not supposed to fall behind."

Addie walked calmly past Bridget, who watched every step we took.

THIRTY

They sent Dr. Lyanne to watch us in the Study room after dinner, which had never happened before. Mr. Conivent didn't belong in the cafeteria. Dr. Lyanne didn't belong in the Study room—not as a watcher.

But both Mr. Conivent and the nurses had disappeared to places unknown, and we were left with Dr. Lyanne. She was no longer the woman we'd seen in the examination room, falling apart. She'd pieced herself back together again, was hard and cool and professional. But there was a glaze over her face that hadn't been there before, a half vacantness in her eyes that made the children bolder than they might have been with the nurses, and certainly more than they would have been with Mr. Conivent. We were supposed to be playing our tattered board games without speaking, but slowly, a murmur of conversation started up. When Dr. Lyanne didn't say anything, just kept her stiff perch on a chair by the door, more and more people started talking, until the room filled with quiet chatter.

Addie didn't look up when Devon came to sit next to us. We were on the ground, half hidden by a table and set of chairs, a good six or seven feet from the nearest person, Cal.

"You have everything," Devon said in that way of his, making a sentence sound halfway between statement and question.

Addie nodded. Cal had snatched a pack of cards and was building and rebuilding a house from them, never so much as flinching when they fell down. His movements were still clumsier than they should be, though his eyes were clearer, more alert. Did that mean they'd taken him off his medication?

<Doesn't matter> I said. *<He's leaving with us tonight.>*

Then, hopefully, he would be fine. He would recover. He wouldn't be irreparably damaged in some terrible way.

Addie looked toward the front of the room, at the clock hanging above the door. Seven forty-five. Not too long now.

<Where did she go?>

It took me a second to realize who Addie meant. But the empty chair was answer enough.

"Addie?" someone said behind us. Kitty clutched a board game, the worn box crumpling in her fists. "Do you want to play?"

Addie managed a smile as she patted the ground beside us and Devon. "Sure. Could you set it up?"

Kitty nodded. Addie glanced back over toward Dr. Lyanne's empty chair.

"There," Devon said, tilting his head to speak into our ear. I saw Kitty's eyes flick up from the game board, but only for a moment. "By Mr. Conivent's desk."

Dr. Lyanne moved around Mr. Conivent's desk. Anyone who wasn't paying attention like we were would have thought she belonged there. But we knew how to read Dr. Lyanne now. And we were hybrid, surrounded by hybrids. We were attuned to every change in voice, in movement, in expression. We saw the tension in her hands as she opened one of the desk drawers and pulled out a small cardboard box.

"What's she doing?" Addie whispered.

Devon didn't reply. He was staring at Dr. Lyanne, who had set the box down and opened it, revealing smaller white containers inside. She lifted them out and set them aside, reaching for what lay at the bottom—a sheet of paper.

"It's a package," he said.

He was right. We could just make out the post office's stamp on the side. It had to be what Jackson had been carrying earlier, when he'd slipped us the screwdriver and the map, when he'd been arguing with the nurse about finding Mr. Conivent, because only Mr. Conivent could sign for these packages.

Why could only he sign?

<Because they're private things?> Addie said, looking away from the desk.

<Then why send them here?> I said. *<If they're so private, why not send them to his house?>*

Kitty had finished setting up the board. She picked a game piece and placed it at *Start*, then offered the handful of pieces to Devon. He took one and put it on the board next to hers.

Dr. Lyanne still stood by the desk, her eyes darting up and

down that sheet of paper. Addie had turned to tell Kitty she could go first when the door opened. She tensed, her words never leaving our throat. Mr. Conivent stood on the threshold. But he'd turned to say something to the man behind him.

Jenson.

Our eyes shot back to Dr. Lyanne. She'd noticed the door, too. In a flash, she shoved the piece of paper in her lab coat pocket and stepped so she blocked the package from view.

Mr. Conivent and Jenson glanced at her, and Mr. Conivent nodded. She nodded back, easing down a little so it seemed like she was just resting against the desk as she surveyed the room and the children.

But Mr. Conivent frowned, even as he continued his conversation with Jenson, and after a moment, he gestured for the other man to step into the Study room. They entered, talking as they drew ever closer to Mr. Conivent's desk and Dr. Lyanne and the package I was 100 percent sure she wasn't supposed to be looking through. A pair of security guards followed them into the room, but stopped by the door. Maybe Jenson needed protection from us kids now. Or maybe Dr. Lyanne was already in trouble.

<It doesn't matter, Eva> Addie said before I could say anything, but our eyes flew between Mr. Conivent and Dr. Lyanne. Beside us, Devon had gone still.

<Of course it matters> I said. *<He'll catch her. And Jenson will catch her. And they'd—>*

I wasn't quite sure what they'd do, but neither Mr. Conivent nor Jenson was pleased with her to begin with, and—

<*I don't care. We* can't *care, Eva*> Addie said. To Kitty, she said, "You go first. Do you have the dice?"

Kitty nodded and cupped her hands together, shaking them up and down. Devon looked at us out of the corners of his eyes, but Addie turned resolutely to the game board. There were only a few more hours to go until lights-out. Until the hospital emptied but for us patients and the skeleton staff. Until our escape.

We didn't need anything more from Dr. Lyanne. She'd given us the codes to the basement rooms.

But—

Mr. Conivent and Jenson had almost reached us, and we were pressed against the wall about halfway between them and Dr. Lyanne. Somehow, I had to stop them—give her time to put everything back. I could just go up to them and say something. But what could I say to keep their attention riveted on us and give Dr. Lyanne enough time?

There was a flash of red and white in our peripheral vision. Cal's card house had fallen again.

Cal.

<*Eva*> Addie said warningly.

<*I can't let them catch her*> I said. <*She helped us, Addie. We owe her.*>

<*We don't owe her anything!*>

"Cal," I said. The word slipped from our lips with resistance, but not as much as I'd expected. Devon raised his head. Kitty stopped shaking the dice.

"Eli," she whispered.

Cal had looked up at his name, frowning, wary. I hadn’t even realized the significance of what I’d said. *Cal.* When was the last time someone had called him by his real name?

“But he isn’t Eli,” I said. “Is he?”

Kitty averted her eyes and let the dice drop. One of her hair clips had slipped loose. “He’s whoever the doctors say he is.”

“No,” I said. “No, Kitty—”

<Eva> Addie said. *<You’re putting him in danger. You realize that? If you ask him and we screw up, and someone finds out he was helping us . . . Lissa helped us, and look what happened to her and Hally.>*

I hesitated. She was right. But Mr. Conivent was only a few feet from the back of the room now, paused as he pointed out a child to Jenson, and I could see Dr. Lyanne clutching the edge of the desk.

“Cal,” I said. “Cal, could you do me a favor?”

“What’re you doing?” Devon said.

It was getting easier now. Every word took specific concentration, but I could do it. “We have to distract Mr. Conivent before he reaches his desk. Dr. Lyanne—”

“Now isn’t the time to think about her,” Devon said.

“She helped us,” I said. “She gave us the code to Hally’s room—”

He fell quiet, and I didn’t wait for whatever he might say next. “Cal,” I said, “could you—could you distract everyone? Just for a few minutes.” Then a thought struck me. They drugged Cal when he and Eli fought. They might drug him again. Now, when the clarity was just coming back into his eyes—

Cal crouched over his cards, his lower lip pushed out. He was only eight. Younger and smaller than Lyle. Only a little older than Lucy. I'd been insane to think to ask him something like this, put him in the way of even more harm.

Our shoulders dropped.

And then Cal screamed.

His cry sliced the room right open—deep down, past the uneasy stillness and straight to the chaos within. I lurched backward, Kitty scurrying beside us. Devon half raised his hands to his ears.

An entire deck of cards slammed into the wall, followed by an abandoned board game. Cal screamed again. Cards flew everywhere. White. Red. White. The other children in the vicinity scrambled out of the way. The security guards by the door stared but didn't move. Maybe they didn't know what they were supposed to do with a small, shrieking boy.

Mr. Conivent turned.

I grabbed Kitty's hand and ran for the far wall as he came toward Cal, his mouth grim. Jenson stayed where he was. I dared a glance at Dr. Lyanne. She was half turned, stuffing the white containers back into the cardboard box.

Cal stopped screaming just as Mr. Conivent tried to seize him, ducking and darting out of reach. The sudden silence hurt. Mr. Conivent's jaw tensed. He made another grab at Cal, and again, Cal slipped out of the way. They regarded each other, the boy and the man, neither saying a word.

And then Mr. Conivent sighed, as if this had all just been the world's biggest inconvenience. He turned to Jenson with a look like *Kids. What can you do?*

Dr. Lyanne was by the bookshelf now, her hands at her side. The package was no longer on Mr. Conivent's desk.

I took a long, shuddering breath and looked at Devon. He slowly leaned against the wall, his fingers unclenching, pressing flat against his legs. Then Kitty squeezed our hand. When I didn't immediately look down, she pulled on our arm until I did.

"What?" I whispered, but then I followed her gaze, and I didn't need to ask any more.

Mr. Conivent was heading toward us.

He saw the small yellow screwdriver on the ground the same instant we did.

THIRTY-ONE

Mr. Conivent didn't ask any questions. He didn't hold up the screwdriver and demand to know who it belonged to. He just bent, picked it up, and slipped it into his pocket. Then he gestured toward the security guards, telling them to take us and Devon back to our rooms.

We didn't go quietly. We screamed and fought and kicked and heard Devon fighting behind us. But they were stronger, and they shoved us into our room, that terrible room with the heavy metal beds and the boarded-up window. The security guards stayed outside after throwing us onto our bed, but Mr. Conivent came into the room with us, and I wanted to attack him—I wanted to shove him against the wall—but we didn't. We grabbed the edge of the bed and cried, "Why?"

Mr. Conivent's eyes were hard. "Because I want to see you get out of this one." He came toward us, and we scrambled away from him on the mattress until our back was pressed against the wall. Still he came closer. "I'd like to see you tear the wood from the window with your bare hands, Addie. I'd like to see you knock down that door."

"I'm not going anywhere," Addie said hoarsely. "You don't have to lock me up."

Mr. Conivent stopped at the edge of our bed. "But just to be safe," he said. "I don't want you anywhere but locked in here while Hally Mullan is on the operating table tonight."

We slumped against the wall.

Tomorrow. Dr. Lyanne had told us the operation was tomorrow.

She'd promised us *tomorrow.*

"You could almost say it's your fault," Mr. Conivent said as he backed away, leaving us frozen in our bed. His tone turned chastising, disappointed. "You're the one who nosed around where you shouldn't have. If you'd just behaved, Hally wouldn't have made a misguided attempt to help you. She wouldn't have been chosen."

He closed the door behind him and left us in the aftermath of his words.

We tried the window. But not until we'd pounded and pounded and pounded on the door. Not until we'd tried kicking at it until our shinbone ached. They'd taken away our nightstands, so the only furniture remaining were the beds, and they were too heavy to make good battering rams. Finally, someone outside our door shouted for us to shut up and quiet down. A guard, maybe. Mr. Conivent had left a guard in the hall. There would be no easy escape that way.

So we tried the window. We wedged our fingers into the cracks between the wood and the wall, braced ourself, and pulled as hard as we could. We pounded our fist against the center of the planks, hoping to smash it. The cut on our left hand reopened and leaked blood through the white bandage. But nothing budged. Nothing even cracked.

We went and sat back down on the bed. Everything ached. Our chip lay beside us on the thin mattress, pulsing softly red. What was Ryan doing in his room?

How could we have dropped the screwdriver?

Guilt crumpled our chest, crushing our ribs like scrap metal. The sharp edges bit into our heart. My guilt, my plan—my stupid plan. We'd helped Dr. Lyanne, yes. But we'd lost the screwdriver. And with it any chance of getting out of our room.

I'd thought I was mastering power over our body, but then the tears came, and I wasn't controlling them at all. They seemed to be controlling me.

Tears for our parents, who'd been too afraid to protect us.

For Hally and Lissa, who needed so badly to be protected.

For Jaime, for who it was already too late.

I cried until we were limp, our hair sticking to our cheeks, our vision blurry. Our hands throbbed painfully.

But I said *<We can't give up.>*

<No> Addie said. *<No, we won't.>*

Keep hope.

Keep hope.

I could feel Addie there, huddled next to me. Warm and sturdy and a source of strength.

<We still have the map to the maintenance room>

I said. We put our forehead in our hands, holding our breath to try and stop the tears. <*If we can get out of the Ward, Ryan can still disable the alarms.*>

<*We know the code to Hally and Lissa's room in the basement*> Addie said. <*If we get down there, we can get her out.*>

If the operation hadn't already started. If it wasn't already too late. But it couldn't be. I refused to believe it was. We could still do it. We could still save Lissa and Hally and Jaime and all the other kids—

Where were the other kids? It had to have been more than an hour since Mr. Conivent locked us in here. Everyone should have been back at the Ward by now.

<*They've got to send them back eventually*> I said. <*And when they do, they have to open this door to let Kitty and Nina in.*> I looked toward the blank stretch of wall beside the door. <*If we stood there—*>

<*We could what?*> Addie said. <*Push past the security guard and just keep running? Even if we make it out of the Ward, we'll be caught before we get off the floor.*>

<*It's late*> I said. <*There won't be that many people in the halls anymore. Everyone will have gone home.*>

But a guard would quickly call an alert, and then the place would be crawling. I knew that. I just wished it weren't true.

<*And they don't have to let Kitty in here*> Addie said. <*They don't ever have to open the door.*> She hesitated, then added <*There's another empty bed.*>

But just as that was sinking in, just as our eyes slid back

to the ground, our shoulders slumping against the wall, a key clicked in the lock, the door opened, and Dr. Lyanne walked in holding Kitty's hand.

I was off the bed before the door was all the way shut again, running toward her, jerking Kitty away from her, hissing, "You lied. You *lied*. You said it wasn't until tomorrow. You—"

"Plans change," she said. "I didn't know."

"You *didn't know—*"

"*Shh,* Addie," Dr. Lyanne said. She still wore her white doctor's coat, and her hair was smooth, brushed back from her face.

"*Why?*" I demanded. "*Why should I?*"

"Because the guard won't let me take you if you're kicking up a fuss," said Dr. Lyanne. "He's by the outer door, but he'll come running if you keep screaming like this. And if he does, I'm leaving you behind."

I stared at her, then down at Kitty, who looked at us with so much confused hope in her eyes I couldn't speak.

"I called Peter," Dr. Lyanne admitted, as if that were a failing, as if even now—even in the middle of this—it felt wrong for her to contact her hybrid brother. "He knows the time. He'll be there, at the side door. They'll have vans—" She stopped. Looked at us. "I'm sure you already know." I nodded dumbly. Kitty's hand tightened around our own. "That boy—Devon. He's the one you told Peter's people about, isn't he? He can disable the alarms?"

Was she tricking us? Had she discovered our plan somehow and was trying to—I didn't even know. But if she already knew so much, what was the point of questioning us?

"Yes," I said.

"Then come on," said Dr. Lyanne. She dug something out of her coat pocket and tossed it at us. I had to scramble to catch it before it hit the ground. A key. "For the maintenance room. You still have the map?" I nodded, bending and tucking the key in our left sock, never taking our eyes from Dr. Lyanne's face. The key was colder against our skin than Ryan's chip. "The other kids are waiting. We don't have much time."

"The other kids?" I frowned. "Everyone? Jaime and Hally, too?"

"No," said Dr. Lyanne.

"Then we've got to get them," I said. "It won't take too long, not with the code—"

Dr. Lyanne shook her head. "It isn't that easy, Addie."

"What do you mean?" I said. "Of course it won't be easy, but—"

"You don't understand," she said.

"Then explain."

Dr. Lyanne looked away from us and toward the boarded-up window. "We're not taking Hally."

Addie and I reacted at the same time, disbelief building on disbelief, anger feeding anger.

"What?" I choked on a laugh. "Of course we are."

She shook her head. "Addie, don't you get it? You think this hospital is just empty at night? That everyone just packs up and leaves all the patients here alone?"

"No," I said. "No, of course not—"

"There are *always* doctors here," Dr. Lyanne said, her voice rising. "Always. Always nurses. Always someone making rounds."

"Yes, but—"

"Except," she said. "*Except* on the days when they operate on one of you kids."

I fell silent. I couldn't be hearing this. She couldn't be saying this. But she was. She was, and she kept on talking.

"Addie, people go to see. People go to watch. Not all the doctors, but a good number of them. The review board will all be there. And the nurses will be thinned out, too; they'll need them in the operating room, so there will be fewer in the halls. I can tell them I'm taking the kids for an exam. It'll be suspicious, but as long as they don't—"

"No," I said. "*No.*"

"Hally's surgery is giving us our chance," Dr. Lyanne said.

"No." I didn't scream it. I didn't shout it. But I said it, and our voice was steel. "Never. We don't leave her behind. And what about Jaime? He's down there, too. Are you abandoning him? *Again?*"

Dr. Lyanne took a step toward the door, a dangerous flush in her cheeks. "When you grow up, Addie, you'll realize that sometimes you have to make hard sacrifices so you can—"

"Is that," I said, "what you told yourself when they cut into Jaime?"

This stopped her.

No one spoke.

Kitty's hand squirmed in ours, and it took me a moment to

realize she wanted us to let go. I looked down at her, but she was focused on Dr. Lyanne. I released her hand. A few short steps took her to the woman's side. Kitty wrapped the fingers that had just been entwined with ours around Dr. Lyanne's.

"Take me out of here," she said, watching Dr. Lyanne with those wide, dark eyes, that pale, almost fae-looking face. "Take me out of here, please. Let Addie go to the basement. And just get the rest of us out."

THIRTY-TWO

It took an eternity for Dr. Lyanne to unlock Ryan's door. I had to hold myself back from snatching the keys from her hand and doing it myself. If we had any hope of making it to Hally before the surgeons did, we had to move fast. There was the tightness in our chest, too, the pinch I knew would lessen, just a little, if I could see Ryan and know he was okay.

Then the door was open and he was jumping out of bed, and in five steps I knew it was Ryan, not Devon, running toward us, confusion all over his face, and I reached up, wrapping my arms around his neck and burying my face in his shoulder. I felt his heart beat beneath his shirt, *thump*, *thump*, *thump*-ing just as fast as mine. The heat of his chest in the chill of the hospital. There was a second—but only a second—before his arms wrapped around me, too.

"Eva," he murmured into my hair. I nodded, and his arms tightened. "What's going on? What's happening?"

"We've got to run," I said.

The halls were still half lit, but empty. Our footsteps echoed, our shadows trailing us like burnt ghosts. Every once in a while, we'd pass a window, running through a patch of moonlight before plunging back into the darkness. Darkness and light. Darkness and light.

Then we reached the stairwell, and there was no light at all. Our hand hovered over the railing, ready to grab hold if I stumbled, but I didn't. We just kept running and running and running. Ryan was sometimes beside us, sometimes a little ahead, sometimes a step behind. By the time we reached the basement landing, we were out of breath.

Yellow emergency lights lit the basement like a danger zone, and we couldn't help slowing our pace. Other than a faint buzzing, all was quiet and still. The silence amplified our breathing, the rustle of our clothes, the sound of our footsteps on the tiled floor. We passed by door after door. I peeked in all the windows, catching glimpses of examination tables and surgical lights on long, plastic arms—flashes of our nightmares. But no Hally. No doctors. Wherever they were, it wasn't in this wing of the basement.

<B42> Addie said, as if I could have forgotten. *<We've got to get Jaime.>*

It didn't take long to find the right room. The emergency lights bathed both us and the stark, sturdy door. They had cut into the boy behind this door. For no good reason, no good reason at all—

And he was the only survivor.

I could barely enter the numbers in the keypad. I got it wrong the first time and was terrified to try again. What if we had only a certain number of tries? What if an alarm went off if you did it wrong too many times? But Addie said <*Calm, Eva. Calm*> and I took a deep breath and did it again. The light flashed green, and—almost light-headed with relief—I yanked the door open.

"Jaime," I said. "Jaime, wake up. We have to go."

He woke with a start and a cry. I leaped backward, ramming into Ryan. He took hold of my waist, steadying me, just for a moment. Then I had to tear myself away again so I could go closer to Jaime.

"Shh, shh," I said, reaching out to him. "It's just me. Do you remember me? I came the day before yesterday. We talked through the speaker."

He neither nodded nor shook his head. He said nothing. But there did seem to be a light of recognition in his eyes.

"Can you get up, Jaime?" I said. "We're going to take you out of here. We're going to go upstairs, okay? Trust me, Jaime."

He nodded, pushing aside the blankets and slowly moving his legs until they hung over the side of the bed. He managed to stand by himself, but he swayed, and I was about to reach for his arm when Ryan grabbed it instead. Jaime looked surprised, and Ryan nodded at him.

The other boy gave him a lopsided smile in response. He seemed smaller now that I could see him more clearly—small, with a shock of curly, dark-brown hair and ashen skin. Skinny. And bearing that long, curved incision line.

I was closing Jaime's door behind us when we heard the screaming.

Ryan pressed Jaime to the side of the hall. "Stay here—"

I was already running, flashing past him.

Lissa screamed again, and this time there was a word in the terror. She cried for her brother. I careened around the corner, flying down the hall. Up ahead, I could see a glow of light. Not yellow emergency lights but brilliant fluorescent ones. The kind that lit Nornand's other floors.

The next corner brought me to a white-lit hall, everything gleaming, almost blinding. There was only one door open, and the screaming came from within. I darted inside, Ryan a step behind me.

One guard, his back to us, arms spread. Two nurses, one holding a syringe, both wearing gloves. And a girl, thrashing and screaming and screaming and screaming and—

Ryan surged forward. I bolted after him. He shoved the security guard aside—hard. The man slammed into the wall. The nurses looked up, pale-faced and wide-eyed. Lissa's glasses had fallen onto the ground, the white rhinestones glittering in the light.

Ryan and I reached the nurses at almost the same time—he grabbed the nurse still clutching Lissa; the other, the one holding the syringe, had already stumbled back a step. I latched on to Lissa's arm. We yanked them apart.

The security guard had recovered his footing. I felt his hand close around our shoulder, and without thinking, without thinking at all, I smashed our foot into his knee. He grunted. I rammed our elbow into his face and that, *that* made him let go. There was blood. Blood and his shocked, pained cursing. One of the nurses tried to seize Lissa again. I saw the flash of the syringe, and then Ryan knocked it out of her hand. His shoe came stomping down on it, nearly snapping the needle—bending it beyond repair. He jumped forward and scooped Lissa's glasses from the ground, tossing them to her. She slipped them on. And there we were, the three of us, the six of us, in the middle of the room, surrounded by the nurses and the guard, panting. Sweat gleamed on pale skin. The guard had taken his hand from his nose, blood dribbling on his lip. It made our stomach revolt, but we couldn't think about it. We had to fight, still. We had to fight past them and out the door and then run, run, run.

The door. If we could just make it to the door—

For a moment, just a moment—a millisecond—everyone was still. One second. A snapshot of fear and sweat and blood.

Then the siren went off.

It sliced through everyone's concentration—everyone's but mine.

I already grasped Lissa's wrist. Our eyes met Ryan's, then flashed to the door. We ran. Everyone's attention snapped back to us, but it was too late. The room was small. We barreled through the nurses, darted just out of reach of the guard, and made it to the door, gasping. I whirled around. Slammed the door shut. And with Ryan and Lissa helping me hold it shut against the nurses' and the guard's banging, I entered the code in the keypad, locking it.

The siren wailed and wailed. The same siren we'd heard our first day here. The one they'd tested us with. The one that had pushed me from our bed, now broadcasted for the whole hospital to hear.

I had a feeling this time, it wasn't a test. This time, it was real. Something had gone wrong. Very wrong. No one in Lissa's room had contacted anyone; none of them could have reported us. So it had to be the other kids and Dr. Lyanne. Something had happened to them.

The guard was still pounding on the thick door, his shouting muffled, barely audible over the siren's keen. Ryan gripped our arm. Lissa's clutch on our hand hurt, her nails digging into our bandaged palm. But the pain helped me think, even as it shot sparks of fire up our arm.

"Come on." I jerked them both after us. "We've got to get Jaime. Then upstairs. *Now.*"

Jaime staggered toward us as soon as we came into view. He was in his night clothes, and he looked like a ghost in the corner, his dark hair in sharp contrast with his white pajamas. Lissa grabbed his arm with her free hand, pulling him behind us. But he stumbled—he stumbled and cried out and fell and we had to stop.

<There're people coming> Addie said.

We could hear them. Rushed footsteps and garbled words. Back down in the direction we'd just come.

But Jaime could only go so fast, even with Lissa and me half carrying him between us. Ryan rushed back to give us a hand, and the three of us slowly, achingly slowly, helped Jaime into the stifling darkness of the stairwell.

<The alarms> Addie said as we hobbled. *<Ryan's got to go turn off the alarms—>*

<Forget the alarms. They already know something's going on.>

The siren wailed its unearthly noise until I thought our heart would burst. It reverberated in the stairwell, covering up the noise of our feet against the steps. Only one floor to go.

Lissa slowly pushed open the door on the first-floor landing, and we all peered across the dim lobby. There was only one hall leading away from it. The side door would be down that hall somewhere. It couldn't be far. And the lobby was still deserted, still safe . . .

I released Jaime.

Ryan reached for us. "What—"

"I have to go upstairs," I said. "I've got to make sure the others got out."

Lissa gaped. "Eva, that's *insane*."

<Eva> Addie said. *<Eva, we have to get them to the side door.>*

I tried to swallow, but our throat was so dry. "Something's wrong. I have to go check. I just—Kitty. Cal. The other kids . . . they—"

"Eva—" Ryan said.

"Side door," I said. "Across the lobby. Just keep going until you find it—it can't be far. Tell Jackson I'll be right there."

"*No*," Lissa said. Her hair was wild from the struggle in the basement, her cheek scratched, her eyes gleaming. She tried to grab our hand again. I pushed her forward.

"You've got to go, Lissa. You've got to get Jaime to the door before they come. He can't go fast. You've got to start *now*."

Still, she hesitated. She shook her head. She looked toward her brother.

"Go," he said. "Please, Lissa. Go. We'll be there in a second."

Lissa wavered a moment longer. Then she nodded. I watched her slip into the darkened lobby, melting into the shadows, clutching Jaime.

"I'm going," I said to Ryan. If I hadn't been so stupid and lost the screwdriver, everything might have been different. Everyone might already be in Peter's vans, zooming away to safety. This chaos, this uncertainty, was my fault. "I have to go. You can't stop me, Ryan."

"Then I'm going with you," he said, and held out his hand.

I took it. We darted up the stairs. We'd just hit the third-floor landing when the lights snapped on—full strength.

<They know we're here> Addie said. *<They know what we're doing, Eva. Eva—we've got to go.>*

I shook our head. *<No. No, we can't.>*

"Eva," Ryan said, "if the lights are coming on, then they're going to be searching the halls. Even if the others haven't gotten out already, there's no way we're going to be able to sneak them past the guards."

I bent down, slipping our free hand into our sock and pulling out the key I'd hidden there. The bandage on our palm slowed us down, but I managed it. "Then we'll have to turn off the lights. All of them." I pressed the key Dr. Lyanne had given us into his hand, along with Jackson's map. "It's on the topmost floor. There's a door, a maintenance room—"

"Shut off all the lights," he finished.

We stood in that barren stairwell, the siren screaming in the background. And suddenly, he laughed, shaking his head. "God, Eva. Do you keep everything in your socks?"

I wasn't sure whether to laugh back or start crying. I sort of felt like doing both, so I did neither, just pushed him toward the next flight of stairs and smiled and said, "I'll see you soon, okay? Down at the door. I'll meet you at the side door."

He nodded, his own smile strained.

The siren stopped.

Both our smiles fell. What did that mean?

"Go," I said.

Ryan ran up the stairs. I took a deep breath and pushed open the door to the third floor.

THIRTY-THREE

The silence was eerie. Echoes of the siren still rang in our ears. I almost missed it. At the very least, it would have covered up the noise of our footsteps as we hurried down the corridor. It would have masked the sound of our breathing. We felt naked and exposed as we moved through the hall, caught under the bright lights.

I walked as quickly and quietly as I could, but our school shoes hadn't been made for sneaking around. They clicked softly against the floor. Finally, I slipped them off and held them in our hand.

Maybe if I hadn't, it would have all happened very differently.

Addie and I had almost reached the end of the hall when we saw her—fairy girl in her Nornand blue. And Mr. Conivent, gripping her arm.

Neither noticed us.

Addie pressed our back against the wall next to an abandoned cart, just peeking around the corner. Mr. Conivent was only three or four feet away, but he had his back to us.

"Where are the others?" he said. Kitty closed her eyes when he shook her. "If you ever want to go home, Kitty, you'll *tell* me."

I struggled against Addie.

<*Wait*> she snapped.

"I don't know," Kitty said. "With Dr. Lyanne and the security guards. Bridget—Bridget wouldn't go and the nurse came and then she called the guards and—"

He shook her again, snapping her mouth shut. "I don't mean *them*, Kitty. Where are Devon and Addie?"

"I don't know—"

The cart next to us was empty but for one of those metal pans, the kind Dr. Lyanne and Dr. Wendle had used to carry their medical instruments. Slowly, Addie bent down, setting our shoes on the ground. She reached over and grasped the tray in both hands.

"I *swear*," Kitty said. "I swear I don't know. I—"

I couldn't stand it another second.

I whirled around the corner and smashed the tray into Mr. Conivent's back. He roared. Kitty screamed. Her eyes were huge, her face ashen. But she didn't freeze up. She wrenched herself free and careened toward us. I grabbed her and pushed her behind us, scrabbling backward. Mr. Conivent regained his balance and twisted around, the veins in his neck harsh against his skin.

His eyes were ice. His face frozen. Gone was the sleekness, the smoothness. He was all jagged, fractured edges.

But when he spoke, his voice was still silk.

"Addie, there you are." He smiled. Then, slowly, he reached for the walkie-talkie in his pocket and murmured, "Third floor. East wing. Now."

Our heart galloped.

It was a stalemate now. Kitty stood behind us, and there was a good three or four yards between us and Mr. Conivent. If he lunged forward, I'd have time to leap back, and then he'd be off balance for me to attack. If Kitty and I turned to run, we'd be vulnerable to being tackled from behind.

Stalemate.

"We're leaving," I said. Our throat was so dry the words barely scraped through. I took a cautious step backward. "We're leaving, Mr. Conivent."

Mr. Conivent barked into his walkie-talkie again, "Did you hear me? I want you here *now.*" Then, to us: "Addie—"

"I'm not Addie," I said. I stopped creeping backward. "I'm Eva."

My name bubbled up my throat, sweet and clear.

"Don't be ridiculous," Mr. Conivent said.

I laughed. "Ridiculous?"

"You're sick," he said. "You're a sick, destructive child, and you don't understand—"

"I'm not sick," I said. He made to speak again, but I cut him off. "I'm not sick. Or broken. I don't need to be fixed or cured or whatever it is you want to do." I took a long, deep breath. I seemed to be the only one in the hall still breathing.

"Addie," Mr. Conivent said, louder. The velvet had gone from his voice.

"I'm *not Addie,*" I shouted.

The lights went out.

I flew forward, swinging and feeling the metal tray connect against Mr. Conivent's skull so hard our bones vibrated with the blow.

<*Eva*> Addie screamed.

I backed away. He hadn't cried out. Mr. Conivent hadn't cried out when I struck him and now—

The emergency lights flickered on, bathing everything in the same sallow light as the basement.

Mr. Conivent lay crumpled on the ground. A doll. Nothing but a rag doll.

Oh God.

Oh God.

I dropped the tray. It smashed to the ground, the crash ringing and ringing and ringing through the halls.

Oh God.

A small, cold hand slipped into ours. Kitty. She pulled us away from the crumpled body. One step. Two. Three. We had to go. We had to go. Peter was waiting.

I nearly crushed Kitty's hand in ours but she didn't complain. We ran back in the direction Addie and I had come, heading for the stairs.

Ryan met us on the landing, almost crashing into us. "Did you find them? Were they there? Did they get out?"

Then he saw Kitty. She barely seemed to be holding herself together. Her hair was stuck against her cheeks, in her mouth. She clutched our hand. We felt her shaking.

She shook her head. "Bridget—Bridget wouldn't go . . ." Her voice broke, but she pieced it back together before going on. "We ran into a nurse, and Dr. Lyanne said she was taking us somewhere, but Bridget said she was lying. She said something suspicious was going on, and—" Our hand ached from her grip. From the strength of it. "Everybody ran, but the nurse, she called the guards. She pulled the alarm, and—I was with Cal, but he got caught and—there were so many people. I hid until they all went away." She took a quick, sharp breath. "I want to get *out* of here, Addie. I—"

"You are," I said. "You are. Right now."

I looked at Ryan. I thought of Cal and the other kids, even Bridget, but I looked at Ryan and I knew there wasn't time. Not if we wanted to get Kitty and Nina to safety.

"Another time," he said softly. "We'll find them, Eva. All of them."

But for now, we had to go.

Ryan's manipulations had killed the lights in the lobby, too, but the emergency lights still glowed and security guards' flashlights crisscrossed the air. They shouted to one another, *No one here. This area's clean—*

We crouched in the doorway of the stairwell, masked by the semi-darkness, staring out into the mayhem. Hoping, praying, that Lissa and Jaime had already made it to the safety of Jackson's promised vans.

Ryan touched our shoulder, pulling us from our thoughts. *On three*, he mouthed. I took Kitty's hand and squeezed it.

One.

Two.

Three.

We were almost, *almost* across the lobby when one of the guards shouted after us. We didn't slow down. I tightened our hold on Kitty's hand.

We ran. Straight ahead. Dead end. Turn left. And there. There—the exit sign glowing red at the end of the long hall. The security guard shouting for us to *stop, stop right now—*

And Jackson. Jackson materializing out of the dimness, a man behind him. He reached for me, beckoning us faster. The man lifted Kitty right off her feet. And then we were outside, we were in moonlight. We were tumbling into a black van, nearly falling on top of Lissa, who threw her arms around us, and there was Jaime in the back and Ryan jumping in after us, Jackson slamming the door before scrambling into the passenger-side seat.

We pulled away, tires screeching, just as the security guard burst into the parking lot.

THIRTY-FOUR

Everything happened so fast.

The drive, the airport, the flash of identification that bore our picture but neither of our names. All passed in a blur of color and engine noise. Before we knew it, we were back on an airplane, Jaime murmuring in the seat next to ours.

Kitty stared out the tiny window, her palm pressed against the plastic pane. Lissa slept. Devon—he was Devon now—stared down at his hands until he, too, fell asleep.

Odd, to think this was only our second time up in the air. We felt no excitement. Only weariness.

Before the airport, there had been a tiny motel room where we'd changed out of our Nornand blue and into clothes that barely matched and didn't fit. We'd combed our hair, washed our face, stared at our reflection, our hollow eyes.

The man, we learned, was Peter. He was even taller than Jackson—sturdier—and we could see Dr. Lyanne in the set of his face, the ash brown of his hair. He'd smiled at us, but we'd been too exhausted to really smile back, though we tried. He was the one who removed the bandage from our forehead as we bit down on our lip and tried not to wince, then replaced it with a smaller, square Band-Aid. The bandages on our legs were easier to cover up with pants, our hands with too-long sleeves. There was a worn baseball cap for Jaime, to hide his incision mark and the staples in his skull. But there wasn't anything that could be done about the cut on Lissa's cheek, the bruises and Band-Aid on our forehead. I let our hair fall over our face, curtaining it as best I could.

Peter and Jackson came with us onto the plane but sat a few rows down. There had been another man, but he'd taken a different flight. He'd been the one driving the second black van. The empty one that should have held the rest of the kids. The ones we didn't save.

We landed in a city by the ocean. Everything was a noisy, overcrowded dream. We had no luggage. There was no one waiting for us at the airport. Everyone piled into a huge van, and the ride was spent in silence, the stars cold and sharp where they poked through the black swaths of clouds.

We reached the apartment a little after dawn. Two women waited at the side of the road, one in her mid-twenties, the other about our mother's age. They laughed and chattered until our van pulled to a stop.

Peter and Jackson climbed out. Jaime leaned against the window, whispering stories to himself, his hands twisting in his lap. Devon sat beside him, silent. I wished for Ryan, who would have smiled at me, who wouldn't have closed himself off to the rest of us. But Ryan wasn't there, and so I looked away, trying to focus on the world outside the window.

The road was empty. A gentle pink-and-yellow haze hung in the streets, illuminating and obscuring them at intervals. I let our eyes wander over the apartment building, tall and cast from red brick with a great metal fire escape winding up the side. Peter, Jackson, and the women spoke quietly in the shadow of a street lamp.

Suddenly, I realized what they were discussing.

"No," I pushed the car door open. Lissa jerked from her daze. Peter's last sentence faded on his lips.

"No," I repeated. "You're not separating us."

A bubble of silence grew, round and hard.

The younger woman gave us a hesitant smile. Her cappuccino-colored hair curled like steam around her face. It would be too suspicious to keep all us kids together, she said. We'd all be close, she promised.

We refused.

In the end, they gave in and all five of us kids crammed into Peter's small apartment. It only had two bedrooms, so all of us girls shared one room while the boys took the other. Kitty hardly woke as Peter carried her up the stairs and into the room, laying her on the bed. Jackson went in search of extra blankets and pillows so Lissa and I could construct makeshift beds on the floor. No one changed. There was nothing to change into but the uniforms, and no one ever wanted to touch those again. We were all too tired anyway, collapsing into tangles of weary limbs.

I just barely kept Addie from screaming aloud when we woke, hours and hours later, from nightmares of Cal on the operating table, scalpels tracing bloody lines across his face. Lissa murmured next to us but didn't awaken.

Slowly, I lay back down, reaching under our pillow and extracting our chip. We were so used to having it there, now, after all our nights at Nornand. The softly pulsing light was comforting. Our heartbeat slowed until the two rhythms matched, beating in sync.

Then the red flashes began to quicken.

I'd pushed our blankets off and sat up before I realized what I was doing. I was moving so much easier now, a far cry from the painful steps I used to take. Maybe it was a side effect of the Refcon that had made things so difficult before.

Addie was quiet as I stepped carefully over Lissa and darted for the door.

Ryan waited for us in the hallway. For me.

"Eva," he said, and then my arms were around his neck, my head on his shoulder.

"Are you okay?" I said.

He laughed. "I was going to ask you the same thing."

"I'm fine," I said, my voice muffled against him. We sank down together, neither of us letting go, his back against the wall. He was quiet. I finally let go, leaning back so I could see his face.

"What?" he said, at first solemn and then grinning hesitantly when I started to smile. "What's so funny?"

"I know it's you," I said, laughing, and then laughing harder because it was all so absurd. It hurt to laugh, but it hurt more not to. Ryan tried to shush me, but he was laughing, too.

Our laughter was tight, breathless, wild. We held our breaths, covering each other's mouths until we could get back under control. "It's dark, Ryan. I can hardly see your face. But I know it's you."

He smiled. That much I could tell, even in the blackness. His hands were still on our shoulders, his face little more than a foot away from mine.

"And you know it's me," I said. He nodded. "How do you know it's me?" I swallowed, suddenly shy. Suddenly aware of how close we were, how I was practically in his lap, how I'd never been this close to anyone before in my life. A dark, uneasy feeling snuck into me. I stiffened and looked away. But the uneasiness wasn't mine. It didn't belong to me, and I tried to shove it aside.

"Eva?" Ryan said. His hand moved down my arm, his fingers curling around my wrist. "Eva?" he said again, softer. He leaned toward me, trying to meet my eyes. I forgot everything else.

There was a moment like a hiccup in time. Inexplicable. And then his mouth was against mine, his lips soft and urgent. It lasted a second. A blink. A beat of the heart. He pulled away and said nothing. I grabbed his arm. This time, I kissed him and was so light-headed I would have fallen if we weren't already on the ground.

But something twisted inside me. Something flinched, sharp and brittle. Something cried out, and before I knew what I was doing I'd jerked away, gasping for air—"*Addie. Addie, Addie*—"

She said nothing, but I heard her cry, and I started to shake. I moved away and Ryan didn't try to stop me, just looked at me, just watched me, and I thought he understood. He didn't get up, but he touched my hand right before I turned around, and for just one more moment, there was just me and there was just him, and no one else in the world.

But it lasted only a second. Because I was never alone, and neither was he.

I fled to the bathroom. I could already feel my control slipping as Addie's emotions swirled stronger and stronger. By the time we shut the door, we were crying.

<I'm sorry> Addie said. *<I'm sorry. I'm sorry. I tried—>*

<It's okay> I said, because what else was I supposed to say? She was Addie. She was the other half to me. She was more important than anyone.

<I just never thought . . .> She covered our face with our hands, trying to muffle her tears. *<I never thought—>*

Never thought she'd have to watch, feel, as we kissed someone she didn't want to. That had been my private fear. My burden.

I didn't know what to say.

By the time we ventured back out into the hallway, Ryan was gone.

The days dripped by. One. Then two. Then a week. Peter wasn't often home, though when he was he brought his friends with him—the young woman with the cappuccino hair, the older one with the horn-rimmed glasses, a man with skin the color of nutmeg, a girl with ballerina poise. Jackson, who never arrived without a smile for Addie and me. They'd gather at the dining room table, conversing in hushed tones for hours. Once, on our way to the kitchen, we heard the other man ask how we were doing.

They're recovering, Peter replied.

Recovering?

I guess we were.

Ryan and I didn't avoid each other, exactly. We were just never there. I told Addie I was too tired to take control, and whenever we looked at or spoke to or even passed the boy with the dark curly hair and the darker eyes, I knew it was Devon, not Ryan. He and Addie didn't say much to each other. If Hally or Lissa noticed, they didn't comment. They were quieter than they'd ever been, spending a lot of time alone, or with Jaime. But as the days passed, they started smiling again, just a little. Then more and more.

There were always groceries in the fridge: milk, eggs, apples. We found peanut butter and bread in the pantry, and for a while, we all lived off sandwiches. No one complained. Jaime's tremor never went away, but he smiled and helped us make lunch, laughing when we caught him licking the peanut butter off the butter knives. Sometimes we found him murmuring to himself, shuffling his fragmented sentences around as if he hoped to piece together the twin soul he'd lost. But other times he was bright and happy, and I could see how he'd captured Dr. Lyanne's heart like no other Nornand patient had.

Then came the day when the doorbell rang and it wasn't the

young woman with the cappuccino curls or the man with the dark skin. It was a tired woman with ash-brown hair in a loose ponytail, carrying a single suitcase and wearing uncomfortable-looking shoes.

She and Peter looked at each other for a moment, their faces so similar and so different, all at once. Then she looked at us and Hally sitting at the table, eating breakfast. The others hadn't woken up yet.

Dr. Lyanne gripped her suitcase and stepped inside, pausing just beyond the threshold. There was a tremor in her mouth that she quickly quashed. She said nothing, as if daring someone to judge, someone to say she couldn't go any farther, that she had to leave. But Peter just moved out of her way, a smile brushing his lips.

We sat on the fire escape. Over the last dozen days, we'd started spending more and more time there. It was the only way to get real, direct sunlight without leaving the apartment, which we weren't allowed to do yet. Of course, it was almost sunset now, so we wouldn't be getting a tan, but the air was still warm.

We used to spend a lot of time on the fire escape when we still lived in the city. The air had been chillier there, the streets busier, but the fire escape had allowed the same sense of peace and freedom it did now. We'd forbidden Lyle from following us, had claimed it as our own spot, and whenever he'd thrown a fit about it, Dad had nearly always taken our side. Maybe he'd understood our need for space, or maybe he'd wanted to keep Lyle away from us, or maybe he'd just thought the fire escape was too dangerous for a little boy—I'd never know. But right now, I'd have given anything to have our little brother here, flinging himself about the small space with his usual lack of abandon, calling us to look at this or that.

I'd have given anything to know Mom was just beyond the window, checking from time to time to make sure we hadn't managed to hurt ourself somehow. I'd have given anything to know I'd be seeing Dad tonight, that our family would take us back and we'd all somehow run away and be safe somewhere. Except, even then, there would be Ryan. There would be Ryan and his family, and there would be all the other hybrid kids in all the other hospitals, all the other institutions, to think about.

The window slid open behind us, screeching a bit as it always did, the hinges whining for oil.

"The others are calling you for dinner," Dr. Lyanne said, and I nodded.

She lingered at the window, looking out at the red sky like we were. Before I realized what I was doing I said, "Haven't you come out here yet?"

She hesitated, then edged her way onto the fire escape. Her heels made her wobble, and I hid a smile.

"It's pretty," I said, turning back to the busy streets far below, the cars zooming by in clouds of exhaust, the people crossing this way and that. Addie preferred portraits to landscapes, but maybe one day she'd humor me and paint the scene beneath us. There wasn't any point in hiding that part of her anymore.

"It is pretty," said Dr. Lyanne.

A moment of silence stretched and stretched. Finally, I said, "What happened at the hospital?"

Dr. Lyanne leaned against the railing next to us, her hair loose around her shoulders. It hid some of her face's sharper lines. "Nothing really," she said. "The children are gone."

"Gone?" I stared at her. "Gone where?"

"To institutions."

I looked away. "And Mr. Conivent? Dr. Wendle? What about them?"

Sometimes, when Addie and I didn't have nightmares about scalpels and crinkly white butcher paper stained with blood, we dreamed about Mr. Conivent lying motionless on the floor.

Dr. Lyanne's lips thinned. "I don't know. The surgeries were technically legal. They never acted without parental consent. But—" she said as our mouth fell open. "But everyone knows that if news gets out about this, there's going to be backlash, legal or not. As far as the review board—the government—is concerned, Nornand clinic was a complete failure." She laughed bitterly.

<Mr. Conivent's all right, then> Addie said. *<She would say if he weren't. If he were . . .>*

If he were dead. Because that was the fear that dragged down our limbs. That somehow, in our panic, we'd hit him too hard or in the wrong place. That we'd killed him.

"They're all scrambling to save their own skins," Dr. Lyanne said. "But everything will get buried. Everything will be erased. A few years down the road and it's going to be like it never happened."

I laughed so sharply Dr. Lyanne flinched. "Except Jaime. And Sallie, and all the other kids who *died*. That's going to stay. That's never going to be erased. And all those kids who didn't get out. They're still stuck. They're still in danger." I closed our eyes for a moment, gripping the iron railing. "Might have been different," I said.

"You saw me at Mr. Conivent's desk." Dr. Lyanne was still looking out at the bleeding sky. "That was your screwdriver he found, wasn't it?"

I said nothing.

"Thank you," she said. "For distracting him."

"It was Cal," I said. "Not me." Down below, a couple of teenagers strolled by in a big group, far enough away to be faceless. But I could read the levity in the way they moved. I turned to Dr. Lyanne. "Was it important, at least?"

She was quiet. "It showed me Peter wasn't lying." Finally, she looked at us. "That paper, Addie—"

"Eva," I said.

It took her a second, but she said it. "Eva. That paper had codes on it, each for a different country. Medication from different places is coded based on region. Of course, you've got to have special access to know which number codes for what, but—"

"But what?" I said.

"The medication in that box came from overseas, Eva," she said. "And I don't think it's just medication. I think we're getting parts from them, too. The plans for our machines. The technology for our equipment. All from overseas."

I had to hold on to the railing because our knees had gone soft.

The vaccines. Were they shipped here from some foreign country, too? Some hybrid country?

If they were hybrid, why were they helping the government exterminate us?

"How can anything the government's told us about the rest of the world be true if *they're* the ones sending us supplies?" Dr. Lyanne said. "Eva, they're better off than we are. They've got to be. At least some of them."

Some of our earliest memories were of the film clips of the wars, the bombs falling, the cities in flames. Even in first or second grade, they hadn't shied away from telling us about the destruction and the death overseas. The hybrid countries, engulfed by chaos and never-ending wars, always ready to launch into a new battle at the slightest provocation. Supposedly, the Americas had ceased trade—had cut off any sort of communication, really—since the years right after the invasions. We'd been taught there wasn't anything worth trading for over there, nothing worth seeing.

Europe. Asia. Africa. Oceania. All hybrid, all devastated, all burning.

"All lies," Dr. Lyanne said so quietly I didn't know if she meant to speak to us or to herself. "Everything. Anything they tell us could be . . ." She quieted. Pushed herself away from the railing. Took off her shoes so she didn't wobble on her way back to the window. Left us by the edge of the fire escape sinking in our shock, wishing we were standing on more solid ground.

And suddenly, I thought of the man in Bessimir. The hybrid at the center of the storm of angry people, the one who'd been accused of flooding the history museum. The one who, from some angles, looked like our uncle.

Those pipes. How many times have we said to get those pipes fixed?

He hadn't done it. Maybe. Probably. Perhaps.

What mattered was that it *didn't* matter. He might never have stepped foot in that museum in his life, and it wouldn't have made a difference. Because our government lied. Because our president lied. Because our teachers lied. Or didn't even know the truth of what they doled out in class, of what marched across their blackboards, lay bound in their textbooks.

"Michelle," Dr. Lyanne said.

I didn't need to ask. Apparently, the question was obvious enough on our face.

"You asked me if I remembered her name," Dr. Lyanne said.

<The night in the basement> Addie said. *<After our fall.>*

What was she like? we'd whispered. *Your other soul. The one you lost. Do you even remember her name?*

"It was Michelle," she said, and the words dissipated in the warm, salty air.

THIRTY-FIVE

We'd never been in the ocean before, never tasted the salty water as we jumped in the waves, never felt the sand shifting underneath our feet. I splashed Hally and she threw back her head, shouting with laughter. The wind whipped her hair into her face. Kitty and Jaime were searching for seashells in the sand, their backs to us. None of us had bathing suits, but that was okay. We had the whole summer ahead of us. We had the summer after that, and the summer after that, and the one after that.

The days were getting hotter and hotter. When the sun was searing and brilliant, it could almost burn away our coldest memories of Nornand's white halls. Lyle, I thought, would love this to bits. I pushed the thought away. It hurt too much.

I sloshed my way through the surf, the bottom of our shorts dripping, our shirt plastered to our skin. The cuts on our legs had scabbed over, and the salt water didn't aggravate them. Even the old gashes on our hand and forehead only stung a little when a wave splashed against them. They'd scar, but that couldn't be helped.

Jackson had come with us, though he stood a good distance from the water. Unwilling, perhaps, to insert himself into our group. He waved at me.

<Always that same grin> Addie said. *<Like he's perpetually got something stupid to smile about.>*

"Having fun?" Jackson said as I splashed from the water and drew closer. The deep blue of the ocean washed out the blue of his eyes, making them seem almost transparent. I smiled, then looked away again, because he wasn't the boy I'd been looking for.

The sun made me squint, but I found Ryan easily. He stood at the edge of the water, a dozen yards from where Hally and I had been. His shoes were still on. The wind made his hair fly up a bit in the back, and my grin grew wider, then faded.

"What's the matter?" Jackson said.

"What?" I said. "Nothing."

"A girl doesn't look like that when nothing's the matter," Jackson said. He laughed. "He doesn't know you like him?"

I flushed and didn't turn to face him. "How do you know I like him?"

Jackson just laughed again.

"Well, he knows," I said. I didn't even have to concentrate to remember the kiss in the hallway, the warmth of his mouth, the pressure of his hands. A kiss snatched in the dark that was enough to outshine all the sun at the beach.

"He doesn't like you back?" Jackson said doubtfully.

Ryan's back was to us. He glanced at his sister, then turned to the ocean, the wide, gleaming expanse of it.

"No," I said. "No, that's not it." Addie stirred but didn't speak. I didn't want to say anything, either, because how could I without sounding like I was blaming her? I wasn't blaming her. This was simply the way things were.

"It's not just about us, though, is it?" I turned away from Ryan and met Jackson's eyes. He was tall enough that I had to crane our head back to look up. "Addie . . ."

Jackson's smile drooped a little. "But Addie doesn't have to be there."

"Of course she does." I frowned. "That's the point. We're hybrid. We're never alone. We—"

"You've never disappeared and come back?" Jackson said.

I stared at him.

The sun beat down on us, hot, hot, hot.

"Never?" he said quietly. "Never made yourself go to sleep? Left Addie alone?"

The summer of our thirteenth year. I'd slipped away for hours. No medication. No drugs. Just me, wanting to disappear.

"But—" I said.

"It takes practice," Jackson said. His eyes were gentle now. "A ton of practice, if you want to really get it down to a science. But it's normal, Eva. It's what everyone does. I thought you knew."

How could we have known? Who could have told us what was normal and what wasn't? I'd spent my whole life gripping on, terrified to let go.

Hally called Kitty and Jaime into the water, laughing as

the two dropped their shells and obeyed without even bothering to kick off their shoes.

<*Eva?*> Addie said.

<*We don't have to talk about it now*> I said. <*Please, let's not talk about it right now—*>

It was too much for right now. For this day. This moment. And Jackson must have understood that, too, because he didn't say anything else, just smiled at me when I tried to smile at him. I left his side.

Ryan was still by the edge of the water.

I approached him gingerly, afraid he'd become Devon before I could reach him. But he didn't shift. He just watched me.

"Hey," he said once I was only a few feet away.

"Hi," I said and stepped closer. My toes sank into the sand.

Ryan closed the last few feet. The water lapped at his shoes, at my bare feet. "You've been talking with Peter."

It was true. I'd started joining his meetings with his friends, listening in on what it meant to be hybrid and free and fighting in this country. Asking him if what we'd heard about the countries overseas was true. If they were really thriving, really sending us supplies.

It was. They were.

The other children's faces still haunted our dreams. Bridget. Cal. Shunted off to another hospital. Another institution. Stuffed into another uniform.

But that was what Peter and the others were working on. Destroying the institutions. Freeing all these children who were abducted from their homes. Whose families could never speak of them again.

We were a part of that now.

"Ryan!" Hally shouted. She laughed, waving at us. "Eva, what are you doing? Get over here."

Ryan grinned at me. I smiled back. He took my hand and pulled me deeper into the water, the waves pushing and pulling us, back and forth, back and forth.

"Your shoes—" I said, laughing, but he didn't stop. He laughed, too, and I felt lighter than I'd ever felt before. Full of sunlight and air and clouds.

I closed my eyes, my hand tight in Ryan's. His grip oriented me just like it had that day so long ago when I lay blind and immobile on his couch—frightened and confused and under everyone's control but my own. I let the sunshine soak into my skin.

Addie was warm and radiant next to me, making up half of *us*. But I—I was Eva, Eva, Eva, all the way through.

ACKNOWLEDGMENTS

After ten minutes of staring at a blank page, I suppose it's time to take the plunge and begin. It's hard to know where to start. Getting a book to readers is very much a team effort, and so many people have worked together to wrangle *What's Left of Me* between covers and out into the wild. If I named each and every one of them, the list would take me months to draft and you days to read!

So with many apologies to those I cannot credit by name, my unending thanks go out to . . .

. . . My parents, first and foremost, for loving me so much, for being forever there when I need them, for telling me I am capable of accomplishing whatever I dream of.

. . . Alyssa G. and Kirstyn S., who were the very first people to see a word of *What's Left of Me*, reading pages as I wrote them. Your encouragement drove me to keep going, even when all of us should have been studying for IB exams. ☺ I once jokingly told you guys you'd be on the acknowledgments page if this old story ever got published, and hey, it did, and hey, here you are!

. . . The ladies of Publishing Crawl, who are the best writing buddies (and most wonderful friends) anyone could ask for. Huge thanks to Savannah Foley and Sarah Maas, especially, for reading at least four or five separate drafts of *What's Left of Me* apiece, sometimes in less than twenty-four hours, and never letting your patience fray.

. . . All the other wonderful people who read early drafts of the book for me, helping me wrestle the story into a semblance of what it is today. Thank you for your notes and your support. I've so appreciated each and every one of you!

. . . My agent extraordinaire, Emmanuelle Morgen. I don't know where I or the Hybrid Chronicles would be without you! I've so loved working together and look forward to many more years. A big thank-you goes to Whitney Lee, too, who allowed the Hybrid Chronicles to hop across oceans and see publication all around the world.

. . . My fabulous editor, Kari Sutherland, and the rest of the team at HarperCollins Children's. Thank you all so, so much for everything. Kari, your insights and suggestions, comments and critiques made *What's Left of Me* such a stronger story.

. . . And last but not least, a certain Ms. V. Patterson—who possibly does not remember me, but whom I recall fondly—for being my first introduction to any sort of professional writing, for guiding a twelve-year-old through submitting short stories, for not telling me I was too young, and for convincing me I had something to offer the world.